BROKEN WISH

A MIRROR NOVEL

Other books in THE MIRROR series:

Shattered Midnight by Dhonielle Clayton

Fractured Path by J.C. Cervantes

Splintered Magic by L.L. McKinney

BROKEN WISH

A MIRROR NOVEL

JULIE C. DAO

HYPERION

Los Angeles   New York

Text copyright © 2020 by Disney Enterprises, Inc.

All rights reserved. Published by Hyperion, an imprint of Buena Vista Books, Inc.
No part of this book may be reproduced or transmitted in any form or by any means,
electronic or mechanical, including photocopying, recording, or by any information
storage and retrieval system, without written permission from the publisher. For
information address Hyperion, 77 West 66th Street, New York, New York 10023.

First Hardcover Edition, October 2020
First Paperback Edition, September 2021

10 9 8 7 6 5 4 3 2 1
FAC-025438-21204
Printed in the United States of America

This book is set in Cochin, Century Gothic Pro/Monotype;
Citrus Gothic/Adam Ladd; New Old English/K-Type
Designed by Marci Senders

Library of Congress Control Number for Hardcover Edition: 2020002172
ISBN 9781368046398

Visit www.hyperionteen.com

SUSTAINABLE
FORESTRY
INITIATIVE

Certified Sourcing

www.sfiprogram.org
SFI-01054
The SFI label applies to the text stock

To Melody Marshall and Marisa Hopkins,
the best writer friends and cheerleaders I could ask for

BROKEN WISH

A MIRROR NOVEL

AGNES'S FAMILY

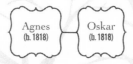

Agnes
(b. 1818)

Oskar
(b. 1818)

MATHILDA'S FAMILY

Mathilda

JANUARY 1848. HANAU, GERMANY.

Agnes saw the gift by the light of the moon.

She glanced back at the cottage, expecting to see Oskar's worried face at the door, but her husband must have still been dozing by the fire. A cheerful glow crept from the shutters and illuminated the snowflakes drifting down from the sky, and, for a moment, Agnes almost turned back, the way Oskar would want her to. Instead, she retrieved the basket that had been left at the gate. She peered at the contents: a note written on finely milled paper; a handful of muslin tea sachets so fragrant she could smell their sweetness on the chill air; a bundle of snowdrops tied together with a frost-blue ribbon; and a jar, a *glass* jar, of honey like precious sunshine.

This basket was the latest in a series that had come every week since October, one gift for each humble offering Agnes left by the towering hedges of the house between the willows. She had never met the occupant, but she knew from these presents that their mysterious neighbor was not poor. *Or unkind*, she thought, gazing up the snowy hill where the woman lived. Last week, Agnes had left her some fresh goat cheese rolled in herbs and mentioned in her note that Oskar had caught a terrible cold. Clearly their neighbor had remembered, judging by the tea and honey.

"This is a mistake," Oskar had said grimly, when two pairs of knitted woolen socks had come in exchange for Agnes's sourdough bread and butter. "People already wonder why we bought this old cottage next door. Let's not risk our good name by associating with her."

Agnes noticed that fearing for their good name hadn't stopped him from wearing the socks, but she decided not to mention it. "I don't believe for one minute that she's an evil witch like everyone says," she had told him. "I *do* believe, however, in being good to our neighbors. She could just be old and lonely."

Oskar had relented, kissing his soft-hearted wife with an affection that had not faded over ten years of marriage. Agnes still sensed his disapproval, but she didn't know how she could stop corresponding with their neighbor when her gifts were so kind and her notes so amusing. When they had first moved in last September, Agnes had baked molasses cookies for everyone who lived nearby, knowing how important it was to Oskar to start off on the right foot in this new town. She had never dreamed that leaving baked goods at the house on the hill would begin such an unusual friendship.

Now, she reached for the message in the basket.

> *To my friend Agnes:*
> *Thank you for the delicious cheese. I put it on some oat bread with a drizzle of honey and feasted like a queen. I think I can taste the friendliness of your goat in it, and I even like her name, Johanna. You asked for my opinion on what to name her baby. What do you think of Honey? I have enclosed some for Oskar's cough. I do hope he is feeling better.*
> *Your friend,*
> *Mathilda*

Agnes chuckled at the suggestion for the baby goat's name, and then noticed a single line of writing all the way at the bottom of the note, like a timid afterthought:

BROKEN WISH

Would you please join me for supper tomorrow night?

She read it three times to make sure she hadn't imagined it. They had exchanged dozens of messages by now, and every time she had tried to invite Mathilda over for tea, the woman had politely declined, citing some excuse or other. It had made Agnes pity her even more, knowing that she had likely heard the distressing rumors about how the old woman on the hill flew to the moon on a willow branch, or could make a hundred poisons from the blood-scented flowers of her night garden, or cursed the hearts of men as revenge for the lover who had left her on their wedding day. No wonder her poor neighbor was reclusive, with such cruel gossip being spread around town.

Agnes did have to wonder, however, where the stories came from. As a child, when she had asked her mother if fairy tales were real, her mother had replied: "The truth of a tale lies in where it took its first breath," meaning that a story transformed with each retelling until its origins faded. But this cryptic answer had always made Agnes think of fairy tales as uncomfortably alive, with clawing roots buried deep in dark winter forests.

Shivering, Agnes went inside and set her neighbor's basket on the table, rubbing her tingling hands in the warmth. Oskar was still asleep in his chair by the fire, so she went to the shelf and took down a little wooden box in which she had been keeping Mathilda's notes. Growing up, she had always wanted a friend to write letters to but had never found anyone, and these messages with her sweet neighbor meant more than she would admit to her husband. As she carefully added the new note to the box, she couldn't help rereading some of the old ones.

Paper was a luxury she and Oskar couldn't afford, so Agnes had been scribbling on the backs of Mathilda's notes. And though she was sure her neighbor could buy as much paper as she liked, the woman had tactfully followed her lead, squeezing elegant script into every corner of each note until it was filled, and then sending a new one on fresh paper. As a result, Agnes had both her own messages to Mathilda as well as Mathilda's to her.

> *To my new neighbors:*
>
> *I was pleasantly surprised to find your gift by my hedges this morning. Thank you for the delicious cookies, which disappeared much too fast. I am glad that poor little cottage, which has stood empty for too long, now has such kind people living in it.*
>
> *Please accept this woolen blanket and my own special rose and chamomile tea, made from the plants in my garden, as housewarming gifts.*
>
> *Gratefully,*
> *Mathilda*

Dear Mathilda,

Thank you for the lovely blanket and tea. My husband, Oskar, and I enjoyed them both. I hope you did not feel obliged to send something back. And since you enjoyed my cookies, I am enclosing a second bigger batch for you. Would you like to join us for supper one day? I am always baking and you would be more than welcome, as we haven't met many neighbors just yet.

Your neighbor,

Agnes

To my kind neighbor Agnes:

How quickly you discovered my sweet tooth. I'm sorry to say that the only thing I can bake well is cake, so I am sending one I made for you and Oskar. I hope you like cinnamon and dates, and it should pair well with that tea I sent. What other sweets do you like? And where did you live before? I'm afraid I don't leave my house much, but I am so grateful for your invitation.

Your neighbor,

Mathilda

Agnes smiled as she flipped through the messages. Exchanging notes with Mathilda felt as easy as chatting, for the woman had so many charming stories to tell: chasing a family of stubborn rabbits out of her garden, following a new knitting pattern for socks that turned out to be some kind of tent, and baking mishaps with her mischievous cat that liked to steal and hide her spices all over the house. There was always a caring inquiry at the end of her notes. How did Agnes and Oskar like their new home? Did they have any family nearby? Did they have enough blankets for the long winter, and would they like her to knit them a few more?

And for the first time in her life, though they had never met in person, Agnes felt that she had a close friend—someone she could trust, someone who would listen and give thoughtful advice.

Dear Mathilda,

I feel low today. I saw a woman and a girl at market. The child was crying her heart out, with her little hands pressed over her eyes, and her mother knelt down to hug her until she felt better. I couldn't look away. I noticed everything about them: how the child tucked her head into her mother's shoulder, how their hair was the exact same shade of brown, how their dresses were made from the same fabric. I imagined the woman sitting up late at night, cutting the cloth with care so there would be enough left over for her daughter.

I went home and I wept and wept because there is no little head tucked against me and no tiny dress to sew beside my

*own. Forgive me for burdening you with my silly, small sad-
nesses, but I feel somehow that you might understand.*

Your friend,

Agnes

To my friend Agnes:

**No sadness of yours could ever be small or silly to
me. You are a person who has much love to give, and
you deserve much love in return. Tonight I send you
mine, along with a honey cake and some lavender tea
that I hope will help soothe you. Will you write again
tomorrow and let me know if you are feeling better?**

Your friend,

Mathilda

As the weeks went by, Agnes had also confessed why she and her
husband had moved to Hanau. Oskar had a secret shame: His parents
had never been married. When Oskar was born, his mother had left
him with his father, who later wed and had a legitimate son, Otto.
All his life, Oskar was treated as lesser than Otto, and when their
father died, Otto inherited the family farm and all the money. Heartbroken, Oskar had saved up carefully for this move and this cottage
so that he wouldn't need to rely on his brother's charity. Agnes knew

her husband would be *furious* with her for sharing this, but Mathilda had no one to tell.

It was why they had needed a fresh start and a new town where they could put down roots and earn respect. *And why he doesn't want me associating with Mathilda*, Agnes thought guiltily.

As if he had heard her thinking about him, Oskar gave a loud yawn and stretched. "How long have I have been dozing?" he asked, giving her a drowsy smile. "I didn't mean to fall asleep on you. I guess fixing the shed took more out of me than I expected."

"It's all right." Agnes closed the box, then came over to him and kissed his unruly mop of wheat-colored hair. "My poor, hardworking husband. It's high time you went to bed."

He got up obediently, and his eyes fell upon the basket. "Another gift from the witch?"

"Don't call her that," Agnes chided him. "Not when she has been so kind to us. Look, she sent flowers and tea and honey, and invited us to supper at her house. I think we should go."

"I don't know— Is that *glass*?" Oskar broke off, distracted by the honey jar. He held the lovely object in his work-roughened hand, watching it glint gold and peach and amber in the firelight. "Where would one find honey this time of year? How can she afford such luxuries?"

"She must have harvested it last summer. And we always suspected she was wealthy."

"But why settle in a humble village like this, then?"

Agnes tossed her heavy flaxen braid over one shoulder, exasperated by his determined dislike of the woman. "I don't know, dear, but we can ask her when we go over for supper."

Oskar set down the jar. "Listen to me," he pleaded. "Whether or not the rumors are true, people fear and hate this woman. If they see us befriending her, they may hate us as well."

"They won't."

"How do you know that? How do you know it won't be like Mannheim all over again, where we can't go to market without being looked at and whispered about?"

"I see the reason in what you say," Agnes said gently. "I do. But no one here knows about Mannheim, and I see such kindness in this woman. I know what it is to be lonely." She looked around their cottage, in which she baked and brewed alone each day. It was cozy and comfortable, but it, too, was an empty womb, without any hope of laughter or little pattering feet. She put her hands on either side of Oskar's face. "And if we find out she *is* a witch, we need not have anything to do with her again. Besides," she added playfully, "aren't you curious?"

After a pause, in which Oskar took in her determined expression, he sighed. "All right. *One* supper," he conceded, and they sealed the agreement with a kiss.

2

The following night, when Agnes and Oskar approached the hedge surrounding Mathilda's house, the wooden gates stood open. Iron lanterns illuminated a path between drooping willow trees, positioned like sentries on either side. Agnes was struck by the absence of even a flake of snow on the property, as though winter itself feared to walk here.

Oskar's hand tightened in hers. "We can still turn back."

"Don't be silly," Agnes said, pulling him through the gates, but even she could not deny that there was something unnerving about this place, a certain resonance that lingered in the air. *Like a fading note of music*, she thought, *played on a pipe to lure the listeners onward.*

It was a beautiful, wild space. All along the hedge grew plants of every kind: shrubs dotted with mauve berries, fragrant alabaster flowers, and trees that draped fleecy leaves over the grass like the train of a bride's dress. Peppermint, rosemary, and thyme spiced the air, and a granite fountain issued a trickle of water that tinkled like fairy bells. It looked like a garden lost in time, a place that could lull someone to sleep for twenty years while the world spun by outside the hedge.

A surprisingly small cottage stood in the center of this wilderness. But where Agnes and Oskar's home was made of mushroom-colored wood, Mathilda's had been built from dove-gray stones, and she had panes of pretty colored glass set into black lead frames for windows. Warm light shone out from the curtains, and a little stone dog stood on the doorstep.

The door opened and Agnes held her breath, suddenly shy at the prospect of meeting the person to whom she had bared her heart in writing. She had pictured Mathilda as an old, frail lady with a gray bun and a sweet face lined with wrinkles, so when her neighbor emerged from the cottage, Agnes had to lean against Oskar in shock. The so-called witch, who by all accounts was loathsome and malevolent, looked about twenty-five, not much younger than Agnes herself. She was small and slim, with rich black hair tied with a frost-blue ribbon, and freckles sprinkled like cinnamon across a pale, heart-shaped face. Her light brown eyes crinkled at the corners as she gave them a shy smile, her hands fluttering at her sides as though unsure what to do.

"Hello," she said timidly. "You must be Agnes and Oskar. Won't you come in?"

Agnes opened her mouth, but no sound came out. They followed Mathilda inside, moving slowly as though in a dream, and were enveloped by a pleasant warmth that smelled of savory stew and honey cakes. Mathilda reached for their coats and they handed them over, unable to stop staring at her. For a moment, they all stood in a bashful silence by the door. And then Agnes burst out laughing, and Oskar joined in. So *this* was the old witch the town feared half to death!

"I'm glad to meet you, Mathilda," Agnes said warmly. "Oskar and I have enjoyed your generous gifts, and your notes have made my winter much brighter."

The young woman's face shone. "I feel the same way," she said, holding out her hands, which Agnes squeezed. "Please sit down and make yourselves comfortable. Supper will be ready in a moment." She tightened the cream-colored apron over her blue flannel dress and bustled over to the fireplace, where two large pots were bubbling away. "I can't tell you how nice it is to have friends over at last. It's always so quiet in my house."

Agnes and Oskar sat down at the kitchen table, which had been set for three people, with deep-blue crockery and real silver. The cottage was as neat as a pin, with a blue-and-white rug on the floor that matched the soft-spun blankets and cushions on the chairs, one of which was occupied by a fat ginger cat. A thick leather-bound book lay open on a side table, a pen resting between the sheets of rough-edged paper as though Mathilda had been writing in it when they had knocked. Pretty porcelain figurines lined the mantel, and a thick purple velvet cloth covered a painting hanging over it, likely to keep off the dust.

"That's some beautiful detailing," Oskar said, pointing at the walls, which were carved with a pattern of willow trees. "I've never seen woodwork to equal it."

"Thank you," Mathilda said, her face lighting up. "My home isn't large, but I like it to be cozy and attractive, since I spend so much time in it." She poured them mugs of barley water and ladled a thick, steaming stew of root vegetables into three bowls, then cut into a fresh, crusty loaf of sourdough bread. She moved nimbly around the kitchen, her cheeks pink and hands graceful.

Agnes exchanged glances with Oskar. Had the townspeople ever even *seen* this woman? But then again, the gossip had never mentioned her age, and perhaps Agnes had heard *witch* and assumed she was an eccentric old lady. "How long have you lived in this cottage?" she asked.

"Oh, it's been a long while now," Mathilda said.

Oskar sniffed suspiciously at the stew. When Agnes frowned at him, he picked up his spoon and took a cautious taste, his eyes widening as he swallowed. Quickly, he took a second, bigger spoonful, and then a third. "Were you born in Hanau?" he asked Mathilda.

"No, I wasn't." Mathilda carried over a heavy plate of sausages, cabbage dumplings, and potatoes and chives swimming in golden butter. "I'm sure you'll find it a nice, quiet, little town."

Agnes speared a piece of buttery potato, which melted in her mouth like a cloud. "Do you have any family nearby?" she asked.

Mathilda's sad little laugh made her heart ache. "None still living. All I have is my cat and my cottage. Your house stood empty for years, and it's so nice to see it lit up at night now."

"I'm glad we came, too," Agnes said sympathetically. "Do you ever go into town? I've never seen you at market. People should see how sweet you are."

"No, never. It isn't pleasant for me, and I can get everything I need from my garden or the forest or the market in Hainburg."

"Hainburg?" Oskar echoed, pausing for breath. He had now finished his entire bowl of stew and wolfed down at least half a dozen sausages, by Agnes's count. "Going there and back by carriage is a whole morning and afternoon. Do you own a horse?"

"No. But it's a nice walk when the weather is fine."

Agnes understood. Hainburg was distant enough that no one there would know the gossip about Mathilda, so she could shop and walk about freely. *The same reason we left Mannheim*, Agnes thought, hoping Oskar would make the connection, too, and feel more charitable toward their neighbor. But clearly curiosity had gotten the better of her husband.

"What happened between you and the town?" he asked bluntly.

Agnes frowned at him again, but Mathilda answered at once. "They blame me for some odd incidents. Years ago, I had a run-in with the butcher's daughter. Lina never liked me—there was a young man she fancied who preferred me instead—but she was especially cruel that day. She followed me into the hat shop and said rude things and laughed at me until I ran home without buying anything. I didn't hear what happened to her until afterward."

"What happened?" Oskar and Agnes asked together.

"As soon as Lina got home that day, she began choking. Her parents called the physician, who discovered a toad stuck in her throat, and for some reason, they accused me." Mathilda's pretty, heart-shaped face darkened. "The physician removed the toad safely, but for seven nights, Lina coughed up something else. A newt, a rat...even a baby snake once."

Agnes clutched her throat. "Goodness! But how could they blame you for such a thing?"

"It's easy to place blame where there is dislike, and Lina's parents knew how she felt about me." Mathilda folded her hands in her lap. "Another time, some of the boys in town thought it would be fun to tear down my hedges. They wanted to see what I was hiding, they said, and took their fathers' axes and destroyed part of my wall. I had just come up the hill and I was so frightened at the sight of them waving the axes at me, I dropped my shopping and ran inside. They laughed at me and stole my bags and ate the candy I had bought."

Agnes shook her head in disbelief. The people they had met so far had been lovely and welcoming, and she could not imagine them being so cruel.

"What happened next?" Oskar asked.

"The following morning, the boys all came down with a terrible sickness," Mathilda replied. "It turned out there had been enough rat poison in the candy to fell an ox. But no one blamed the confectioner from whom I had purchased it. All fingers pointed to me."

Agnes looked from Oskar's grim expression to Mathilda's downcast face. There was something odd about the line of the woman's mouth that troubled Agnes, a faint upward tug at the corner that was not *quite* a smile. Perhaps Mathilda did not deserve to be blamed... but had she enjoyed these incidents? After all, they had happened to people who had been unkind to her.

"After that, I started getting blamed for everything," Mathilda went on. "Too much rain, too little rain. Broken carriage wheels, dead crops, bread gone bad, cracks in the bridge, and even children who went missing." There was such sadness in her eyes when she looked up that Agnes felt guilty about what she had been thinking. "Now you know why I want nothing to do with Hanau. I have nowhere else to go and I prefer to keep to myself here."

"I understand, and I don't blame you," Agnes said.

Mathilda patted her hand. "Enough serious talk now. I hope you both have a little room left for tea and honey cake. I baked enough for you to take home."

Oskar, who had been grave and silent throughout her speech, spoke at last. "I think we should get back. Thank you for the meal." He got up abruptly and went to get their coats.

"A little dessert won't hurt, dear," Agnes said, taken aback by his lack of manners. "And you know honey cake is my favorite. My mother used to serve it with cream."

Mathilda gave her a faint smile. "I always wanted a daughter to spoil with cake and cream, but that doesn't seem likely to ever happen. I have the highest hopes for you, though."

Oskar spun around. "I beg your pardon?"

Agnes got up and placed a soothing hand on his tense shoulder. "It's all right. I told Mathilda about how we've hoped for a child in vain these ten years."

"We shouldn't trouble our neighbor with these private matters, my love." He wrapped Agnes's coat around her, his face pleading. "Come, let's just go home."

Mathilda's voice rang out. "I wasn't saying it to be kind. I meant it. You are my friend now, Agnes, and you will be a mother, too, if I have anything to say about it. I can help you."

Oskar clenched his jaw. "I don't think you have anything to say on this subject."

"Please, Oskar, don't." Agnes's heart raced as she turned back to Mathilda, whose face was bright with determination. "What do you mean you can help us? How?"

"Surely you've heard plenty of gossip about me by now?" Mathilda asked bitterly, as she wrapped a small, crumbly brown cake in flannel. "Well, the rumor that I have a gift for herb lore and medicines happens to be true. Back when I wasn't the town pariah, I helped cure everything from broken bones to broken hearts. I've been trained as a healer and I know about midwifery, and people were glad enough to benefit from my skills before they turned against me." She came slowly toward Agnes, who felt Oskar's hands tighten on her shoulders. "I know a tonic that might help you. That's all," she added, holding out the wrapped cake.

Agnes took it, feeling its soothing heat between her hands. Mathilda must have been keeping it warm all through supper, and it was just like her to be so thoughtful and considerate. Agnes looked into her pretty face and desperately wanted to trust her. The air next to her skin tingled, as though destiny had arrived and wanted her to know it was there.

But Oskar's hands were still tight on her shoulders. "I don't feel comfortable discussing this with you," he told Mathilda flatly. "You can't go around making these outrageous claims. I won't have you raising my wife's hopes. It's no better than lying to her."

Mathilda's gaze remained on Agnes, calm and gentle. "You're the only person in *years* who has bothered to treat me like a human being. You've given me hope that not everyone is terrible, and that my loneliness won't last forever. You deserve what you wish for," she said. "All it would take is a simple tonic: three ingredients, taken by you in three sips on each of three separate nights."

Something in her voice made Agnes believe her, against all reason and what her rational mind knew to be true: that no drink could give her the child her heart hungered for. But the tingle in the air and the chill down her spine suggested there was more to Mathilda than what they saw. Whether it was good or bad—whether Hanau was right about her—she didn't know. "We don't have any money," Agnes heard herself say. "We can't pay you."

Behind her, Oskar yanked open the door.

"I don't need money," Mathilda said, with a small smile that broke

Agnes's heart. "The price would be for you to keep writing to me and have supper with me every month. I've felt less lonely with you around, and I know you feel the same. Don't decide now. Just think about it."

Agnes hugged the warm cake as Oskar pulled her out the door. "I will," she said, and the last thing she saw before the door closed was Mathilda's light brown eyes wet with tears.

And then she and Oskar were hurrying through the garden and back down the hill.

O skar cursed under his breath when they reached home, for standing at their door with a basket of pastries were the Braun sisters, the nosiest busybodies in town. Both women were in their sixties: Sophie was a widow with a grown son in Stuttgart, and Katharina, who had never married, was the town's midwife. She had told Agnes once that she had chosen her profession because the juiciest bits of information often came from women in childbirth. "The poor dears are so racked with pain," she cackled, "they don't even know they've revealed the *true* father of their baby!"

Agnes knew that of all the townspeople, Oskar would have *least* wanted the Brauns to see them coming from Mathilda's house. She forced a smile. "Good evening, ladies."

"What were you doing up there?" Sophie demanded. Her bulging blue eyes cut from them to the hill. "You didn't eat anything the witch gave you, did you?"

Agnes felt Oskar biting back his irritation and patted his hand. "We paid her a quick call. Would you please excuse us? Oskar's getting over a cold, and we shouldn't stand out here long."

"What was her house like?" Katharina asked. She was all sharp angles from her chin to her elbows, in contrast to her soft, round sister. "Did she change her appearance in front of you? Frau Werner says she once saw the witch's hair go from black to golden in minutes."

"Kat! Be quiet," Sophie snapped, then turned back to Agnes and Oskar. "You *mustn't* be seen with that woman. You're new here, so you don't know, but the Werners and the Bergmanns—the most important families in Hanau—hate her because she cursed young Frau Bergmann once! She made toads and snakes and I don't know what else fall from Lina's lips!"

"Don't forget Lina's cousin nearly died eating that poisoned candy,"

Katharina added. "The Werners were up in arms about that, but as soon as Georg Werner proposed a mob to roust the witch from her house, he fell deathly ill. A coincidence? I think not."

"You're a nice young couple and we like you, so we won't tell anyone. We wouldn't want people to think you were in league with the witch, would we?"

Agnes's stomach twisted at the fear on Oskar's face. He had worked so hard to buy them this cottage and move away from the old scandal, and now she had spoiled their fresh start. She had put them in this position, and now the gossips knew. "One of our goats escaped its pen last night," she blurted out, and everyone looked at her in surprise. "It damaged the woman's hedge, and we wanted to make amends with some milk and cheese. That's why we went up there."

At once, the Brauns broke into relieved smiles.

"Oh, you poor dears," Katharina cried. "No wonder you looked so distressed just now! We almost thought you didn't want to see us!"

"So you've never associated with her before this?" Sophie asked.

Agnes swallowed hard. "No," she lied, pushing away the image of Mathilda's notes and her light brown eyes, wet with tears. "This was the first time we had anything to do with her."

"Well, no harm done, then," Sophie said, patting Agnes's arm. "Tie your goats securely and don't leave your house for a few days. It was wise to appease her with a gift, but you don't want to keep reminding her of what happened. Lord knows that witch can hold a grudge!"

"We'll do that," Agnes said weakly.

"Well, since that's been cleared up, we wish you a good night," Oskar told them.

"Good night," Katharina said, handing Agnes the basket. "And next time you go to the tavern, Oskar, be sure to tell of your experience to Jacob and Wilhelm Grimm."

"Who are they?"

"They're professors in Berlin, but they were born in Hanau," Sophie explained. "They're back all week to visit and collect stories about witches. Something about a volume of children's tales they're compiling. Frankly, it sounds like nonsense to me."

"But if these Grimms can make a living from it, I say good for them!" Katharina added, as the sisters disappeared down the path.

Oskar went inside without another word and Agnes followed, glancing up the hill before she closed the door. The iron lanterns by the gate were still lit, illuminating a figure in a hooded cloak, which slowly turned and headed back toward the hedge wall. Agnes wondered if Mathilda had seen everything, if she could guess at what had passed between them and the Brauns. Her stomach clenched with guilt at the memory of Mathilda's notes filled with care.

"I can help you," the young woman had said, so confident, so sure.

It was silly to think a tonic could erase years of heartache and bring the child they wanted desperately. And yet it sounded so simple: just a few sips and a few suppers with a kind woman who longed to be friends. If it didn't work, what was the worst that could happen?

But if it *did* work . . .

Agnes closed her eyes, imagining a head with sunny curls, eyes as blue as Oskar's, and chubby hands touching her face. A little voice calling her Mama and squeals of delight blending with Oskar's great shout of laughter as they played. She felt her husband's arms wrap around her tightly, and only then did she realize that she had been sobbing.

"Go see her again," he said gruffly. "Go take that tonic and find out what happens."

Agnes looked up at the good husband she knew with all her soul would be a good father, and saw that his bright blue eyes were wet, too. "But the Brauns . . ."

"Hang the Brauns." He put a big, callused hand on either side of her face. "I know you. If you don't do this, you will spend the rest of your life wondering. Witch or not, I think that woman does care about you. So let her help you, if you want her to. Just promise me one thing."

"Anything."

Oskar touched the thin band of gold on her right hand. "Promise me on my mother's wedding ring that when you've gone to her three

more times and are done taking the tonic, you will never see her again."
The fear and worry had returned to his face. "Whether or not it works,
give me your word you will end the friendship when she's through.
Please, Agnes."

She looked at the ring he had put on her finger ten years ago.
"Mathilda's price for helping me was my friendship," she said slowly.
"You're asking me to use her. And lie to her."

"You know what my life was like back in Mannheim. My father
committed the sin of not marrying my mother, but I got all the punishment." He shook his head. "I can't let that happen to the children we
might have. I can't see them suffer like I did. You heard the Brauns:
We'll be shunned if we associate with the witch, and I don't want to
risk our lives here."

Agnes stared at him, her chest tight with shock. "I don't know if
I can promise you that, Oskar. How can I live with knowing that I
tricked a good woman—and I do believe she is good—into helping me?
What kind of example would that be for our children, if we had any?"

Oskar bowed his head.

She exhaled. "Let me think about it some more. It's late, and we
should get to bed."

But after tossing and turning for hours, Agnes still didn't know
what to do. If she did what Oskar asked, she would break Mathilda's
heart. If she accepted Mathilda's deal, she would risk turning Hanau

against them. And if she did neither, it would be just as Oskar had said: She would spend the rest of her life wondering.

After breakfast, Oskar went out to tend to the animals, and Agnes watched him from the window. She didn't know anyone who had a better heart than her husband, and his suggestion that she betray Mathilda had truly shocked her. Yet it would accomplish everything they desired: They might get their baby *and* stay in good standing.

Only Mathilda would suffer.

Agnes's eyes turned upward to the hill on which her neighbor might have been gardening, petting her cat, or sitting by the fire. *If I lied to her,* she thought, *her situation wouldn't be much different from what it is now.* Mathilda would still have her cottage, with that garden and that cat and that fire. She would go on sewing and cooking and walking all the way to Hainburg to buy what she needed. She would just do it all without Agnes.

"No, I can't," Agnes said aloud, as the temptation grew and grew. "I can't do that to her."

But even as she dove into her daily tasks, trying to distract herself, a small voice insisted on lingering at the edges of her mind. It whispered, *You can.*

The next evening, Agnes went back up the hill. There was no moon and no sound except the lonely cry of an owl and the crunch of her boots on the snow. Oskar had stayed home, afraid that other neighbors might come calling, and had sent her off with a hug and a kiss. They hadn't said another word about his request, but it had hung in the air between them like a thick curtain. And now, panting slightly as she climbed the slope to Mathilda's open gate, Agnes still hadn't made a decision. *I'll know when I see her*, she told herself.

Whatever she decided, she would be open and honest and business-like with Mathilda, not emotional. But her resolve faded the minute she came to the woman's cottage, which shimmered in the cold with a kindly light. And when Mathilda appeared at the door, her face full of gratitude and relief that Agnes had come back, it was impossible *not* to feel emotional.

"I'm glad you're here," she said, hugging Agnes. "I've been cooking all day. Come in."

Inside, a fire blazed in the hearth and Mathilda's ginger cat blinked in recognition as Agnes took a seat at the table. A floral smell tinged the air from a vase of snowdrops resting on a thick, leather-bound book on the mantel. The pure white flowers contrasted well with the purple velvet that protected the painting on the wall. One corner of the fabric had slipped, and Agnes noticed what looked like an ornate gold frame. The young woman must be even wealthier than she and Oskar had thought.

"My husband's still getting over his cold," Agnes said, as Mathilda stirred the pot over the fire, her cheeks glowing from the flames. "He's sorry to miss another good dinner of yours."

Mathilda gave her a wry smile. "You don't need to lie. I know Oskar would rather swim in the freezing river than come again, and it's all right. All that matters to me is that you're here."

Agnes searched for some apology, but all that came out was "You're my friend."

"And you're mine," Mathilda said, her eyes shining as she poured them two mugs of piping-hot ginger tea. Her long, wavy dark hair had been tied back with a frost-blue ribbon and cascaded over the shoulder of her dark green wool dress. She wrapped her hands around her drink, her eyes soft. "I know what people think of me. And contrary to what they believe, I *have* had friends before. I've even fallen in love, once. But it didn't work out."

"Why not?" Agnes asked gently.

The young woman fixed her with a steady gaze. "Because to love me is to choose a life of isolation. I was born to stand apart, and few people want to do that." She looked into her tea, searching for words.

"Humans are social creatures. They want to be accepted by others, and if that means going along with what most people think, then that's what they'll do. I think Oskar is like that, and he isn't wrong to be. It's the safe path."

"He had a hard childhood." Agnes felt the need to explain. "We left much grief behind in Mannheim."

"I don't blame him. If I were Oskar, I wouldn't befriend me, either. But I don't get to be him, or you, or anyone else, however much I want to be." A shadow passed over Mathilda's face. "I almost didn't write to say thank you when you first baked me cookies. I thought, *I can't subject this poor woman to that.* But I'm glad I did, and I found such a kind person who doesn't let other people's opinions scare her."

Agnes's gut twinged with guilt, remembering the lie she had told the Brauns.

"So will you let me help you?" Mathilda asked, her face bright. "Will you allow me to make the tonic for you, and see what comes of it?"

Here was the moment Agnes had felt certain would reveal what she ought to do. But no answer, no decision appeared—only a hope so sharp it felt like hunger. "You sounded so certain the other night. Can you really do all that? And how? How is it that physicians and apothecaries Oskar and I have seen over the years couldn't help us, and you can?"

Mathilda laughed. "Some might call it magic," she said, and Agnes couldn't tell from her playful tone whether she meant it or not. "I was raised by a woman who taught me everything I needed to know. She was a great healer; she showed me how to help people."

"And she succeeded?" Agnes asked anxiously, as her neighbor got up to fill two bowls with a spiced pot roast and root vegetables. "She helped someone have a baby?"

"Yes, and delivered it, too."

The answer filled Agnes's chest like air. "How many times did she do it?"

"Just once," Mathilda said, handing her a bowl. "The next day, she was driven out of the town where she lived. It was her reward for helping that woman, who did nothing to defend her. Just cuddled her baby and put her out of her mind. So my mentor never did it again."

Agnes stared at her food. Oskar had suggested she betray Mathilda in just the same way. But the tonic had worked before; it had gotten someone else a baby, and it could help her, too.

"You don't need to worry about me," Mathilda said, misinterpreting her expression. "The people of Hanau have left me alone for years. They might talk and abuse my name in the market and the tavern, but no one has come up this hill in almost a decade."

"Yes." The word escaped Agnes without thinking.

Mathilda paused in the middle of sprinkling pepper on her vegetables. "Yes, what?"

"Yes, I'd like you to help me."

The young woman went still. "And you agree to my terms? If I help you, you'll promise to continue to write me and have supper with me?"

Agnes swallowed hard. "Yes. I promise."

The smile on Mathilda's face was like sunshine over the frozen hills. Agnes tried to return the smile, even though she had made the split-second decision without knowing whether she would be loyal to her husband or her neighbor in the end.

But underneath the warring emotions—and the feeling that she had started something from which there was no going back—she felt hope and joy for the first time in years, and she clung to them with everything that she had.

4

Once the supper dishes were cleared away, Mathilda began gathering the ingredients for her tonic. "They all come from my garden," she explained, laying bundles of leaves, roots, and tiny flowers on the table. They released a dark, earthy smell when she rubbed them between her fingers. "The materials for this tonic have to be gathered at night. The moon happened to be just right the evening you and Oskar came over, so I collected them after you left."

Agnes studied the plants, touched that Mathilda had begun

preparing to help even before they had given her an answer. "Didn't you say the tonic would have three ingredients only?"

"Three active ingredients, yes, but they have to be delivered in a special solution." Mathilda pulled more bottles from her cabinets. "They can't be taken as they are, because their properties are strongest when mixed with other agents."

"You learned all this from your mentor?" Agnes asked, impressed. Her mother had taught her how to read and write, which was more of an education than most girls of her age and class had, but she was awed by how much knowledge Mathilda seemed to possess.

"Yes. She always said that magic relies on balance." Mathilda chopped the leaves into neat, precise slivers. "People think it's as simple as making things appear from out of nowhere but don't understand that it all has a cost. We never take without giving back in return. We *can't*."

"What's the cost of helping me, then?"

Mathilda smiled. "Why, the promise you just made me, of course. A promise is like a contract," she explained. "I gave my word to use my magic to help you have a child, and in return, you gave *your* word to continue writing and visiting me. It's an easy exchange for us because we're already good friends. But I assure you, there can be serious mishaps."

"What do you mean?"

"There's power in a promise, no matter who you make it to. The most powerful are made when magic is involved. If you break one of *those* promises, you release its energy into the world."

Agnes found that she was holding her breath. "What happens then?"

"No one knows. Where magic gives, it can also take—in ways that no one can foresee."

"And that affects people like you, too? People with ... magic?"

"Of course." Mathilda chuckled. "The promise I regret breaking the most is the one that took away my ability to sing. I used to have a voice like a nightingale, but now I can only croak."

"And there's nothing you can do about it? You have to accept the consequences forever?" Agnes asked. "That seems very harsh."

Mathilda shrugged. "Those are the rules. But I know I don't have to worry here. I trust you," she added, leaning over to pat Agnes's hand.

Agnes couldn't help it—her hand jerked guiltily away, but Mathilda didn't seem to notice as she picked up a pestle and ground the dry ingredients together in the bowl. Every now and then, she added a few drops of water, and slowly the mixture became a deep purple paste.

"You add it like a dollop of honey to a cup of tea," Mathilda said, sprinkling in a bit more water. "There's lavender and sugar in there to make it taste better. You need to drink all of it in three sips. Do this on each of three nights. Tonight will be the first."

"Why three?"

"It's a powerful number, like seven. It appears in all sorts of potions, poultices, spellwork . . ." Mathilda dusted off her hands and went to get the kettle. She poured boiling-hot water into a pretty cornflower-blue teacup filled with dried lavender flowers, then stirred the paste into it. "Here you are. Blow on it first, so you don't burn yourself."

Agnes accepted the cup with trembling fingers. The tea had turned an attractive shade of lilac, and she could see her own wide, anxious eyes in it. She had the odd sensation that all the world held its breath as she stared at her reflection. Once she drank this tonic, there would be no going back. She would have to decide, at the end of it—no matter what happened—whether to continue her friendship with Mathilda or betray her.

Perhaps Oskar had been afraid of this woman for a good reason. Perhaps people didn't gossip about her without just cause. Because try as she might, Agnes couldn't think of any way to describe all this talk of spellwork and power *but* witchcraft, plain and simple. She shivered, wondering whether the creatures in Lina's throat and the poisoning of the troublemakers had been accidents, or something worse.

"Don't be afraid," Mathilda said gently. "The tonic won't hurt you."

Unless I break my promise, Agnes thought.

"It will help you, because one good deed deserves another," the woman went on, and there was such kindness and trust in her eyes that Agnes found it difficult to look at her. But she forced herself to, and for a moment, she felt as though her soul was bared before this strange, elegant, solitary person. She wondered if loneliness was another unwanted consequence of magic, another price Mathilda was paying for a broken vow.

I could go, Agnes told herself. The cup steamed, smelling of dewy spring mornings. *I could return to my husband and never see her again. No harm done and no promises broken.*

But whenever she closed her eyes, she would see that child with Oskar's bright blue eyes. She would hear that little voice calling, *Mama, Mama,* and feel that tiny hand reaching trustingly for her own. And she would know, with every painful beat of her heart, that it was not real.

That it would never, ever be real.

Unless . . .

Before her courage could fail her, Agnes picked up the cup and sipped. Within the tonic, she tasted secrets she had never told a living soul, winter nights by the fire as her mother combed her hair, and lullabies with words she had long forgotten. Her entire life passed down her throat, burning her insides, and she felt an overwhelming rush of both joy and melancholy.

"Two more sips," Mathilda encouraged her, and Agnes tipped the cup to her mouth again. The liquid scalded her all the way down, and she gasped for breath and then, at a nod from Mathilda, took her final sip. The cup slipped from her hand, and she only vaguely registered Mathilda catching it before it could shatter. "Good. How do you feel?"

"Fine," Agnes said, though her head swam and the cottage seemed to be tilted on its side. She looked around in a daze and noticed that the velvet over the mantel had slipped a bit more, revealing a dark glimmer as though oil and canvas did not hang there, but a sheet of silvery glass.

"The tonic will make you a bit drowsy, so let's get you home," Mathilda said kindly. She helped Agnes slip her arms into the sleeves of her coat and buttoned the front for her. "You'll feel wonderful in the morning, with a great deal of energy. Come back at the same time tomorrow evening and I'll have your second dose ready, all right?"

"All right." Agnes's knees wobbled as she opened the door. She had never had a sip of ale in her life, but thought this might be what it felt like to be drunk. "Tomorrow evening."

The walk back down the hill was a blur, and then she was home, where Oskar, pale and worried, helped her into a chair by the fire. He knelt in front of her, asking over and over if she was all right as she blinked away her confusion.

"I took the tonic," she heard herself say. "I'm going back tomorrow night."

"Do you have to?" Oskar asked tensely.

"Yes. What's wrong?"

"Katharina Braun came a few minutes after you left. She must have just missed seeing you go up the hill, thank god. She brought us a chicken pie." He pointed to a covered dish on the table with a desolate little laugh. "I had to make something up about where you were. I wanted to say you were in bed sick, but she would have wanted to come in and see you."

The murky, dazed feeling dissipated, and in its place was fear. "What did you tell her?"

"That you had forgotten to buy something for supper and had to run into town." Oskar ran a weary hand over his face. "She asked why she hadn't passed you and I said you were still learning the routes, so perhaps you'd taken the wrong path. I don't think she believed me."

Agnes took one of his hands in hers and felt his pulse thundering. "You have no reason to lie that she knows of," she said reassuringly. "And she accepted my story about the goat escaping and damaging Mathilda's hedge. She hasn't the faintest idea I went back up the hill."

"But what am I going to say when she comes back tomorrow?" Oskar asked. "She and Sophie want to call on you and get your recipe for those molasses cookies. I can't make excuses for two more nights...." He got up and paced before the fire, his features strained with anxiety. "They're watching us now. They're curious. And if they knew the truth... My god, Agnes, the way these women gossip. In the few minutes before I got rid of her, I heard all about a failed marriage, a truant child, and a family in ruin, and I didn't even know who these people were! That's how it will be when the Brauns find out you've been seeing the witch. It will be all over town." He stopped pacing. "We have to leave Hanau."

Agnes's heart clenched at his helpless panic. "Oskar..."

"But how are we going to afford to leave?" he went on, raking his hands through his hair. "We spent every last penny on this cottage and the hired wagon for our furniture. Good god, I'll have to go to Otto. I'll have to swallow my pride and let him help us like he offered to...."

"Oskar!" Agnes cried, and he finally stopped talking. She got up and took his face in her hands. "Listen to me. There is no need to go to your brother for help or for us to leave Hanau. I truly believe Mathilda can help us. She's given me hope for the first time in a long time, and I *need* to go back twice more. I need to finish taking this tonic. We can't stop now."

"If the Bergmanns or the Werners hear of it..."

"No one will hear. Because the friendship will not continue." The words shocked Agnes, though they came from her own lips. She shivered, as though Mathilda might have somehow heard her. "I love you, Oskar. You are my husband and my priority. I wish there was another way. I wish I didn't have to hurt Mathilda. But I don't want to keep running, so I'll end it with her." She closed her eyes, picturing the gifts and messages that had made her so happy.

Oskar wrapped his arms tightly around her, his sobs muffled in her hair.

"I have to keep taking the tonic," Agnes said, her voice breaking, and she felt Oskar nod. "Tomorrow morning, I will find Katharina and bring her my recipe. I'll tell her I'm coming down with your cold and not to come over for supper until next week. That should hold her off. I will go back to Mathilda two more times, and then never again."

"Thank you," her husband whispered.

Agnes closed her eyes, feeling exhausted with the weight of the decision, the friend she would have to betray, and the consequences— unknown and uncontrollable—that she would have to face for her broken promise. *Where magic gives*, Mathilda had explained, *it can also take—in ways that no one can foresee.*

But it was a sacrifice Agnes had to make for Oskar, and for the family they hoped to have. It was the only thing she could tell herself to make it feel any better.

To my lovely friend Agnes:

I was expecting you last night! I hope nothing is the matter. I wanted to see how you were feeling after taking the third dose. Sometimes the tonic can make you feel sick to your stomach. I'm worried that this is the case, since you have always come when you said you would.

Here is a package to make you feel better, with some mild biscuits and hard candies I purchased for you in Hainburg, along with my own ginger tea and honey. Please drink plenty of tea and water and get rest, and do not worry about writing me back until you feel better.

With great affection,
Mathilda

To my dearest Agnes:

How did you fare with the biscuits and candy? Did the ginger tea help? I hope you've been able to keep food down, poor thing. I think you must be very ill indeed, since it has been five days without any response. Here is another blanket I made for you. Stay warm!

This snowstorm is truly horrible, and if it weren't for that and my fear of annoying Oskar, I would have come down to see you already. Please write back when you can.

Your concerned friend,
Mathilda

Dear Agnes,

It has been a week and a half since I last saw you. Is anything amiss? I was in the garden gathering winter berries for a pie yesterday (yes, you've inspired me to try something other than cakes!) and I heard voices down the hill. Imagine my relief when I saw you with Oskar, looking perfectly well. I'm glad the tonic's effects did not linger, but I hope you haven't been troubled by anything. I suppose something has happened with Oskar's brother, or perhaps someone else in your family, to occupy your mind?

Please write to me soon. I will send over a berry pie tomorrow if it turns out all right.

Your friend,
Mathilda

Dear Agnes,

How did you like the berry pie? I hope whatever has been troubling you is over. It must have been a very bothersome family matter for you to not write back for so long. I'm glad we are nearing the end of February. That warm day we had was such a blessing. Perhaps if we have another one, you might be able to come up and have tea? We can sit in the garden, and Oskar is of course invited, though I feel certain he won't wish to come.

Please write back soon. I badly miss your company.

Your friend,

Mathilda

To Agnes:

I am not sure what to think. I have neither seen nor heard from you in over a month, and I am beginning to despise myself for the doubt I've had about you. I know in my heart that you are good and loyal, and you would never go back on your word or use me for my magic. I can only conclude that Oskar is preventing you from seeing my gifts and messages, or perhaps persuading you to ignore them.

Whatever the reason, my heart is breaking. I know our friendship means as much to you as it does to me, and I hope you will reconsider. I am glad that Hanau is taking to you and Oskar so well. Every time I look out of my gate, it seems you are entertaining a new guest for tea or supper. Was that Frau Werner herself the other day? Such an important person coming to call on you must have made Oskar very happy.

Please write, Agnes. At least send a little note if you are unable to see me.

Your friend,
Mathilda

5

"You look lovely this morning, Frau Heinrich," a neighbor called as Agnes strolled by. She waved in thanks at the woman, swinging her basket as she entered the crowded market.

It was the first week of April, and winter had begun to ebb into spring. Icicles still frosted the trees like fairy glass and the sun shone weakly upon the frozen earth, but there was a freshness in the air. Agnes breathed it in, feeling more invigorated than she had in a long time. She had been cooped up indoors for too long, and though she

and Oskar had frequently invited new acquaintances over for a meal—
many of whom brought presents of meat and pastries—even entertaining had grown tiresome.

Distractions don't last forever, Agnes reflected, then silenced that train
of thought. She had left the house to get her guilt off her mind, not
linger on it.

She took another deep, cleansing breath before stepping into Herr
Steiner's bakery, which was full of people. The shop took up the first
level of the Steiners' home. Rich, golden apple strudel and flaky, jam-
filled tarts covered one table, while another held buttery biscuits and
cookies of every kind. A counter ran alongside one wall, displaying
dozens of beautifully made cakes, and Agnes headed toward it as the
crowd dispersed. One of Herr Steiner's tall, dark-haired daughters
was carrying out a tray of piping-hot cinnamon cakes, fresh from the
oven. Agnes closed her eyes and inhaled, thinking how much it smelled
like Mathilda's house.

So much for not lingering on her guilt.

For one wild and fleeting moment, she considered buying a cinnamon cake to bring to Mathilda's house as a peace offering. They
could eat it in front of the fire with cups of lavender tea and the cat
dozing at their feet, and chat together as before. But Agnes knew, with
a tightening in her gut, that she would not be welcome there again,

not after coldly ignoring all of Mathilda's attempts to reach her. The kind gifts and notes had stopped coming in March, and she had not known whether to feel relieved or heartbroken. While they had arrived at regular intervals, she had been able to fool herself that Mathilda still cared, but their absence meant that she had, at last, understood Agnes's betrayal of her.

"Agnes! How wonderful to see you," trilled Katharina Braun, pushing past a group of women to stand beside her. "Beautiful day to be out, isn't it?"

"It is," Agnes said, forcing a smile. "Are you looking for a cake as well?"

"My mother taught me never to come to a party empty-handed. I suppose that's why half these people are here, looking for something to bring to the Bergmanns'. My money is on Frau Bauer buying that enormous rhubarb cake. She's from the city and they do love to show off."

Last week, Oskar had danced with joy at the invitation to the Bergmanns' Easter party. It was proof that he and Agnes had been welcomed as worthy, respectable people. Agnes had found it harder to be happy, imagining them all celebrating while Mathilda sat alone in her cottage.

"... but when they went up the hill, the witch was completely gone!"

Agnes's attention snapped back to Katharina. "I'm sorry, what?"

"My dear, where is your mind today?" the woman asked playfully. "You seem a hundred miles away. I asked if you saw the boys go past your cottage, and you nodded!"

"What boys? Could you repeat the story?"

"The Schmidt boys. They celebrated Franz's birthday yesterday, and one of them dared him to pay the witch a visit," Katharina explained. "They all came with him, of course, hoping to see her curse off his fingernails or some such nonsense. But when they went up there, the gates were open and the house was empty, like she had never been there at all."

Agnes's chest tightened. "She's gone?"

"Yes, and I hope for good. It's better that way, if you ask me," the woman said lightly, picking up a box of white sugar–dusted cookies. "No one wanted her here. She cast such a dark cloud over the whole town. Maybe now you and Oskar will get some *decent* neighbors... though who knows if anyone would want a house that's been occupied by a sorceress!"

Deep down, Agnes had known that betraying Mathilda would mean never seeing her again, but still the hollow ache of loss gnawed at her. Mathilda's disappearance felt odd and unfinished, like reading a book only to skip the final pages. A story without an end. Never again would Agnes read one of her charming notes or receive a kind and thoughtful gift from her.

"My dear, you *are* distracted today," Katharina scolded her, and too late, Agnes realized that the woman had asked her a question. "What's gotten into you?"

"I've been cooped up for too long, I think," Agnes said apologetically.

Katharina's eyes scanned her slowly from head to toe, then slid to Agnes's belly, and then she smiled like a cat that had gotten into a saucer of cream. "Well, well, so that's the reason. I no longer blame you, my dear," she said, laughing. "When were you going to tell me? Or were you planning to keep it a secret until you could no longer hide it, you sly thing?"

Agnes's heart seemed to stop beating. "What do you mean?" she croaked.

The woman patted her arm. "Give me a few months and I'll be able to tell you if it's a boy or a girl, based on how low you're carrying."

Agnes stared at her, speechless, feeling as though someone had poured a bucket of melted snow over her head. She pressed one hand over her belly, inside her open coat. "Can it be true?" she whispered, leaning against the counter for support. "How can you guess that?"

"I didn't guess. I'm a midwife, I know it for certain. I've tended to women in the family way for as long as you've been alive, and there's no hiding a babe on the way from me. But, my dear," Katharina added, her eyes wide, "don't tell me you didn't know?"

Agnes shook her head, her breath coming in gulps as she gazed down at her stomach. It was true that she hadn't bled for months, but after so many disappointments, she had taken it to be simply a peculiarity of her body. She had not allowed herself to hope.

"Can it be true?" she repeated, her eyes filling with tears as she thought of telling Oskar.

Katharina took her hand and squeezed it. "Congratulations, Agnes. I'm happy for you and Oskar. You've been delightful additions to our town, and I'm glad you will add a third."

The tears spilled down Agnes's face as she hugged the woman. How could she and Oskar have ever called the Brauns busybodies? They were wonderful, lovely people, particularly Katharina. "I hope you'll be one of the first people I introduce my baby to," she said, her voice trembling with emotion, and the midwife's smile split her face as Agnes rushed out of the bakery without buying anything she had intended to. She ran all the way home, and when she reached their cottage, she could hear her husband whistling as he fed the animals out back.

"Oskar!" she cried joyously. "I have to tell you . . ."

The rest of her sentence died in her throat when she saw the basket sitting at the gate.

It was made of pale, woven straw, with a frost-blue ribbon tied around its handle. A piece of blue-and-white-checkered flannel covered the gift inside, but Agnes could see a note with familiar handwriting peeking out from the folds. Her knees trembled as she bent to pick it up.

To my former neighbor:

I am well. I have gone elsewhere and will not trouble you again, knowing what a burden my friendship has been to you. I wish you had been the person I thought you were, but I see now that you are just like everyone else. To say I have been bitterly disappointed would not do justice to the heartbreak you caused me. I suppose I ought to thank you for reminding me why I should never trust anyone. I wonder if you meant to use me the whole time.

But it doesn't matter now. You have chosen to break your promise, and you can only hope that the consequences will be kind. It is out of my hands entirely.

In this basket, I enclose a gift I was making for you when I thought you were still my friend. I don't want it in my possession anymore.

Mathilda

Agnes pressed her fist against her mouth, her shoulders shaking with sobs as she read the note again. There were several splotches on the page where tears had marred the ink, and they hurt even more than the words. She imagined Mathilda weeping at her table as she wrote this last angry good-bye, while down the hill, she and Oskar went carelessly on with their lives.

Tears blurred her vision as she reached for what lay in the basket under the flannel. It was a beautiful baby girl's dress of blush-pink wool, embroidered with little yellow flowers.

"Back from market so early? I thought you'd be gone longer," Oskar said cheerily, coming around the side of the cottage. He stopped short at the sight of her. "What's wrong?"

But Agnes could not find her voice.

She held up the baby's dress from Mathilda, hoping it would do all the talking for her.

DECEMBER 1855. HEINRICH FARM, HANAU, GERMANY.

Elva slid out of bed and put on her slippers. Last month, for her seventh birthday, Mama and Papa had given her this little bedroom all to herself, with its pretty yellow curtains and a big window facing the barn and the river Main. She was glad she didn't have to share a room with her brothers anymore. Rayner, who was five, would hear her sneaking out and demand to come, too, and that would wake up little Cay, and then Mama would be upset. But Elva was a big girl now, so she could come and go whenever she liked...as long as her parents didn't know.

She crept down the corridor, moving noiselessly past the boys' room, and sat at the top of the staircase. The downstairs was bathed in cheery light, and she could hear the grown-ups talking and laughing. She lowered herself a few steps to catch a glimpse of the party and gasped.

How pretty the ladies looked! They wore festive dresses of ruby and green and deep gold, and the men looked nice, too, with their dark coats and groomed mustaches. But Mama looked the loveliest and Papa the handsomest, Elva thought, swelling with pride at the sight of them standing before the fireplace. Mama wore blue ribbons in her hair that matched Papa's sparkling eyes as he laughed at something Herr Steiner, the baker, was saying.

"A toast, Oskar!" someone called, and several other men voiced their agreement.

Papa raised his glass. "Dear friends and neighbors, thank you for joining Agnes and me on this final night of the year. We wish you good fortune ahead—as much good fortune as we have had. Eight years ago, we were penniless, with only a cottage, a cow, three goats, and each other." He looked at Mama, and she slipped her hand into his. "Now we have three children, a new home and farm, a few more cows and goats...and considerably less peace and quiet."

Everyone laughed.

"Don't forget the chickens and the horses, Papa!" Elva clapped her hands over her mouth as the adults laughed even harder, swiveling their heads to the staircase where she perched.

"Why aren't you in bed?" Mama exclaimed, but Papa grinned and held out his arms, so Elva ran right into them. He picked her up and kissed her, and she giggled as his whiskers, which were the same bright gold as her hair, tickled her.

"I want a sip of that, please," Elva told him, pointing at the amber liquid in his glass.

Papa shook his head. "Whiskey is a grown-up drink, my love. But you can hold it quietly for me while I finish my toast, all right?"

"All right." Elva felt proud in her father's arms, holding on to his glass as all the adults looked at her. Papa began to speak again, his deep voice rumbling against her shoulder, and she amused herself by looking at the guests through the whiskey. It turned them all funny shades of burnt orange and copper, like the autumn leaves she and Rayner loved to roll around in, and the glass made their faces look blurry and wobbly.

She held the drink closer, wrinkling her nose at the smell, and looked inside. She could see her own face in it. She blinked an eye, and so did her reflection. She blew a kiss, and so did the Elva in the glass. She wiggled her eyebrows, and as she did so, she noticed something funny about her reflection's chin. There was a dark spot that looked just like a little black horse.

As she watched, entranced, her reflection disappeared and in its place was Papa's barn. The horse wasn't one of Papa's, though, and it had been tied to the door of the goats' pen. Elva frowned, wondering what a strange horse was doing with her father's goats. The rope was just short enough that the animal couldn't reach a bale of hay stacked against the wall. It strained forward, pulling the rope taut, and Elva saw the door of the goats' pen begin to tremble. And then, all of a sudden, it burst open and the startled goats began running out!

"Papa!" Elva cried, sloshing the whiskey over her father's arm. "The goats are escaping!"

"What on earth...?" He set her down and took the glass away, wringing out the soaked fabric of his jacket into the fire.

"Someone must be falling asleep," Mama said quickly, and the guests chuckled.

"I wasn't dreaming, Mama!" Elva stamped her foot. Everything she saw always turned out to be right. Once, she had looked into a rain puddle and saw some naughty boys stealing their chickens, and it had happened a month later, exactly as she said. She had even seen Uncle Otto in her water basin, breaking his leg as he fell from the roof of his barn, and Mama and Papa had doubted her until a letter arrived later that week. "I saw it, honest! There's a big black horse in the goats' pen and it pulled the door open, and they're all getting out!"

Herr Steiner stopped laughing. He was a big, jolly man who always gave Elva an extra cookie when she and Mama went to his bakery. "Come to think of it, Oskar," he said ashamedly, "I did put Gunnar in with your goats. I came late and the other stalls were all taken. It might be worth looking in on them.... I'll go...."

"It's all right, Herr Steiner," Elva said. "You shouldn't have tied him to the door, though."

Mama and Papa both looked at Elva, their faces now stern, serious. She clung to Papa's leg, wondering if they were mad at her. Mama kept glancing at the guests like she was scared.

"I'll go with you," Papa told the baker, and they put on their warm wraps and went out.

"My daughter's bedroom faces the barn," Mama told the others in a bright voice that didn't sound like her own. "Isn't that right, darling? You must have seen it all happening from your window." She excused herself and swooped Elva up, hurrying upstairs with her.

"Mama, I *saw* it in the glass. I wasn't making it up!"

"Quiet, now. Don't wake the boys." Her mother set her down and knelt in front of her. "I believe you. But, my dear one, it's not right to see things this way."

"It's not?"

"No. People aren't supposed to know when something is about to happen. It's not normal to see the future." Her mother looked so scared and worried that Elva felt upset.

"I'm sorry, Mama," she said in a small voice. "I didn't know it was wrong."

Mama hugged her tight and kissed the top of her head. "It's not your fault, precious. I'm not angry with you. But if you ever see anything like that again," she said, pulling away a bit, "and other people are around, keep it to yourself until you can tell me or Papa privately. Don't tell anyone outside of the family, because it might scare them. Do you promise?"

"I promise."

"Now be my good girl and get back into bed. Can you do that for me?"

Elva padded away to her room, but as soon as Mama got downstairs, she heard Papa and Herr Steiner come back into the house. The baker returned to the party, and Mama and Papa stayed talking quietly by the stairs. Elva couldn't help it—she snuck down the corridor to listen.

"The animals are safe," her father said. "I told Hans she saw it from her window."

"That's what I told everyone else," Mama said, sounding relieved.

"I'm not sure he believed me. He kept asking how she knew where he had tied his horse, since the goats' pen isn't visible from the house." Papa sighed. "I should have known better than to give her my glass. I wasn't thinking."

There was a noise like Mama sucking air through her teeth. "This can't keep happening, Oskar. I feel as though bad luck has been following us for eight years, and this odd... *ability* of Elva's is just another thing to add to the list."

"We've had quite a bit of good luck, too," Papa pointed out.

"Always two good things, followed by one bad thing. Over and over and over." Elva heard the soft sound of Mama's slippered feet pacing. "*She* told me three is a powerful number. Maybe all magic comes in a pattern of threes, including its consequences."

"Agnes..."

"The day I found out I was having Elva, Honey was born," Mama said, and Elva's ears pricked up at the mention of their sweet goat. "And then a wind came out of nowhere and swept my washing into the trees. Every shirt and sheet lost when we couldn't afford to replace them."

Papa was silent as her feet continued pacing.

"The year our corn grew twice as tall as you," Mama went on, "you bought the horses for next to nothing, and then a blight killed our apple trees. The week Rayner was born, we had an enormous wheat harvest, and then all the bread I baked went bad within *three* hours.

Every time something good happens, I hold my breath, wondering what terrible occurrence will come next."

"I don't deny there has been a strange pattern, my dear, but it could be a coincidence."

"No. This... this *curse* is because of me. And it's my fault Elva is the way she is, not Mathilda's or anyone else's." There was a long pause. "I need to go find Mathilda. Perhaps she won't be too angry to listen."

"No. Absolutely not."

"But she's our chance to make Elva normal," Mama pleaded. "Even if she can't stop the rest of it, maybe she can make Elva just like any other little girl. We know she hasn't gone far, not with the signs up all over town warning people to stay away from the 'witch of the North Woods.'"

Elva clutched a fold of her nightdress, frozen where she stood. A trickle of fear crept like a spider down her back. Were Mama and Papa going to send her to a *witch*?

"You're not thinking clearly," Papa said. "You cut ties with her long ago, and no one would make the connection now. What if someone sees you visit her? After all these years, after how careful we've been to build up our respectability..."

"What if someone were to find out about Elva? All it takes is one evil gossip." Mama's dress rustled as she peered nervously into the other room at their guests. "I'm frightened, Oskar. It's so easy for someone to be accused of being a witch. Girls and women who are pretty, who are rich yet unmarried, who are passing through town, who hum songs the church doesn't like."

"Agnes, calm yourself. We won't let anything happen to Elva."

"I won't look for Mathilda if it upsets you, but at least promise me that if her path and mine should cross, you will support me in seeking her help. I don't want Elva to be different."

Papa sighed heavily. "I promise that we can ask her to make Elva normal if the opportunity arises, but that is all. *You* promised *me* you would end all association with her long ago, and I know you don't want our reputation sullied any more than I do. Come, we've been away too long. Let's get back to our guests."

Within moments, the grown-ups were all talking and laughing again, and Elva went slowly back to her room. It wasn't right, Mama had said. It wasn't normal for Elva to see things happening before they did. And now people might think she was a witch like that lady her parents mentioned, and no one would want to play with her or come to her house.

Elva's chin quivered. She had upset Mama and Papa. She didn't want to look at water ever again. She would try to close her eyes whenever she took a drink or washed her face or splashed in the rain with her brothers. That way, she wouldn't worry her parents, they wouldn't have to send her to the witch, and no one else would know she wasn't normal.

After all, she had promised Mama.

And as Mama always said, a promise was a promise.

APRIL 1865. BAUER FARM, HANAU, GERMANY.

Elva had never seen anything as pretty as the Bauers' barn decorated for the Easter party. Earlier that day, after church, Papa, Rayner, and Cay had gone over with the other men to clear the space for dancing. They had pushed the heavy barrels, firewood, and hay into the corners and dragged in tables and benches for the food. And then Frau Bauer and her three daughters had covered every surface with jars of wildflowers and tiny twinkling candles. As soon as the sun went down and the musicians began to play, the barn looked almost magical.

"Come on, Elva! Let's see if you can keep up!" cried Peter Bauer, as the fiddle sang over the harmonica, horn, and flute. He took Elva's hand and spun her into the crowd of men keeping rhythm with their feet and women twirling their colorful skirts to the melody.

Elva saw Mama and Papa sitting with the Bauers, all smiling broadly as they watched her and Peter dancing, and she tossed her head. Whatever their parents hoped, she and Peter thought of each other as siblings and would never marry. *Besides*, Elva thought, *I'm only sixteen. And there are* so *many other handsome young men to dance with!*

As soon as the song ended, Karl Bergmann asked her to dance. And then his older brother, Kurt, back from university and *oh, so sophisticated*, claimed the next set. Then Stefan gave her his hand, and after him came Anton and Daniel and Lukas and Georg.

She loved the way they watched her dance, her new blue-and-cream dress swirling around her. But she hadn't worn it for them, and she hadn't pinned starflowers all over her long, bright gold hair for them, either. It was for someone else, and he wasn't even here....

"Elva Heinrich," said Freida Bauer, when Elva finally sat down to catch her breath, "do you plan to keep all of the men to yourself tonight? I would hate you if you weren't so sweet."

Elva laughed. "And if I weren't your closest friend."

Freida reached over and carefully repinned one of the tiny white flowers in Elva's hair. "I see we're wearing Mama's best cream ribbons tonight. For whom, I wonder, hmm?"

"Hush!" Elva stole a glance at her parents, who were safely out of earshot. "It was all for nothing. I haven't even seen him all night."

"He *is* a farmhand. Maybe he's still out in the fields, working," Freida suggested. "Anyway, what do you want with Willem when all of these other good-looking young men have eyes only for you? Don't pretend to be modest. You're the prettiest girl here, and your papa has a thriving farm. All of the gossips are placing bets on who catches you."

"What about *you*?" Elva poked her lightly in the ribs. "This is *your* papa's party, and you're every bit as pretty. Karl Bergmann looked at you the whole time he danced with me."

"Liar!" Freida squealed, looking delighted.

"And here comes the sugar bread," Elva said slyly. Frau Steiner and Frau Bauer were carrying in a platter with a gigantic golden-brown loaf. "I hope your Karl gets the copper ring."

They put their arms around each other's waists and giggled. They weren't the only two to do so. All around the barn, every unmarried girl over fifteen blushed and whispered to friends and looked at one or two—or even three—prospective young men as the sugar bread arrived.

The special sugar bread made an appearance every Easter, no matter who hosted the barn dance. The women of the village all contributed eggs, sugar, flour, and butter to the making of the dough, and then the hostess would slip a little copper ring inside before she baked it. A large slice would be given to every unmarried young man at the party, and whoever found the ring won the right to kiss the girl of his choice.

"Silence, please!" Herr Bauer clapped his hands for attention. He had the same rosy cheeks and dark hair as his daughter, Freida, and his eyes shone like hers as his wife and a few other women began cutting into the bread. "Will all of the unmarried men please step forth?"

There was laughter, teasing, and some shoving as the young men gathered before their host. One by one, they accepted a slice of the sugar bread from Frau Bauer, and an air of tense anticipation hung over the room as they began eating.

Stefan, who stood not far from Elva, had the nerve to wink at her as he bit into his bread. She tried to give him her loftiest expression but collapsed into giggles when she met Freida's eyes. Stefan was bold and daring and handsome, and nothing scared him—last year he had nearly broken his neck trying to ride his father's most aggressive stallion. Every girl in Hanau had scratched her initials with his into the loving tree, the oak by the river Main that had sheltered generations of lovers, and Elva was sure he would *definitely* know how to kiss.

The only problem was, she had been hoping to save her first kiss for someone else—someone who, it seemed, still had yet to arrive.

The barn was silent . . . and then . . .

"Ha!" A big hand popped into the air—a hand that was attached to a very nice arm, tawny and thick with muscle. It waved a shiny copper ring for Herr and Frau Bauer to see, and the room exploded into piercing whistles and cheers. The man's back was turned to Elva, and through the crowd of hopefuls she could see only a gray work shirt stretched over broad shoulders. When the other young men moved away good-naturedly, leaving him alone in the middle of the room, she recognized the red-brown hair and the line of his square jaw. He turned in a slow circle, studying the guests, and his dark eyes gleamed with triumph when he found her. Elva's heart leaped.

"Willem Roth," Herr Bauer said, clapping him on the back. He faced the guests with the air of an auctioneer. "A worthy, honest, and hardworking young man. Eighteen years of age and a farmhand in my employ. Ladies, do I hear any starting bids?"

The barn roared with laughter and Willem's face turned pink, but he did not take his eyes from Elva. She didn't realize she had seized Freida's hand and was squeezing it with all her might until Freida gave a squeak.

"Well, Willem, you've found the copper ring and earned a kiss. Who will it be from?"

"Elva Heinrich," the young man said, his voice ringing throughout the barn.

People began clapping and hooting, and a few of the other girls murmured enviously as Elva, face hot, rose to her feet. She had dreamed of this moment since first meeting Willem, but now that it was here, she didn't know if she wanted it to happen in front of everyone in Hanau. In front of her *parents*. But Mama and Papa didn't seem bothered, and both were smiling.

It's just a kiss, she told herself, as her feet carried her across the room. *A silly tradition.*

Yet when Elva looked into Willem's kind eyes, everything faded away. The Bauers' barn, her parents, and the guests seemed to disappear, and all that was left was the two of them. She stood shyly before him, keeping an arm's length between them. He hadn't seemed quite so tall and imposing whenever they had chatted on the riverbank. She had to tip her head back to look at him, and the corners of his eyes crinkled at her when he saw the white starflowers, his favorite, in her hair.

"Hello," he whispered.

"Hello," Elva whispered back.

He reached out and took her right hand, and it was all she could do not to gasp at the touch of his skin. His hand was warm and callused as it slipped the copper ring onto her finger. Her heart thundered as he pulled her gently to him. They were closer than they had ever been before. The heat and the solidness of him made Elva feel giddy and faint. He smelled like hay and fresh air and sunshine. His eyes shone as he lowered his face a few inches above hers.

"May I kiss you?" he asked softly, for her ears alone.

"Yes, you may." Elva couldn't help laughing at his lovely, old-fashioned manners, and as she beamed up at him, he caught her mouth with his. As rough as his hands were with work, his lips were as soft as silk and tasted of the sugar bread he had just eaten.

And despite the whole town watching and her desire to show him she was self-possessed and mature, both of her traitorous knees buckled beneath her at once. She would have collapsed right there at his feet if his arm hadn't gone quickly around her waist.

Elva hid her face against his chest as the entire room erupted with laughter. She felt the deep rumble of Willem chuckling, too, as he kept his arm tightly around her.

"Now *that's* a kiss!" someone yelled.

"Come on, strike up a tune for Willem and Elva! We'll see if they dance as well as they kiss!" Herr Bauer cried, and the musicians began playing a lively song.

Elva relished the feeling of being in Willem's arms as he twirled her around. Other couples soon joined them, shielding them in their own little world. "I thought you weren't going to come tonight," she told him, trying to keep her gaze on his eyes. Her knees had already betrayed her; if she kept looking at his mouth, she didn't know what her lips might do.

"How could I not come, knowing you'd be here? I'd swim across the river if I had to." Willem lowered his lips to her ear, and the feel of his breath on her neck sent a delicious tingle down her spine. "Walk down to the water with me. I've a mind to practice that kiss again."

Her heart began to race again at once. "Now?" she asked, giggling.

"No time like the present," he said with a devilish wink, dancing her to the barn door.

They pushed through the crowd of dancers and slipped into the cool evening air. Elva hoped her parents hadn't noticed her leaving with Willem. A moonlight stroll on the night of the party was as much a tradition as sugar bread, judging by how many young couples were shyly holding hands and talking—or not talking much at all—in the shadows of trees, but Elva knew Mama and Papa wouldn't understand. They wanted her to have a chaperone at all times, even if it was just one of her brothers. She stifled a laugh, imagining Rayner's disgust if she asked him to join her and Willem on their romantic walk. Cay, the sweeter of the two boys, might agree more readily and perhaps even move apart to give her privacy.

"Are you cold?" Willem gazed at her, and all thoughts of her family faded at once. She loved the crinkles at the corners of his eyes and the slow curve of his smile, like a secret meant only for her. His arm brushed hers, solid and warm. "I can go back and get a shawl for you."

"I'm all right, thank you," she said, blushing when his eyes flickered to her lips. Her heart gave a tug of anticipation, wondering when he would kiss her again. She had never seen him at night, and never alone—they had always met in the sunshine with Rayner or Cay or Freida lingering nearby. In the shadows, Willem's face looked elegant and grown-up, far from the boy who had laughed and joked with her on the riverbank.

A starflower slipped from her hair as they walked, and he caught it before it could tumble to the ground. "I've loved these since I first saw them," he said, touching the fragile white petals. "It's because they only grow in Hanau, which reminds me of how my father always wanted to move here before he died." He glanced sideways at her. "When I saw these in your hair the first time we met, it felt like fate. The other farmhands always tease me for taking my lunch hour alone, but that day, I'm glad I did."

Elva's breath hitched when he gave her his warm, slow smile again. "It's been a whole year since we met," she said playfully. "Do you still remember which tree it was?"

They had reached the river at the end of the rough stone path. The water gleamed with the stars and the spring moon, like a dark blue ribbon embroidered with constellations. All along the riverbank, great oak trees stretched their branches toward the sky and one another, creating a soft canopy of shadows. Elva saw the famous loving tree about a hundred yards to the left, tucked in a blanket of wildflowers, but Willem moved confidently to the graceful willow nearest them.

"I was in this tree, dreaming. When I opened my eyes, you were sitting by the trunk."

"Freida was there, too," she pointed out.

"I didn't see anyone but you. You wore a blue-and-white dress like that one, with your hair all over your shoulders like sunshine. I thought I had pulled you right out of my dreams."

Elva ducked her head shyly. She remembered everything about that bright April afternoon: the warm tree at her back, the wildflower garlands she had woven, and the handsome farmhand who had jumped down from the branches to talk to her. Other young men had never dared speak to her without her father's permission, but this one had been new to Hanau and hadn't known any better, and he had been funny and charming and kind.

"I couldn't stop looking at you," Willem said softly, "just like I can't stop looking at you now. Elva..."

She couldn't remember crossing the short distance between them. But in a split second, the whole universe became Willem's arms wrapped tightly around her and his gentle lips moving on hers. She supposed she had flung herself at him and ought to be embarrassed, but it was dark and the moon was shining and a fragrant spring wind blew, and he didn't seem to mind one bit. They gasped for breath through their noses, not wanting to break the kiss. It might have lasted for a few minutes or an eternity, for all she knew.

Finally, Willem pulled away. "I've wanted to do that for a whole year."

"Me too," Elva confessed, thrilling at his soft laugh. "I'm glad you came to Hanau."

"It was the first place I thought to look for work when my parents passed away. I didn't know I'd find you, too." Willem hugged her close to him and leaned back against the trunk of the sheltering willow.

Elva listened to the comforting thump of his heart. "Tell me about your parents."

"Papa was a blacksmith. A hardworking one, but all of our money went toward Mama's medicine. She was sick for a long time, and when she died, Papa seemed to forget how to live."

"He must have loved her very much."

"More than anything. When he died, too, I told myself I would fight to have a good life. I would never starve or go cold or see a loved one suffer without medicine again. Herr Bauer says I work harder than any of his farmhands, and it's because I know what it is to be hungry."

"I think that makes you brave, Willem Roth," Elva told him, her heart swelling with pity and admiration. "And I think your mama and papa would be proud of you."

He bent to kiss her again, and as he did so, they heard a rustling noise and turned to see a piece of paper nailed to the trunk of the tree. It was a notice for yet another missing child, the latest of several who had been disappearing from Hanau and the surrounding towns for years.

"This one's only ten. One year younger than Cay," Elva said sadly. "His poor parents."

"Do you know the family?"

She shook her head. "They must live on the other side of the river. Mama and Papa had a cottage there once when I was just a baby." She studied the drawing of the boy, with his big eyes and button nose. "It says this boy was last seen near the North Woods."

"What is it about that place?" Willem asked, shaking his head. "So many children vanish there. Why are they going in to begin with?"

"Because it's big and beautiful and perfect for hide-and-seek," Elva said. "Mama and Papa took us on a picnic there long ago and Cay keeps begging to go back, but they're afraid he'll go missing, too. Remember poor Ben Schmidt?"

Willem shook his head.

"It must have been before you came to Hanau. He was an old man who wandered out of the woods one day, claiming that he had been missing for over sixty years. Apparently, he had gone in to pick mushrooms for his mother and never found his way back out until now."

"It sounds like one of the Grimms' tales." Willem glanced at the piece of paper again. "For a moment, I thought that was another notice about the witch. They're nailed up everywhere and Herr Bauer hates them. He's been making us remove them from his trees and fences."

"Mama hates them, too." Elva thought of the day she and her mother had passed a fence covered with dire warnings—"Stay Away!" and "Avoid the North Woods or Perish!"—and drawings of a crone with soulless black eyes. Elva had never seen her gentle mother so furious. Neighbors whispered for weeks afterward about sweet-tempered Agnes Heinrich ripping the notices to shreds. *It's vicious, the gossip people dream up about those who are different*, she had seethed to Elva. *Promise me you'll never be so unkind.*

"Maybe it's true, what the notices say," Willem suggested. "The witch *does* live in the North Woods. She could be the one taking all of these missing children."

"What on earth makes you say that?" Elva asked, taken aback.

"I don't know. I guess a lonely hag would be the most likely culprit, wouldn't she?"

Stunned, she freed herself from his arms. "You can't say things like that without proof. You can't just accuse a woman of kidnapping simply because there's been awful talk about her."

He stared at her in astonishment. "Elva, everyone says she's evil, and the North Woods are on that side of Hanau. I was just putting two and two together."

The breeze no longer felt soothing, but chilling with the lingering touch of winter, and Elva wrapped her arms tightly around herself. "Mama says gossip is the work of the devil," she said. "It's beneath you, Willem. I thought you knew better."

"I'm sorry," he said contritely. "I was only repeating what the other farmhands say."

Elva turned away, thinking again of the tears in Mama's eyes and the torn-up notices in her hands. "I wish you wouldn't. It's cruel," she said, and found that she couldn't look at Willem. She walked to the edge of the river and looked at the moon's reflection, wondering if she had ruined everything between them. But something about the way he had so freely shared the gossip irked her.

"Elva, I'm sorry," Willem said again, and his remorse sounded genuine. "It was horrible of me to make such an accusation, even as a joke. I'm a fool."

Elva caught sight of his reflection in the water, wringing his hands, and it made her smile. She opened her mouth to say that she would forgive him if he never showed such unkindness again, when something impossible caught her eye in the dark river: ripples of colors and a face she knew well. Everything around her—the star-dappled sky, the willows swaying in the wind, Willem begging for her forgiveness— blurred as the vision in the water came into focus. *Oh no,* she thought, panicking. For ten years, she had tried her hardest to avoid looking into even a glass of water and had pushed away any images that had danced around the periphery of her vision. But *this* scene was so bright, she couldn't tear her eyes away from it.

She saw a sunny day, and a young man with reddish-brown hair sitting in a rowboat on the Main with his fishing line trailing lazily in its wake. "Willem," she breathed, watching as he adjusted the hat on his head. And then he gave a sudden start and sat bolt upright in the boat, frantically reeling in his line. Elva saw the tip of an enormous fish's head break the surface of the water. A wild grin spread over Willem's face, and Elva clasped her hands together excitedly.

The line grew shorter and shorter in his white-knuckled hands, and then the fish burst out of the river, landing in the rowboat with incredible force and soaking Willem's shirt. But he didn't seem to notice—he was staring, slack-jawed, at what he had just caught. It was a fish half as long as the boat, with violet fins and scales of a whole palette of colors: the cornflower blue of the sky, the deep plum of violets, and the lush green of underwater plants.

It was beautiful, like a rainbow.

"Elva! What's beautiful like a rainbow?" a worried voice demanded in her ear. Someone's hand shook her shoulder. "What are you talking about?"

Elva blinked, and the vision was gone. The river reflected only the night sky, and beside her stood Willem himself, looking at her with huge, concerned eyes.

"Did you see something in the river?" he said slowly, studying her.

Her stomach dropped. All these years, she had been so careful not to give anyone an inkling about her strange ability, and now she had lapsed in front of the one person she wanted, more than anything, to like and respect her. "No, of course not," she fibbed. "I just remembered a dream I'd had about you last night. You were on the river, and being here made me think of it."

A twinkle came into Willem's eye. "You're having dreams about me?" he teased. "What were we doing in it?"

"*I* wasn't in it," Elva said, blushing. "Just you. You were in a boat on a sunny day, and you caught an enormous fish." She described its massive size and lovely colorful scales to him.

"You're talking about the Blue Mermaid of the Main," Willem said in amazement.

"The Blue Mermaid?"

"It's a fish of local legend," he said, his eyes darting to the calm surface of the river and then back to her. "They say it's nearly as long as a grown man and only appears on a warm day after a crescent moon. Herr Bauer jokes that any farmhand who catches the Blue Mermaid will receive a pay raise, because it's supposed to bring good luck. You dreamed about me catching it?"

"I must have heard Papa talking about it," Elva said faintly, leaning against the willow tree. She had come dangerously close to revealing her secret. If Willem ever found out, it would be the end of them, forever. He would never bring her flowers or dance with her again.

His arms enveloped her. "Please don't be angry with me anymore. I'm sorry for saying that about the woman in the North Woods. I won't listen to the farmhands' gossip ever again."

He looked so earnest and apologetic that Elva couldn't help smiling. She stood on her tiptoes and kissed him fiercely, her heart full of him. But though she tried to lose herself again in the feel of his lips and his warm arms, her mind was still on the vision of the Blue Mermaid. She didn't know how she would explain it if her "dream" happened to come true. *Maybe it won't this time*, she thought desperately. *Maybe it will be my first wrong prediction.*

She could only hope.

8

"**I** hate to say this, but that's not how fish work." Rayner crossed his arms in an uncanny imitation of their father as he looked down at his siblings. Elva and Cay were sitting at the big oak table in the parlor, stitching one of Elva's skirts. "What on earth would they do with wings?"

"Fly, of course," Cay said, as though it were utterly obvious.

"Fish *swim*." Rayner leveled a look at him that would have made Papa proud. Even when he wasn't trying to emulate him, Rayner was a perfect fourteen-year-old copy of Oskar Heinrich, right down to the blue eyes and the beginnings of a beard. "Birds fly. That's how nature works."

"Well, we're not trying to show how nature works. We're *imagining*, like Mama says," Cay said, as he went on embroidering his fish's elaborate wings. They were jagged at the ends, like a bat's, and Elva smiled, knowing he had been inspired by the natural history book he had just devoured. If there was anything eleven-year-old Cay liked better than trying new things, it was reading all of the volumes in Mama's library.

"Imagining," Rayner muttered. Neither he nor Papa had ever understood Cay, who took up any hobby from sewing to baking to riding with equal alacrity, and had once caught a terrible cold sleeping outdoors to study field mice. "Anyway, you shouldn't be sewing. That's for g—"

"Shouldn't you be helping Papa?" Elva snapped, looking up from the fish she herself was embroidering with violet thread. "If Cay wants to help me sew my skirt, that's his business." Cay grinned at her. Rayner shrugged helplessly at the pair of them but left without further argument.

Elva smoothed out the folds of the skirt. "This is turning out nicely! I think I might wear it to Freida's birthday supper next week." Along with Elva and Mama, Freida Bauer was one of the few people who supported Cay's interest in embroidery. The last time she had come to their house, she had helped him stitch a fantastical purple horse with duck feet instead of hooves.

"I like Freida. She's nice to me. Is that the Blue Mermaid you're sewing?" Cay asked knowingly. He was the only one Elva dared to confide in about her visions. He knew how hard it had always been for her to resist looking at them whenever she did things like bathe, drink water, or help Mama with the washing. But unlike their parents, he found her ability interesting instead of frightening.

"Yes. I can't stop thinking about how close Willem came to finding out about me," Elva said, sighing. "I should have been more careful, but the vision appeared so suddenly."

"He didn't find out, though," Cay reassured her, putting the finishing touches on his fish and moving on to a unicorn. "And he believed you when you said it was a dream. Willem's all right." He paused, then looked up at her. "Except didn't he tell you the woman in the North Woods was kidnapping those children?"

"He was just repeating gossip." Elva frowned. "It's so easy for people to spread rumors. Just because that woman lives alone, everyone makes up stories about her. And children have gone missing in the woods for years and years; there's always someone different to blame."

Two years ago, a young woman had been driven out of Hanau after a pair of missing twins turned up at her cottage. She had been accused of kidnapping, and no matter how much the twins argued in her defense, no one had believed them. She had been forced to leave forever. Before that, it had been a mother and daughter, skillful healers whom the town had turned against because they had saved too many lives, thereby sparking accusations of witchcraft.

Elva shuddered at the thought of Hanau finding out about her visions. For more than a decade, she had lived with the shameful secret of being strange and different. She glanced up to see Cay's keen blue eyes on her. "Now that you've finished reading that natural history book, what will you study next?" she asked brightly, deciding it was high time for a change of subject.

"Fairy tales," Cay said at once. "I want to study where they came from. The Grimms had a theory that some magical objects actually do exist, and I want to hunt for one."

"Which one? A spinning wheel? Seven-league boots?"

"No. A wishing well."

Elva laughed at how typical it was of Cay to be fascinated by anything related to water—ironic, considering how hard she tried to avoid water herself. He had a knack for finding hidden streams and forgotten creeks; he had even discovered an old sinkhole once that the town council had marked upon the official map of Hanau. Mama called him her lucky charm and often joked that if there was ever a drought, she would simply set him loose.

"I'm sure if a wishing well exists, you'll be the one to find it," Elva told him.

Cay grinned, then looked down at his spool of red thread. "This isn't the right shade for my unicorn's mane. It's too orange. Do you think Mama has anything darker, like ruby?"

"Let's go see." Elva led the way to the sunny nook where their mother stored keepsakes and sewing supplies, including bolts of fabric, ribbons, yarn, and other odds and ends.

Cay climbed the short ladder and reached for the basket on the top shelf, which contained Mama's needles and threads. In his enthusiasm, he knocked some books onto the floor.

"Be careful!" Elva urged him.

"Oh, look, there was something behind those books," he said, not listening to her at all. He pulled out a little wooden box painted with autumn leaves. When he opened the lid, they saw bundles of yellowed letters tied together with frost-blue ribbon.

"Cay, don't!" Elva scolded, as her brother eagerly pulled the first letter from the bundle. "What if they're love letters or something?"

"They're signed *Mathilda*. Who's Mathilda?" he asked, still not listening to her. Ever the voracious reader, he had already begun skimming the first paragraph. "Oh, she's a neighbor who lived next door to Mama and Papa. *Little cottage* . . . What cottage is she talking about?"

Elva's curiosity was aroused at once. Mama had always been reluctant to talk about their early days in Hanau. "It's the first home they bought before we were born," she explained. "Across the bridge on the far side of town. They had me there but moved a year later." Against her own judgment, she slipped the second letter out of the bundle. "Here's something about Honey!"

Honey was an old goat that had been with them for as long as Elva could remember. When she died a few years ago, Cay had held an elaborate funeral that he insisted the whole family attend. "What does it say about her?" he asked eagerly, taking the note Elva gave him. "Oh, I think this lady Mathilda was the one who named Honey."

"She made sweaters for Mama and Papa once," Elva said, glancing over the other letters. "And Mama made sourdough bread for her in return. They were friends."

"Here's one where she tells Mama she'd be a good mother." Cay nodded his approval. "She was right. And it looks like she liked the goat cheese Mama gave her."

"I wonder why Mama never talks about her. Maybe she moved away." Elva scanned the dates as they moved through the bundle of letters. "They started writing to each other in 1847, the year before I was born. When is the last one dated?"

He located the letter at the bottom of the pile. "The beginning of

1848," he said, and as he scanned the message, his face grew serious. "It looks like they stopped being friends. She writes that . . . that Mama wasn't the person she thought she was."

"Why? What happened?" Elva asked, stunned.

"She says something about magic in here. I think Mathilda did magic," Cay said, looking troubled. He passed her the letter and there was no denying that he was right, after Elva read the neat script several times. "Papa didn't like her, which explains why we've never heard of her. He doesn't even like it when people talk about that woman in the North Woods."

Elva froze. "Their old cottage wasn't far from the North Woods. What if that woman *is* Mathilda? If they were friends once, that would explain why Mama was upset about the notices."

Cay looked doubtful. "I don't know if Mama would associate with a witch. You know how Papa gets. . . . But maybe they didn't know about her at first." He paused, his eyes widening. "If that woman *is* Mathilda, do you think she could help me with my fairy tale research?"

"Cay," Elva groaned.

"What?" he asked defensively. "She lives in the North Woods, and there are all kinds of strange stories about that place. We could ask her about the family curse, too."

They had long found it strange that their mother was so superstitious about the number three, given how practical she was otherwise.

But every time something good happened to their family, she believed it would be followed by another stroke of good luck and then something *awful*. And more often than not, it was. Even Papa couldn't explain why the pattern had happened over and over through the years, and they had all taken to calling it the family curse. Last year, Mama had barely slept after Rayner found a lost pregnant ewe that belonged to no one, and Papa had sold his famous apples for more money than he ever had before. "Two good things. Something bad is coming next," she had said, making them all nervous, and then she had broken her wrist slipping in the rain.

"I'm not sure even witches can do anything about bad luck," Elva said absentmindedly, flipping through the letters. Her mother had sounded so young, hopeful, and trusting, and Mathilda kind and caring. What had happened between the two of them to end it all, and on such bad terms, as Mathilda's final message seemed to imply?

They heard a door close somewhere in the house, and it suddenly struck Elva that Mama might not have wanted them to know about Mathilda. Quickly, she and Cay stuffed the letters back into the wooden box and replaced it on the shelf behind the books. No sooner had they taken their spots at the table again than Agnes Heinrich swept into the room.

"Come outside," their mother said merrily, her cheeks rosy. "It's an incredible sight."

"What is, Mama?" Elva asked, but their mother only chuckled and led them out to the front of the house. A group of men stood talking and laughing with Papa and Rayner, and Elva spotted Herr Bauer and a few of his farmhands. Willem was standing beside a big red wheelbarrow covered with a cloth, looking as happy and excited as any of them.

"Oh, good, everyone's here," Herr Bauer said, smiling at Elva and Cay. "Come and see our good fortune. Or should I say, *Willem's* good fortune!"

Elva's stomach lurched at the sight of Willem's shirt, which was soaked with water. She already knew what she would see as Willem swept off the cloth with a dramatic flourish: a beautiful fish so large that its head and tail dangled over either side of the wheelbarrow. Its scales glimmered cerulean and sea-foam green and lilac. All it needed to be a storybook mermaid was the face of a beautiful woman and long turquoise hair twisted with pearls. Willem's eyes met Elva's with joyful disbelief, but she shook her head, silently pleading with him not to say anything about the "dream" in front of everyone. To her relief, he seemed to understand.

"The Blue Mermaid!" Cay cried, glancing at Elva.

Papa patted his shoulder. "Willem caught it this afternoon. Isn't it glorious?"

"It shimmers so," Mama said. "I thought it was only a legend."

"You and the rest of Hanau, my dear lady," Herr Bauer said brightly. "We joked about it for years but never believed it would actually be caught. And by Willem, the lucky rascal!"

Elva met Willem's eyes again, and as the men said good-bye and turned to go back to their work, he mouthed, *Walk with me.* "May I go with them as far as the gate? I want to study the fish a bit more," Elva said. Her parents agreed, and soon she found herself walking beside Willem and the wheelbarrow, wondering what to say.

She kept her eyes trained on her shoes. "I'm happy for you. Imagine catching the Blue Mermaid...."

"It happened just as you dreamed. Do all of your dreams have the habit of coming true?"

"It was a coincidence," she said quietly, but Willem stopped in his tracks.

"Then why did you look at me with so much fear just now? You shook your head so I wouldn't say anything in front of the others. If it *had* been a coincidence, we would have laughed about it." A long silence passed. "I think you *knew* for sure I would catch the Blue Mermaid."

To Elva's horror, her eyes filled with tears. Her heart beat a frantic rhythm. Here it was, the moment she would lose Willem forever. No one as wonderful as he was would ever associate with someone like her, a girl with a terrible secret. She waited for him to say as much, to bid her good-bye.

"Please don't cry," he said, his face now etched with distress. "I swear I haven't told anyone. Though I must admit I don't know many people who can predict things before they happen."

Elva bit her lip. Telling him the truth would be a relief, a way to share a part of herself. And she felt sure he would keep it a secret, even if he didn't like her anymore because of it. But doing so would mean betraying her family and breaking her vow to Mama.

She looked up at him, expecting to see fear or judgment on his face, and yet there was only curiosity. "You must think I'm mad," she whispered.

"No. Not one bit. Please...tell me."

The kindness in his eyes broke through her resolve. She sighed, hugging her arms close to her, despite the warm spring air. "Ever since I was little, I've seen things before they happened," she said softly. "Always in water—my uncle breaking a leg, Papa's goats escaping, my brother finding an injured rabbit. But as I grew up, I did my best to make the visions stop. I didn't want anyone to be afraid of me, so I tried not to look. The night of the Easter party, I was careless. I glanced at the river before remembering what might happen if I did."

"And it's all come true? Everything you've seen?"

She nodded, holding her breath.

"Elva, that's amazing," Willem declared. "You saw that I was going to catch the Blue Mermaid, and I did. Imagine if Herr Bauer knew I was always destined to be the one to do it!"

"No!" Elva cried. "No one can know about this. I've kept this secret for so long, and I promised Mama and Papa I wouldn't tell anyone. They're worried I'll be called a witch."

"I'd like to see people try," he said hotly. "What you have is a gift, and it does no harm."

She blinked at him. "You think so?"

"Of course! Ever since the Easter party, I've been borrowing Herr Bauer's fishing rods and sitting out on the river. I never imagined catching the Blue Mermaid before, but I thought I might as well give it a try. You encouraged me, don't you see? *You're* my good luck."

Elva could have kissed him right then and there, though they were still within view of the others. She settled for taking his hands in hers, and the warmth in his eyes was almost as good as a kiss. "And you really don't mind that I'm . . . odd?" she asked.

"You are not odd." Willem squeezed her hands. "You're beautiful and strong and kind. I like everything about you, Elva Heinrich, and it's going to take a lot more than that to scare me off. And today, I feel like *almost* the luckiest man in Hanau."

"Almost?"

"I have a roof over my head and an employer I like, and I have just caught the rarest fish in the history of this town. There is only one more thing I would ask to be truly happy." Willem ducked his head, his cheeks pink. "I'll need to speak to your father about it, of course. . . ."

Elva's stomach gave another lurch, but this time it was a pleasant, swooping feeling.

"I know you're only sixteen," he said quickly.

"Turning seventeen in November," she pointed out, and he laughed.

"And I need time, maybe two or three years, to earn money. I want to build a cottage with a dog lying by the fire and curtains at the windows. How would you like that, my dear one?"

Elva's cheeks flamed as he looked shyly at her. She kept her eyes down, too overwhelmed with joy to speak. She felt like spinning in giddy circles right where she stood.

"Don't answer me now," Willem said gently. "Just think about it. I won't ask your papa until I have enough savings to take proper care of you." He bent his head close to hers but seemed to remember that they weren't alone and cleared his throat, taking a step away. "I should get back. Herr Bauer wants me to show off the fish to all of the neighboring farms."

"I'll think about what you said," Elva told him, and he beamed. He kept his eyes on her as he walked away, turning back several times to wave good-bye. When he was just a speck in the distance, Elva placed her hands on her burning face and laughed. Willem knew her secret, and not only did he still care, but he also wanted to marry her! He wanted her to share her life with him. He loved her for exactly who she was, and he would wait patiently for years to have her. Elva pictured sitting with him by the fire at night, in their own home, talking together the way she loved to see Mama and Papa do on cold winter evenings.

Willem might have caught the Blue Mermaid, but *she* was the lucky one.

She twirled as she entered her house and heard Papa's affectionate laugh. He looked so kind that Elva came close to kiss his whiskered cheek. There was something sweet and almost sad about the way he looked at her.

"Come in here for a moment," he said. "Mama and I would like to talk to you."

"What is it?" she asked, but he simply led her into the parlor, where Mama sat studying the skirt Elva and Cay had embroidered. "Is anything wrong?"

"No, darling," Mama reassured her. "We only wanted to tell you how proud we are of you. You're everything we hoped you would be, and more. I suppose I still thought of you as my little girl up until the night of the Easter dance. We looked up and suddenly you were a woman."

They gazed at her fondly, and Elva felt a rush of love for them both.

"You and Willem Roth make a handsome couple," Papa said, clearing his throat. "Bauer says he's a nice, hardworking boy, and his parents were good people, though penniless. They died of consumption, one after the other. As you can tell," he added sheepishly, "I've taken the liberty of finding out more about him."

Elva's cheeks heated. "Why, Papa?"

"We've noticed for a while now that Willem has taken a special liking to you. I despised him for it at first," Papa said, and Mama swatted him on the shoulder. "But your mother encouraged me to get to know him better, and I'm glad I did. I don't think anyone will ever be worthy of you, my Elva, but Willem comes close. He hasn't spoken to me formally yet, though he has hinted, and seeing you together just now ... well, I'd be happy to see you wed him when the time comes," he added gruffly, and tears sprang to Elva's eyes once more.

"Do you know what this means?" Mama asked, looking wide-eyed at Papa. "Three wonderful things have happened. Your mare gave birth to twins, the weather has been perfect for our corn and berries, and soon our Elva will be betrothed."

"Can this be?" Papa teased. "Has the pattern been broken at last?"

"I think it must. It *has* been more than seventeen years, so perhaps ..."

"More than seventeen years?" Elva repeated, the old letters springing to mind. "Since what, Mama?"

But her mother shook her head. "Never you mind, love. I am happy for you and Willem. But remember what Papa said: We'll be glad to see you marry him *when* the time comes," she added significantly. "You are only sixteen and must not think of marrying for at least two years."

"Yes, I know, Mama."

"And Willem will need to work for a few more years before he can afford a home."

"We know that," Elva said, some of her joy giving way to exasperation. So much for thinking of her as a *woman*; in the span of a few breaths, her mother had shown that she still thought of Elva as a careless child. "We're both happy to wait for two or three more years."

"And as for your . . . issue with water." Mama hesitated, and Papa froze, looking shocked that she had brought up the subject. "You've done well to hide it all these years, and I would normally advise complete honesty with one's husband, but I don't think you need to tell Willem about it. It will have no bearing on your marriage."

Elva bit the inside of her cheek, wondering what they would say if she told them that Willem already knew and didn't care. He would be *her* husband, wouldn't he? And it would be *her* life to share with him alone, just as it was *her* secret to reveal or keep.

"Go on the way you always have," Mama instructed her. "Willem doesn't need to know."

"Well, then!" Papa said hastily. "I'm glad that's been settled. Now, moving on to the matter of where they will live, I'm happy to give them some land. I've chosen the perfect spot."

"Oskar, you don't mean that area in the south fields?" Mama asked, surprised. "Didn't we agree that it's too hilly to build a house? And it's so bare. Elva likes trees."

"Elva will like this plot," Papa assured her. "Besides, Willem can always plant some trees. I have seedlings in mind for him already, and the type of lumber for the new cottage, too."

Elva sat listening to them discuss her future as though she wasn't even there, as if they could plan every detail of her life...and hide the ones they did not approve of. She had thought of her ability as something shameful because it scared them, but now she realized it was as Willem said: Her visions did no harm to anyone. In fact, they were helpful and had even encouraged him to try catching the Blue Mermaid. What if, all this time, she could have been using her powers to quell her family's bad luck?

Perhaps it was time she made her own decisions.

Perhaps it was time to *use* her ability instead of pretending she didn't have it. Mama and Papa wouldn't have to know, and she might even see a glimpse of her future with Willem. Her breath caught at the thought of looking straight into her basin instead of closing her eyes. But it was long past time to access the power she had been given.

And now, Elva thought, *I will decide to do it for myself.*

9

Later that night, when everyone had gone to bed, Elva set her basin on the floor. She knelt beside it, wiping her clammy hands on her nightgown, and tried to find her determination again. *The visions are mine to do with as I like*, she told herself. Of course she was nervous. Of course it felt wrong, because she had been taught to think that way. She hadn't dared to look into a glass of water for ten years, and now she was about to call forth her visions on purpose.

Elva took a few deep breaths, then looked right into the water.

She saw her reflection: a round, lightly freckled face, with the wide blue eyes and dimples she shared with Mama and Cay. She tucked a strand of blond hair behind her ear, feeling self-conscious, as though someone might be watching her clumsy attempt. She fidgeted, imagining what might happen if Mama came in and saw what she was up to. Why wasn't anything happening?

The vision of Willem catching the Blue Mermaid had come so easily, without her even trying. Perhaps that was the trick; perhaps she was trying too hard. She exhaled and allowed her eyes to unfocus slightly, and as soon as she did so, an image materialized in the water.

It was the bundle of letters written by Mama and Mathilda, bound by a pale blue ribbon. Mathilda's handwriting stood out sharp and elegant against the clean white paper. And then there was a burst of light, in which a hot white symbol blazed into Elva's eyes. She thought it looked like a willow tree, but before she could study it, a new vision appeared.

This time, she saw Cay curled up on the window seat with an enormous book. "Look," he said, his voice as clear as though he was in the room with her, "a story about wishing wells."

The tree symbol blazed again, and then Elva saw herself crouching on the grass by a gray stone well, surrounded by trees. The forest? She leaned closer to the basin of water, trying to see what it was that had captured her attention in the vision, but before she could, the willow tree symbol blinded her once more and the image changed.

She saw her parents' fields and orchard beneath an angry night sky that swirled with clouds. It was so realistic Elva could feel the bone-chilling wind raking through her hair and smell the impending rain. A fiery spark of light erupted in the heavens, and the trees shook with the fury of the storm. Rain poured down as branches snapped, crops were torn up, and the barn became a whirling wreckage of splintered wood, flung all over the devastated farmland.

"No," Elva whispered, riveted by the awful scene. "This can't be."

The *Farmers' Almanac* had predicted a dry season, but even if Papa hadn't taught her how to read it, Elva thought she would still sense something unnatural and deeply *wrong* about this storm. There was so much rain, it looked like the river had crept up and swallowed all of Hanau. Lightning cracked the sky again, illuminating the ruined barn, and Elva felt certain that such damage would have killed some of the animals inside. It was the type of disaster that would strip Mama and Papa of almost everything they had worked for over the past decade.

Elva fell back, dizzy and panting, and the trance was broken. Her body trembled with cold and nausea. She closed her eyes to get the room to stop spinning, and behind her lids she could still see the strange tree symbol, burning like a white-hot brand. After a moment, she got shakily to her feet, averting her gaze from the basin of water as she paced beside her bed.

"What will I do?" she asked in despair. "What *can* I do?"

She knew from experience that her visions always came to pass, which meant there was no doubt this storm would come. What a terrible disaster...almost like a punishment. *Or a curse*, Elva thought, stopping in her tracks. Just that afternoon, Mama had been so happy and hopeful that the odd pattern of bad luck that had pursued them had been broken.

Elva stared out at the calm night sky. Over the years, she'd had the sense that Mama was holding her breath, waiting to see what would happen to even out any good fortune. Perhaps this awful storm was it. And if so, it would be Elva's duty to warn them—except then they would know that she had gone against their wishes and broken her promise to bury her powers.

She groaned, frustrated. Even now, when she could help her parents prepare for the worst, she was worried about having disobeyed them.

Her mind raced as she sank onto her bed.

If she told Freida, it would only frighten her, and the girl couldn't keep a secret to save her life. Telling Rayner was out of the question, because he would go straight to Papa, and she didn't want to burden Cay with this knowledge. As for Willem, who loved her, such an evil vision might even change his mind. Predicting the Blue Mermaid had been one thing, but seeing such a catastrophe was quite another.

There was no one she could confide in. No one who could help.

She rested her head on her knees, thinking hard. And in the whirl of her frantic thoughts came a single image: Mama's secret letters tied up with blue ribbon, each paper marked with a flowing signature. *Your friend, Mathilda.*

Elva lifted her face.

Mathilda might just be the rumored witch of the North Woods, the woman hated and feared by all of Hanau, including Papa himself. And yet Mama had secretly kept her letters all of these years. If anyone knew anything about being different, it would be Mathilda.

"Yes," Elva whispered.

Mathilda had once cared about Mama, and though it had ended long ago, she might just be willing to help the daughter of her former friend. It was worth a try to venture into the North Woods and find her, if she really was the witch. If she turned Elva away, Elva would be no worse off than she was right now.

And if she didn't turn her away, together they might figure out what to do about this awful storm . . . and stop it from happening.

After breakfast the next morning, Elva attacked her chores with an energy that impressed even Rayner. "What has gotten into you?" he asked, wiping his forehead. "You've cleaned out more stalls in an hour than I have all week."

"I want to finish early so I can go stitch my skirt," Elva lied, and as expected, the mention of sewing bored him at once. He went to get water for the horses as she continued raking out the stables and putting in fresh, clean straw. Her hands were stinging on the pitchfork by the time she finished, and she took a moment to help Cay, who was struggling under the weight of a large bucket of feed. Together they distributed the food, then led the horses back in and brushed their coats as the animals fed. "When we're done, I have to go on an errand for Freida," she told Cay, with a jolt of guilt, knowing she was using his fondness of Freida to her advantage. "It's something to do with her young man, and she doesn't want her mother to know. So don't tell Mama, all right?"

"I won't," he said agreeably.

"Just tell her I've gone to sketch by the river."

Within half an hour, Elva was walking toward the Main with a basket over her arm, her sketchbook on clear display in case anyone saw her. She might have laughed at the amount of thought it had taken to make this short trip across Hanau if she didn't know how furious Mama would be about her search for the witch. She hadn't slept much after that vision of the storm and had stayed up all night thinking about why Mama and Mathilda's friendship had ended.

Elva's footsteps quickened as she passed the town hall, where people liked to gather outside and catch up on gossip. But aside from a few who called out greetings, no one stopped her or asked questions. Thankfully, there were even fewer people when she crossed over the bridge toward the North Woods. Her family never went to this side of Hanau, and on the rare occasions when Mama talked about their old life, she had mentioned that Papa had bad memories of it.

"Your father doesn't like thinking about that old cottage," she had confessed. "It reminds him of leaving Mannheim, and your uncle Otto inheriting everything from your grandfather."

The story made sense, but now Elva suspected it wasn't the only reason Papa avoided the cottage. She was certain he had played a part in the demise of Mama's friendship. *I have gone elsewhere*, Mathilda had written in her final note. And if she was indeed the witch of the North Woods, then she hadn't gone far and there might be a clue to her whereabouts at her old cottage.

The well-traveled path led Elva deep into the forest. Fifteen years ago, Mama and Papa had walked this very route to their new life on the other side of the river. Retracing their steps felt to Elva like walking into memory and time. The trees formed a dense canopy overhead, covering the woods in cool green shade. She breathed in the smell of soil and moss, admiring the wildflowers along the path, and almost wished they had never moved away from the woods. There was something mystical in the way light danced here, as though it were made up of fairies.

"Did you know there's a lot of magic in the forest?" Cay had said once. He had held up yet another heavy book, *A Complete History of Hanau*. "Apparently a lot of people who were accused of being witches went in there to hide. No one's ever mapped it in its entirety because the trees move around and the path changes all the time. Folks say there are tunnels to other worlds and fairy rings and elves who might trick you and replace you with a changeling that looked just like you, so your family would never be able to tell."

Elva had laughed at him, but now, deep in the North Woods with its lilting birdsong and dappled shadows, it wasn't hard to imagine passages out of time and forgotten pockets of magic. She could see why children were attracted to this place, with its wandering paths and graceful trees. *Attracted*, she thought uneasily, *and then lost, never to be found again.*

Goose bumps rose on her arms, and she was grateful when a family of small, slender people with sun-bronzed skin and jet-black hair passed her on the path. Their tense faces relaxed when she gave them a friendly nod and a smile, and one of the children waved at her. Over the past few years, many people had migrated to Hanau from lands in the Far East to seek work or to escape war in their countries. Elva thought these were perfectly sensible reasons, but Papa had explained that not everyone in town welcomed them, and some were even downright hostile.

"That's how people are," he had told her. "Mama and I teach you to respect everyone, but there will always be folks who think we ought to keep to our own countries."

Dismayed, Elva had thought of her mother's volumes of stories from around the world. "But then we would never get to read tales from other places. Or learn other languages or eat those dumplings you love," she had added, recalling Papa's love of the round, flavorful pockets of pork and vegetables that some of their new neighbors brought to sell at market.

Papa had taught her kindness and understanding for others, yet he, too, had once shunned Mathilda for something she couldn't help. Even Willem's mind had gone straight to the woman in the woods when they had seen the notice for the missing child. There was so much suspicion and prejudice, and Elva's stomach hurt at the thought of Hanau ever turning against her.

After walking for a half hour, she stopped to rest beneath a beautiful old willow that reminded her of the tree by the river where she and Willem had first met. The sun was high in the sky when she emerged from the North Woods into a hamlet of shabby cottages. Mama had said that their old home had a rickety wooden gate, into which Papa had carved a daffodil, her favorite flower.

Elva passed gate after gate, looking for it, and finally found it in front of a cottage of mushroom-colored wood, rotted in several places, at the end of the lane. Smoke rose from the crooked chimney, indicating that the owner was at home, so Elva didn't dare linger long. She only ran her fingers over the daffodil before going up the hill to where Mathilda had once lived.

Despite knowing that the woman was long gone, Elva still felt a prickle of apprehension. If the rumors about Mathilda were false, then it was cruel and unfair. But if they were true, then Elva might be walking into danger. *I've come too far to go back now*, she thought.

Swallowing hard, Elva approached an overgrown hedge fifteen feet high. A rusted metal gate hung crookedly off its hinges, and here and there were signs of trespassing: scraps of rotten food, the remains of firecrackers, and holes in the hedge, as though mischievous children had tunneled through it. She sighed at the sad state of the property, for once it must have been lovely.

Inside the hedge stood two majestic willow trees surrounded by a tangle of weeds. Elva's breath snagged when she saw the cottage at the center of this wilderness. It was overrun with flowering vines, making it resemble a giant sleeping under a blanket of greenery. The windows had once held glass in their panes, but most of it had been broken. Shards shimmered at Elva from the grass, reflecting the blue of the sky.

"Hello?" Elva called out. "Is anyone home?"

Glass crunched underfoot as she went up the steps. The door stood ajar, and as Elva came closer, the unmistakable sound of movement emerged from within. She froze, petrified, as a pair of gleaming dark eyes watched her from the room beyond.

10

In the next moment, whatever was watching her moved, and Elva saw the sleek, reddish-brown body of a small fox. It backed away from her and leaped out of one of the broken windows. She let out a sigh of relief and peered in to see that the place had otherwise been long abandoned. A thick layer of dust covered the floor, marred only by the tracks of other animals that had come foraging for food. She guessed that the second, smaller room in the back was once a bedroom.

A musty but not unpleasant smell lingered in the air. Birdsong drifted in and dust motes floated around her like stars. It looked like it had been a sunny, comfortable home, judging from the pretty window glass that had been shattered by unkind hands. She could easily picture a table with a red-checked cloth, cozy stuffed chairs, and soup warming over the hearth.

The image didn't fit at all with what she might associate with a witch.

Elva ran her fingers over the beautiful woodwork on the walls, admiring the willow trees that had been carved from ceiling to floor. It was the kind of craftsmanship Papa admired but could not copy himself. Her eyes followed the carvings down to a floorboard in front of the fireplace, where a large, elaborate willow tree had been etched into the wood.

She bent to wipe the dust from it, wondering why it looked familiar. And then she realized that this carving was what she had seen in the water basin, flashing between visions of her family. It *had* to mean something that it was here, and that she had been the one to find it.

She ran her hands eagerly over the board, noticing how wide the gaps were around it. Slipping her fingernails in, she gently wiggled the board loose to reveal a hiding space beneath.

"More glass?" Elva muttered, as something glimmered up at her from beneath a piece of deep-purple velvet. She lifted away the fabric to reveal a mirror, about as tall as her arm from elbow to fingertips and a little more than half as wide, with an ornate frame that looked like real gold. Mirrors were so expensive that Elva knew no one in Hanau who had one bigger than a man's palm.

Carefully, she picked it up to find that it was lighter than she thought. She had never seen herself so clearly: Every freckle, stray hair, and eyelash was magnified in the reflection. Her gaze held both wonder and fear, and only when colors began to ripple up from the mirror's depths did she remember that she shouldn't have looked so long into a reflective surface.

A vision appeared of a pretty woman standing by the gate of an old cottage, holding up a pink baby's dress. A tall man with bright gold hair gave a shout of joy and twirled her around, and Elva's heart leaped when she realized she was looking at Mama and Papa, many years ago.

"Can it be true?" Mama asked. "Katharina wouldn't lie about this."

"I take back everything I said about those nosy Brauns." Papa's face wore the ear-to-ear grin Elva knew and loved. "We're going to have a child!"

"Mathilda knew this would happen," Mama said softly. "That's why she made this for me. Oh, Oskar, I wish I had been a better friend to her. She made this child possible for us, and all she got in return was my betrayal. My broken promise."

Elva's eyebrows shot up. Mama had always taught them to keep their word. "Promises have power," she liked to say. So this, then, was why Mathilda had ended the friendship?

"You chose to live in peace and be respected in Hanau. She can't blame you for that," Papa said, wrapping an arm around Mama. "She would have done the same in your place."

Mama hugged the baby's dress close to her heart. "I don't know about that. Mathilda knows all too well the price of betrayal where magic is involved. I wonder what will happen to us."

"Don't think of that," Papa urged her. "She's gone now, and good riddance. Don't be sad when we have so much to celebrate!" And he spun her around again, making her laugh.

The mirror flooded with light, and Elva saw again the symbol of the willow tree.

A new vision appeared of a woman sobbing her heart out in the forest. Her pale, heart-shaped face twisted with grief as she sat with her belongings all around her: woven baskets, blankets, mismatched chairs, and a ginger cat, which put a gentle paw on her shoulder. A thick book, perhaps a diary, lay open beside her, its rough-edged pages filled with writing. Elva knew this had to be Mathilda. A knot tightened in her chest at the revelation that the friendship had ended because Mama had feared what the town might think. "She made this child possible for us," her mother had said. But what did Mathilda have to do with her parents having Elva?

Elva shook her head, confused, and then the tree symbol appeared again before a new image of Mathilda materialized. She sat petting her cat in a cottage similar to the one Elva was in right now. "You'll be all I need, won't you?" she crooned to the purring animal. "And I'll never do another kind deed only to be repaid with lies."

The mirror flashed once more.

Mama and Papa were running through the North Woods, their faces stricken with terror. They looked older, more like their present-day selves, and Elva's stomach clenched at the fear on her mother's face. The scene melted into a vision Elva recognized because she had seen it last night in her water basin: It was of herself, kneeling on the ground by an old stone well. But this time, she could clearly see herself weeping and bending over a crumpled, motionless body.

"The price of breaking a promise," Mama's voice murmured from the mirror, dreamlike. "The price of breaking a promise . . . the price . . . the price . . ."

Elva pressed her lips tightly together as the mirror showed once more the wreckage of her parents' farm after the storm: crops uprooted, animals lying dead, the house and barn shattered. Mama sobbing, Papa surveying the damage with tears in his eyes, Rayner clenching his fists.

Flash after flash, image after image.

They came faster now, in wild, dizzying succession, and the visions were of people Elva had never seen: a young man in an odd short-brimmed hat, yelling in a language she couldn't understand; candlelight flickering across the frightened face of a beautiful, olive-skinned girl; and a boy and girl with dark skin and dark hair, running in terror through what looked like frighteningly tall columns of metal and glass. All of them looked familiar somehow. Perhaps it was the shapes of their noses or the colors of their eyes. . . .

The mirror slipped from Elva's fingers.

She fell backward onto the dusty floor, breathing hard as the nausea and dizziness came back with a vengeance. She closed her eyes and pressed her hands over her madly beating heart.

So many visions of fear and anger, sorrow and loss. So much unhappiness, even in the people she didn't know. Elva couldn't even begin to understand what it was all about.

But one thing was crystal clear: Mama had wronged Mathilda and had regretted it for years. And her voice had echoed over and over about a price to be paid for that betrayal.

Elva's eyes flew open.

When she had first seen the storm, her mind had gone to Mama's obsession with their family curse. Now it occurred to her that if Mathilda was a witch, perhaps *she* had cast the curse in response to Mama's broken promise. Perhaps the coming disaster was part of her revenge.

Elva sat up slowly. She *needed* to find Mathilda and make this right—but she had no idea where the woman lived now. The vision had only shown her new home, not how to get there.

Elva groaned and picked up the mirror reluctantly. The last thing she wanted to do was look into it again, but it might be her only chance to find the witch. In the past, she had only ever seen random images, had never asked to see a specific vision. But now she stared at her reflection, trying to will the glass into showing her the way to Mathilda.

Nothing happened.

"Could you please show me where she lives now?" she asked awkwardly, but the mirror still showed only her face. Maybe she was trying too hard again. She inhaled and let her eyes unfocus once more, praying that the need in her mind would materialize in the mirror.

The glass grew warm in her hands as the tree symbol shone bright, and then she saw the forest path she had taken earlier. Fascinated, Elva watched the scene move forward. If it hadn't been for the gold frame around the mirror, she might have imagined herself walking at that very moment and not sitting on a cottage floor at all. She recognized the willow where she had rested earlier. The vision moved past it on the right side, then swiveled back to show that it was gone.

"What?" Elva said, confused.

At once, the scene returned to its starting point. It moved along the forest path again until it reached the willow, then moved around the right side and turned back to show that the tree had disappeared. She stared into the mirror, intrigued and frightened. Perhaps the tree had been enchanted to disorient travelers and keep them from finding Mathilda.

Now there was an interesting thought.

Hanau was full of would-be adventurers who had searched for the witch of the North Woods for years, whether to take revenge for the missing children or simply to make mischief. But however hard they tried, one thing always remained the same: No one ever found her.

Cay might be right about the forest after all, Elva thought, shivering as she recalled his fairy tales.

In the mirror, the vision repeated itself again. But this time, it continued on past a trio of birch trees that stood in a circle, slender and tall, like conspiring fairy princesses with crowns of green leaves. The scene moved to their left, then swiveled back to show that they were gone.

"The disappearing trees are landmarks," Elva breathed, and at her realization, a surge of warmth from the mirror met her fingertips. She understood now what she had to do: pass each marker and then look back; if it was gone, she was on the right path to Mathilda.

After the birches, the scene showed a second willow even larger than the first that exactly resembled the symbol on the floor. The vision flowed past it on the right, and then a small, tidy stone cottage appeared. It was the witch's new home, and now Elva knew how to get there.

She closed her eyes, breaking the trance, as an even stronger wave of nausea crashed through her. She waited for it to pass before getting up on shaky legs. "Thank you," she told the mirror. She felt silly, but it *had* helped her, and she didn't want to offend where magic was involved.

Magic. She had performed real magic. Perhaps she had been doing so all these years whenever ripples and colors appeared in reflective surfaces. The revelation was as thrilling as it was terrifying. *Papa had shunned Mathilda and Mama had cut her off, all because of magic*, Elva thought. And if Elva hadn't been their daughter, they might well hate and fear her, too.

She pushed away the painful thought as she moved to put the mirror back in its hiding place, then hesitated. It might be useful to bring it so she wouldn't get lost; it wouldn't be stealing if she managed to find Mathilda and return it. Quickly, before she could change her mind, she slipped the mirror into her basket and left the cottage.

Back in the forest, Elva retraced her steps to the first willow tree. She walked around the right side of it, just as the mirror had said to do, and paused a few paces away.

She took a deep breath. "If I turn around and the tree is still there," she muttered, "I will go back to Mama, abandon this nonsense, and hope the storm I saw will never come."

Slowly, she turned on her heel.

The tree was gone.

Elva braced herself against a nearby elm, panting. It had worked. It had actually worked. She closed her eyes against another bout of dizziness, wondering if having so many visions in a short span of time had brought it on. When it eased, she set off again and saw the three birches within a hundred paces. This time, she went around the left side, head swimming with every step. When she turned to look back, there was only an empty space where they had been seconds ago.

Whoever Mathilda was, there was no question that her abilities were impressive. *Which means she'll be able to help me*, Elva told herself, forcing her feet onward.

The only problem was, they seemed to be stuck in place.

She attempted to lift her left heel, but it didn't budge. She tried her right, but it, too, was stuck as though she had stepped onto a layer of wet tar. Beads of perspiration formed on her neck as she struggled, trying not to panic. The mirror hadn't warned her about a trap, though it was likely that whatever she was stuck in had been designed to catch trespassers.

Elva decided to take her feet out of the boots and continue on barefoot. But when she bent to unlace them, she heard a menacing croak.

A toad sat watching her from atop a large gray mushroom. The toad was no color she had ever seen in nature before—toxic purple and poisonous yellow swirled across its pebbly skin, and it had baleful bloodred eyes. It croaked again, an angry, threatening sound, as it stared at her.

She noticed suddenly that she was standing inside a ring of huge mushrooms, all gray with red-spotted caps. Her mouth went dry at the slick, deadly sheen on each one. She had gone mushrooming enough to know that eating one of these would kill a person in seconds. She had been so focused on the trees that she had stumbled into their midst without realizing it.

The toad croaked again; its expression was nothing short of murderous. Slowly, it hopped off the mushroom and landed about two feet away from Elva. Then it hopped once more until it was sitting on her boot, glaring up at her. Its legs tensed, preparing to hop again, and Elva knew that this time, it would fly right at her face.

"Oh no," she moaned, trying in vain to move her feet. "Please!"

The toad croaked a final warning, and then its back legs launched it upward.

Elva screamed, but not before she heard someone speak a low, guttural command. She screamed again when she saw the toad suspended in midair, helpless and inches from her nose. Whatever enchantment had been holding her feet in place disappeared. She took the opportunity to run, not waiting to see who had spoken, but was still so dizzy that she hurtled face-first into a tree. The impact sent Elva to the ground on all fours.

For a moment, she remained still, drenched in sweat and feeling so ill that she had no energy to push herself upright. Vaguely, she noticed someone standing over her: a woman in a long flowing dress of deep burgundy wool, with black waves of hair cascading around a heart-shaped face. And then the dizziness overwhelmed her, and everything went black.

When Elva opened her eyes, she found herself lying flat on the grass. She tried to lift her head, but the world gave a sickening lurch, forcing her to quickly lower it again.

The woman was still there, watching her. "Don't move."

"M-Mathilda?" Elva quavered.

The woman gave a single nod and crouched down, her skirt pooling around her like dark wine. She looked no more than twenty-five, which didn't make sense because she had been an adult when she had met Mama almost two decades ago. Her pale, freckled skin was smooth and unlined, and above her rounded cheeks were eyes bright with intelligence.

"This is what happens when you overextend yourself with magic," the witch said. "You should learn your limits so you don't faint and empty your stomach."

"I emptied my stomach?" Elva asked, horrified.

"No, but you will if you keep going on like this. Would you like some water?"

"No, thank you," Elva said, unable to bear the thought of drinking anything at present, especially from a witch who might enchant her with a potion.

The woman snorted, as though she had heard Elva's thought. "Well, you're definitely Agnes and Oskar's daughter. They didn't like accepting hospitality from witches, either." She tilted her head, studying Elva. "And yet their child has magic.... How ironic. There's no other way you could have found me."

"You know who I am?"

"Of course. You're not the only one with an enchanted mirror." Mathilda nodded at Elva's basket. "Mine is the twin sister to *that* one. I made them from the same sheet of glass. I saw you coming, and a good thing, too, or I couldn't have rescued you in time. Silly girl, don't you know a fairy ring when you see one?"

"A fairy ring? The mushrooms, you mean?"

"Never step into a circle of mushrooms or stones. It's extremely offensive. That guardian would have poisoned the life out of you as punishment."

"What guardian? The...the toad?"

Mathilda rolled her eyes. "Who else? Be more careful when you leave. I don't have time to rescue you from every trap in this forest."

"Leave?"

"Did that mother of yours teach you to be a parrot? Yes, I said leave," she snapped. "And be warned: If you tell anyone where I am, they'll encounter worse than fairy rings."

Elva's heart sank. Clearly, the witch was still angry with Mama. "Please, won't you speak with me first? I came all this way looking for you."

"I don't care. I owe you and your mother nothing. Don't think to trespass and then manipulate me into helping you. I'm sick and tired of being used."

"I didn't mean to offend," Elva said quickly. "Of course I don't expect you to tell me anything. I only *hoped* you would."

The witch furrowed her brow. "Why did Agnes send you to me after all this time?"

Elva tried to sit up again, because it didn't seem right to have this conversation lying down. Thankfully, her stomach appeared to have settled. "I sent myself. I found the letters you and Mama exchanged years ago and read enough to understand that your friendship ended because of your magic. I thought you might be the right person to help me."

Mathilda's frown deepened.

"It's just that..." Elva took a deep breath. After ten years of hiding her secret, she didn't think she would ever get used to talking about it. "I've been able to see the future for as long as I can remember. I look into water—into any reflective surface—and I see things that will come to pass...and things that have already happened, too," she added, as a thought occurred to her. "When I used the mirror to look for you, I saw Mama as a young woman. And you crying because of her."

"Who taught you how to do this?"

"No one. The first time was when I was five or six. But I've tried to hide it ever since because Mama and Papa wanted me to."

The woman snorted again. "Of course."

"I knew I had to see you—not just to ask for help but to apologize for my parents, too. Mama kept your letters all these years. She still regrets what she did to you."

"That doesn't mean a thing to me," Mathilda said scornfully. "Her guilt isn't important. I cut her out of my heart long ago, and if she has a magical daughter, that's her problem."

"But you saved me from that toad, knowing who I was," Elva persisted. "You didn't have to do that."

"I don't believe in a child paying for the sins of her mother. I would have done it for anyone else, and that's that. Now I think you should be on your way."

"Please," Elva begged. "Won't you help me prevent something terrible I've foreseen?"

"I don't know why you think I have any answers for you," Mathilda said in a tart voice. "The forest path is waiting for you beyond the willow tree, and for heaven's sake, keep your eyes open this time because I won't be rescuing you again."

She walked away, her dress trailing behind her, and Elva noticed suddenly that they were in a clearing with a cottage in the center. Its pale-gray stones shone against a lush garden with a beehive. Smoke rose from the chimney, and despite the hour, the windows all glowed with soft, comfortable yellow light. Elva was in the witch's sanctuary, and for a moment, hope rose within her. Mathilda wouldn't have taken her in if she was absolutely against helping her.

But when the witch kept walking and didn't turn back, Elva knew it was a lost cause. She would be no better off than when she had left her parents' house. "All right," she called, dejected. "I'm sorry to disturb you. Here's your mirror back."

Mathilda didn't respond, so Elva put the glass on the ground and got up to go. She had walked about ten paces toward the willow tree when she heard the witch tell her to stop.

"You got the mirror to show you how to pass through my enchanted boundary. How?"

"I don't know," Elva said honestly. "I've had visions before, but they were all random. I've never asked to see something specific. Today was the first time I tried."

The witch let out a contemptuous sniff. "No wonder you were half-dead for ten minutes! You need to work up to your magic, girl! You can't just sap your energy all at once."

"How was I to know that?" Elva protested. "That's why I'm here: to learn about my ability and find out how I can stop the terrible things I've seen."

Mathilda stared at her. "You want me to help you *use* your powers? Not to take them away and make you a normal girl, as your darling parents undoubtedly want?"

"You can do that? Make me normal?"

"Of course not! But that's what I assumed you would want." The witch pursed her lips, thinking. "You'd better come inside. I'm not promising anything," she added brusquely, as a hopeful smile spread across Elva's face. "But I want to know what you can do, and what these *terrible things* are that you would risk your own safety to prevent."

"My own safety?"

"Haven't you listened to anything the townspeople have said? Or read the Grimms' tales?" Mathilda asked, striding away. "I could be luring you into my cottage to throw you in the oven. Watch out for the trail of candy in the grass."

Elva couldn't help peeking at the ground. She looked back at the willow tree, wondering if she ought to take this opportunity to go. She could return to Mama and never speak of what she had seen . . . but then she would also lie awake every night wondering if, or *when*, that horrible storm would come.

Put that way, there was no real choice in the matter.

She placed the mirror back into her basket and timidly entered the cottage. The place was homey and bright, and had been built in the same style as the witch's old cottage. There was a large, sunny central room, a fire roaring in the hearth, and a kitchen table covered with jars of bright wildflowers. The ginger cat Elva had seen in the mirror looked up from the windowsill, its deep green eyes narrowing with judgment at her.

Mathilda hung a kettle over the fire and set two delicate porcelain cups on the table. "So you came here despite having heard how dangerous I am?" she asked sarcastically.

"Mama calls it evil gossip, what people say about you."

The witch's eyes met hers for a moment. "You had better take a seat, then," she said ungraciously, cutting two slices of fluffy, deep brown cake that smelled of butter and nutmeg. "Tell me more about your visions. What happens when you look into water—what you're thinking about, how long the images last, and so on and so forth."

Elva obeyed, grateful that Mathilda had chosen to listen. When she described the great storm, the witch set down her fork, intent. "So you see, that storm is why I wanted to find you. I want to know how we can stop it."

"*We?*"

"Yes, with magic." Now that Elva was saying it aloud, it sounded foolish. But she forced herself to continue. "It also occurred to me that perhaps . . . well, perhaps you might be responsible for the storm . . . as revenge against Mama?" She winced, half expecting the witch to fly into a rage.

Mathilda only looked at her calmly. "The only thing you're worried about is this storm destroying your parents' farm, then? You're not thinking of using your powers for profit?"

"Of course not! That never even crossed my mind," Elva said indignantly, and when she saw the witch nod, she realized she had passed some sort of test.

Mathilda handed her a cup of chamomile tea. "I don't know why the storm is coming. It has nothing to do with me. Why would I wait seventeen years to destroy your parents' farm? If I ever wanted to do such a thing, I already would have."

She spoke with such disdain that Elva had no choice but to believe her. "But why can I see it coming? Why do I have this ability in the first place?"

"It may have to do with your mother's broken promise." The witch's hands, wrapped around her cup, were as oddly youthful as her face. "Every magic-wielder has a gift that comes more easily than any other. Yours, I suppose, is seeing the past and future. Mine is potions. I've always had a way with anything that grows from the earth: trees, flowers, roots. When I found out that Agnes desperately wanted a child, I offered to help and she agreed to be my friend in return." She paused, looking severely at Elva. "Every spell comes with a condition laid down by the spellworker. If it's a promise and the promise is kept, the magic will be satisfied because both parties kept their word. Understand?"

"I think so," Elva said slowly. "It's like a contract."

The witch nodded. "Your mother disrupted the balance of magic by breaking her vow. She produced consequences that no one can control."

"Me. I'm the consequence, aren't I?" Elva uttered, slumping in her chair. "You helped Mama have me, but she got a daughter who was more than she bargained for. A daughter who isn't normal."

Mathilda's mouth twisted. "Normal according to whom? To those shrieking villagers who are scared of anything they don't understand?

There are more people like us than you think, my girl. Don't be so quick to disrespect the tremendous skill you've been given."

Elva stared at her, never having heard anyone describe her ability that way. "But is it a gift or a curse? Will I be able to use it to protect my family?"

"I can't tell you what you want to hear," the witch said. "I don't *know* if your power is 'good' or 'bad,' nor do I think it matters. What I *do* know is that magic-wielders have tried to play games with time in the past, and they have always lost. They have killed others or died in the process, or *worse*. Some of them have given up their very souls in the attempt."

Elva shuddered. "So there's nothing anyone can do to amend the future?"

"I didn't say that. I said that no one has been successful."

"It's not impossible, then! You just said I have tremendous skill. If you taught me more about my visions, I could be the first person to change time."

Mathilda shook her head. "I won't encourage you in something so dangerous. I will only consider helping you if you accept this: Warn your family but do not expect to change the future. Too much is affected when you toy with time."

Elva's hope deflated at her resolute tone. The disaster would come, and she would not be able to stop the farm from being torn apart. She would have to watch, as helpless as the rest of them. . . . But at least they could prepare if they knew it was coming. And if she learned how to hone her magic, she might be able to protect them some other way, too. "All right," she said resignedly. "I accept that the storm will happen. Now will you teach me about my ability?"

"I said I would *consider* it. I need time to think." Mathilda crossed her arms. "And *you* need to decide what learning from me would mean for you. You are already going against your parents' wishes. Would you be able to continue doing so? Would you risk the other townspeople finding out about you? Would you willingly enter into the *evil* art of witchcraft?"

"But I don't think you're evil," Elva argued. "Mama wouldn't regret losing you if you were. And you saved me just now, and all this time you could have hurt me, but you haven't."

"Witches aren't all bad, then?" Mathilda asked tartly.

"I don't know anything about witches, except ones in storybooks who lock up princesses and eat children," Elva admitted. "But now that I've met you, I'd like to think they're like anyone else and can choose who they want to be."

"And what have I chosen, then?"

Elva took her in: her dark hair, her well-made clothes, and her strong and lovely face. She seemed to have lived a peaceful, quiet life, yet she had spent all these years hidden among the vanishing trees of the forest. Her old cottage had not been so far apart from the rest of Hanau, and now she might as well be on the moon. She had removed herself entirely from the world.

Elva tried to imagine the same existence for herself, a life without Papa's hugs or Mama's smiles or the ability to walk freely about town.

"I think you chose not to hurt anymore," she said, and surprise flickered on the witch's face.

Mathilda rose and glanced out the window. "You'd better go before it gets dark. I need time to think, and *you* do, too." When she looked at Elva, her expression was almost angry. "You need to consider whether you want to study with someone who would poison children for destroying her hedges or make reptiles come out of her enemy's throat."

"But those are just rumors—"

"No," Mathilda interrupted fiercely. "There are many lies told about me—that I kidnap children, for example. Where on earth would I put them? How would I feed them all? It's absurd. But the poisoned candy, and the snakes and toads from Lina's throat . . . those stories are true, and now you know that they are, from my own lips."

Elva watched the play of emotions across the witch's face, and fear rippled down her spine. At least some of what the Brothers Grimm had written in their books *had* happened.

"I won't apologize for trying to survive," Mathilda went on. "But I want you to know the truth. I want your eyes wide open before you decide to associate with me. Your mother came to the conclusion that I wasn't worth it, and you may as well."

"But she didn't understand. She's not like us," Elva said softly.

Mathilda was silent for a moment. "If you decide you still want to learn from me, come back in three days at moonrise. I will tell you whether I can help you then." She crossed the room and opened a wooden trunk from which she removed a pair of beautiful, flat-soled dancing slippers. They had been fashioned of deep rose-red satin, with ribbons sewn onto each side of the heel, so the wearer could tie them around her ankles and let the ends flutter prettily. "These are for you. They're only a loan," she added sourly, when Elva's mouth opened in astonishment. "Don't go expecting presents just because you've managed to charm me into not throwing you off my property. Put them on."

"But why?" Elva gasped, taking them. The slippers were light as feathers in her hands, and the satin ribbons tickled her wrists.

"I enchanted them to be silent. No one will hear you come or go, and you will leave no tracks behind you. I can't risk anyone following you. And if you change your mind about coming back," Mathilda added, "leave the shoes in the branches of the first willow tree, where they will be well hidden. Just be sure no one is following you, understand?"

"Yes," Elva agreed, with a twinge of pity at how exhausting it must be to forever worry about being found. She slipped off her sturdy boots and put on the slippers, which were lined with fur and delightfully soft. They had looked too small for her, but on her feet, they fit as perfectly as though the cobbler had designed them for her. She tied the ribbons around her ankles and stood, taking a few steps around the cottage. Her feet made not a sound on the floorboards.

"Keep that mirror with you, too," Mathilda said, nodding at Elva's basket on the table. "It is connected to mine, and I will know at once if you tell anyone about me."

Elva opened her mouth to protest at being spied on like a thief, but she couldn't blame the witch for not trusting her. She was, after all, a stranger and also the daughter of someone who had betrayed Mathilda. "Thank you," she said instead. "I'm truly grateful to you."

The witch regarded her with something of the sadness Elva remembered from her vision. "You're very like your mother, you know? You even talk like her. Now go on," she said gruffly. "Before I change my mind. And keep your wits about you in the forest this time."

"Will I be able to find my way back?" Elva asked nervously, gathering up her basket.

"The path you took here will be just beyond that tree," Mathilda said, pointing at the willow. "Walk with your head up, stride with purpose, and don't stare too long at anything odd. You'll be much less of a target for the imps and the fairy rings that way."

"All right. Well, thank you," Elva said awkwardly. Then, with her basket in one hand and boots in the other, she moved out of the door and back through the trees. She gulped when she realized that her feet in the dancing shoes did not even disturb one blade of grass. When she passed the willow, she glanced back over her shoulder, but Mathilda's cottage and the clearing had completely disappeared. The sight of the now-empty space in the forest made her shiver, and she hurried on back to the path.

She could only hope she had done the right thing in seeking out the witch of the North Woods.

12

The next morning, Elva went out to harvest radishes for supper. She worked slowly, digging into the soil to check the roots and pulling the plants out if they were ready. She placed the greens in one basket and the radishes in another, all the while running over the conversation with Mathilda—and her confession—again and again in her mind.

Years ago, when nosy old Frau Braun had fallen ill, Mama had sent Cay and Elva to her with hot soup and sourdough bread. The midwife had told them an interesting story about Frau Bergmann, who had been a Werner before she married and apparently even snobbier as a girl than she was now. The story went that she had offended the witch of the North Woods by refusing to invite her to a party, and as revenge, the witch had cursed her to have spiders, lizards, and other horrible animals come out of her throat for a week. Elva had laughed at the tale and teased impressionable little Cay for believing it. But it seemed Cay had been right to do so.

Elva frowned, tossing another radish into her basket. No one would lie about something like that. Mathilda must have been telling the truth and clearly expected to frighten her off with it. Or maybe it was all a test. Maybe she wanted to see how brave Elva was...or how desperate.

Sighing, Elva wiped her forehead across her sleeve and looked up to see Cay coming toward her. "What are you doing out here? Mama asked you to milk the cows."

He gave her a strange look. "That was two hours ago. I'm all done, so she sent me out here to see if you needed any help."

Elva glanced up at the sky and realized that the sun had already reached its peak. "I was so busy daydreaming, the morning flew by. You can help me bring the baskets in."

Cay picked up the basket of greens and walked with her back toward the house, rambling about a book he had recently read. Elva only half listened, nodding absentmindedly until he said, "The last chapter said wishing wells with the most powerful magic are usually found near trees. So there must be one somewhere in the North Woods."

"What are you talking about?" Elva asked, alert at once.

He frowned at her. "Haven't you been listening? I'm planning an expedition to find my wishing well, and I just know that if I go into the forest..."

Images raced through Elva's mind at a frantic pace: swaying trees, an old well, and someone crumpled on the ground. Her body went cold and she stopped, looking her brother in the eye. "Cay," she said sternly, "you must *never* go into the forest alone."

"I'll be fine," he said, waving an impatient hand. "I've read all the stories. I'll leave a trail of bread crumbs. Well, not *actual* bread crumbs, because that's stupid. But I wouldn't get lost."

"Cay, I mean it," Elva said loudly. "You are not to go into the North Woods for any reason at all. Do you hear me?"

He blinked at her forceful tone. "Yes, I hear you."

"It's dangerous in there. Promise me. *Promise* me," Elva demanded. She wished she could tell him about everything: the fairy ring, the mirror, the vanishing trees, and the witch who had been both Mama's confidante and the poisoner of the candy eaten by the village children. But looking into his bewildered face, she couldn't bring herself to burden him with what she knew. Not yet, not until she had made a decision. "I'm sorry I raised my voice," she added more gently. "I'm worried you'll get hurt, that's all."

Cay frowned. "You've been odd ever since you came back yesterday."

"Odd? What do you mean?"

"Just odd. You didn't tell me how your errand for Freida went, and you've never told me not to go adventuring in the woods before." Cay studied her. "You tell me all of your secrets, but this time you're keeping something to yourself. I can feel it."

"You're right," she admitted, struck by how well her brother knew her. "I had another vision. I saw a bad storm coming, but I didn't want you to worry."

"But the almanac said it would be a dry season."

"I know. But before what I saw comes true, I'm going to try to do something about it."

"Like what?"

Elva bit her bottom lip, knowing she had already said too much. "I'm not sure yet; I want to think through it some more. All right?"

Cay scuffed the ground with his boots. "Are you going to tell Willem?"

"What made you think of that?"

"He's right there."

Willem was indeed waiting for them and chatting with Mama in front of the house. Elva's heart picked up at how handsome he looked: The sleeves of his blue work shirt had been rolled up over his arms, and a lock of reddish-brown hair blew across his forehead in the breeze. As soon as he saw them coming, he hurried to take the heavy basket of radishes from Elva.

"I came to say hello," he said, his eyes shining.

"Why don't you bring those radishes into the kitchen, Willem?" Mama suggested, with an indulgent smile. "And then you can sit out here with Elva for a bit. It's such a lovely day."

In a minute or two, Elva and Willem were sitting on the sun-warmed grass with cups of Mama's honey-sweetened barley water. "What did you end up doing with the Blue Mermaid?" she asked, shyly tucking a strand of hair behind her ear.

"Herr Bauer helped me salt it down to preserve it. He wants to invite the whole town to a fish bake this week." Willem's face took on a mischievous expression. "It will probably taste delicious, and you and I will dance at least three times. But I'm sure you already know that."

"Well . . ."

He glanced at the house quickly, then captured her lips with his, which were sweet and warm. The butterflies danced more frantically than ever in Elva's stomach, and she giggled when they separated. "And you probably knew I was going to do that, too," he joked.

Elva shook her head, laughing. "That's not quite how it works."

"I forgot. You have to look into a reflective surface first, like the river."

"Yes. I even saw something in Papa's brandy once," Elva said, gratified by the way he spoke about her ability, as though it was perfectly normal.

"You're brilliant." Willem kissed her again, and she leaned against his warmth, even though Cay and Mama might see them from the windows. "But I think you were right to keep it a secret. I'd hate people to bother you about it. That is," he added hastily, when Elva pulled away in surprise, "they might ask you to predict things for them all the time, which would be a nuisance. Although you might be able to charge them a fee. Now there's a thought!"

Elva laughed, yet it struck her that Mathilda had said something similar yesterday. She twirled a bright yellow dandelion between her fingers, wondering what Willem would think if she told him she had seen the witch.

"What does it feel like when you see the future?" he asked.

"Strange," she confessed. "Like I'm looking into a small window, and it's all happening in front of my eyes. That evening, I saw you as clear as day in the river. The fish, too."

"Do you hear voices?"

"Sometimes."

"Please tell me if I'm asking too many questions. I don't want you to feel like you *have* to tell me," he added quickly. "I won't be that kind of husband." As soon as the word *husband* slipped out, his face turned bright red, and Elva thought she couldn't possibly adore him more.

"It doesn't frighten you at all, what I can do? Or feel wrong or unnatural?"

"Of course not." Willem plucked a few daisies and braided their stems together. "I think certain people can sense things. Frau Werner's ankle hurt when her twin twisted *hers* miles away. And one farmhand's mother always sends him exactly what he wants to eat, even though she has no way of knowing what he craves. Everything *you* see has to do with people you care about, so maybe it's similar. You worry about them and want only good things for them."

Elva's heart soared as he spoke. Everything he said made sense; even the vision of the terrible storm had to do with her protecting her family. He understood her so well.

Willem blushed again. "Have you seen anything about us? I mean, about our life together?" He fiddled with the cup of water in his hand, looking into it at his own reflection.

"Not yet. But I haven't really tried." Elva's heart sank a bit at his hopeful expression, remembering how sick she had felt after calling up the last vision. "I'm not sure if I can do it. I haven't practiced enough."

"Of course," he said at once. "You don't have to."

"But maybe I should give it a try." She had felt wonderful—and *powerful*—calling up the path to Mathilda's house. Perhaps she could conjure another specific image and not get so ill, now that she knew to stop before she did. "What would you like to know?"

Willem sat up, excited. "How about the cottage I'll build for you? And our family?"

Elva's blush rivaled his as she held his cup in front of her. It had been a long time since she'd had a vision in front of someone else on purpose, and her heart pounded as she tried to relax. She took a few deep breaths, turning her thoughts toward the life they would share.

But when the scene appeared, it was of Willem leaning against a fence, talking to another young man who was short and strongly built, with black hair and light gray eyes. Both were dressed in work shirts and suspenders, and Elva guessed that the other man was another one of Herr Bauer's farmhands. His hands moved eagerly as he spoke. "It'll be easy," he said. "It comes to Berlin at the end of summer, and it would be simple to hitch a ride there. Think about it."

Afraid of getting sick again, she blinked and quickly broke the trance.

"What is it? What did you see?" Willem asked.

"I'm sorry, I didn't see our cottage. I saw something else." She described the black-haired young man and what she had heard him say.

"That sounds like Klaus," Willem said, amazed. "He's brand-new, just hired yesterday, and hasn't been introduced anywhere yet."

Elva furrowed her brow, wondering why she hadn't seen what she had wanted to see. Perhaps she should have asked out loud again. She longed to talk to Mathilda about it . . . but going back to her would mean overlooking everything awful the woman had done.

"I can't wait for that conversation to happen," Willem said gleefully. "Wouldn't it shock Klaus if I told him I knew he was going to mention Berlin?"

"Willem," Elva said, alarmed.

"I'm joking," he reassured her. "I won't tell anyone. Your secrets are my secrets now, too." He braided the last daisy into the chain he was weaving, and then placed it atop her hair like a crown, his eyes so full of love that Elva couldn't help kissing him again.

And after that, they didn't do very much talking at all.

13

Two days later, Elva stood in the kitchen with Mama, struggling to stay awake as they churned butter. "Are you all right?" her mother asked, concerned, as Elva stifled yet another yawn. "You've looked exhausted all day. I hope you're not coming down with something."

"I'm fine, Mama. I just haven't been sleeping very well."

For the past two nights, Elva had woken up almost every hour with her heart racing and her nightgown stuck to her clammy skin.

Last night it had been a nightmare about the storm and having to swim through rainwater to save Cay from drowning. The other night it had been bad dream after bad dream of the stone well from her visions. Each time, a different person had lain crumpled and dead in front of her—Papa sprawled out with his head lolling to one side, Willem lying lifeless on his stomach, Mama staring sightlessly up at the sky. Elva had sat bolt upright after each disturbing image, shivering and crying and sick to her stomach.

They're just dreams, she had told herself. *Not visions of the future.*

And yet how could she be certain? Maybe her ability was now manifesting itself in sleep; maybe everything she dreamed would also come to pass. After the final terrifying nightmare, she had made up her mind to go see the witch again and had packed her basket with the red slippers and mirror. What Mathilda had done was in the past, and Elva cared about the future. If there was even a small chance that she could do something about it, then it would be worth going against Mama and Papa's wishes and risking everything to learn more about magic.

"You should go up to bed," Mama said sympathetically. "I can finish churning alone."

"No, I'll be all right. Honest," Elva told her.

Mama had been in the fields all day, helping Papa and the farm-hands cut the wheat. It was hot, tiring work, and Elva couldn't stand the thought of Mama doing all the churning by herself, too. So she braced her hands on the dash and drove it over and over into the tub, working the buttermilk into a lather with as much energy as she could muster.

"Cay noticed how tired you were today, too. He offered to feed the chickens tomorrow morning so you can sleep in a bit." Mama gave an affectionate shake of her head. "He's a good, steady boy, for all that talk about ogres and wishing wells."

Elva's grip tightened on the dash. "Mama, he's been talking about going to the North Woods alone," she said, ignoring the stab of guilt at revealing her brother's plans. But it was for his own protection. "He thinks he might find a wishing well there."

Mama stopped churning. "What a foolish idea!" she fumed. "I'll speak to him. I don't know what it is about that place. Sometimes I think these folktales do more harm than good."

When they finished, Elva went upstairs and allowed herself one longing look at her bed before sitting on the hard floor. She could not fall asleep, not at moonrise on the third day, when the witch had told her to come back. Once the house had fallen silent at last, she put on her cloak, drawing the hood over her bright hair, and opened her window. Her bedroom was on the second floor above the kitchen, which had a low roof and a drainpipe she could climb. She hooked her basket over one arm, put on the red shoes, and slipped out onto the rooftop.

Her feet made no sound on the shingles, and she landed silently in the grass below.

Thank you, Mathilda, she thought, and with a glance back at her dark house, she headed for the river. Several times, she was forced to duck around the corner of a building or into the shadow of trees whenever she heard voices or horses approaching. The magical red shoes made no sound and left no tracks, but they didn't make her invisible.

Her heart pounded in her throat as she scurried across the bridge and plunged into the North Woods. The forest seemed like a different world at night, vast and full of watchful eyes. The smell of earth and smoky moss hung in the air as she jogged through the trees. Not a single twig crunched beneath her slippers, nor did her footsteps displace any leaf or pebble. She stayed alert, not wanting to get caught in another fairy ring, especially not in this heavy darkness.

Soon enough, Elva found the willow and passed it on the right side. For a moment, she dreaded looking back, worried that Mathilda might have thought better of their association and changed the path. But when she peered behind her, the tree was gone. *She wants me to find her again*, she thought, her heart soaring.

She passed by the other landmarks, and the witch's cottage came into view, looking even more inviting with its bright windows shining against the night. The front door had been left ajar, and Elva pushed it open to find Mathilda sitting by the fire, writing in a leather-bound book with the cat curled up against her side.

"So you've returned," the witch said sourly, though she couldn't quite hide the look of pleasure on her face at the sight of Elva. "I suppose you'd better come in and have a seat."

Elva pulled out a loaf of apple-cinnamon bread from her basket. She had baked an extra one earlier and squirreled it away before Mama could see. "This is for you," she said shyly. "I saw your beehive and thought you might like to eat this with honey, since you have a sweet tooth."

Mathilda harrumphed. "What makes you think I have a sweet tooth?"

"You served me cake when I was last here."

"And you didn't eat a bite of it. Did you think I would enchant you?"

Elva blushed. The thought had, in fact, crossed her mind.

"Put it on the table," the witch went on, looking amused. She closed her diary, set it aside, and picked up the blanket she was knitting. "And come here."

Elva took the seat facing Mathilda. It was a comfortable rocking chair piled with soft blankets much like the one the witch was currently working on. The cat turned its inscrutable green eyes upon Elva, who smiled at it and then felt unreasonably hurt when it did not smile back.

"So, knowing the full truth about me and what I have done to people in the past," the witch said, "you have decided that you wish to learn from me anyway?"

"I have."

"And if I poison you?" Mathilda asked sarcastically. "Or put toads in your throat?"

Elva swallowed hard. "I've decided to take that risk."

The witch fixed her with a stern gaze. "Then I will come quickly to the point. Three days ago, you trespassed at my old cottage. You stole a mirror belonging to me, performed magic beyond your ability to determine my location, and then trespassed *again* at my new home. You demanded that I answer your questions and help you hone your inexplicable magic."

Elva's mouth opened to argue, but the witch held up a hand to silence her.

"As a result of all that, I have decided to help you." An unexpected smile crossed her face at Elva's shocked expression. "But let us be clear: I'm only doing so for two reasons. The first is that someone I loved, who trained *me*, would not want me to turn you away. The second is that your ability is greater than any I have seen in someone so unschooled, and I fear you may destroy Hanau in your clumsy attempts to use your powers. And as much as I despise this town, I live here and would prefer that you not raze it to the ground. Do you understand?"

"Yes, ma'am," Elva said, as calmly and politely as she could. But inside, she felt like getting up and dancing until her red shoes fell apart. The witch wanted to help her!

"And let us also make *this* clear: I will not be teaching you to play with time. What you see in the visions will happen, yes? And you will not attempt to change it?" Mathilda asked, her voice stern, and Elva gave a reluctant nod. "Very well. Now that you understand all of that, I'd like to see what you can do. Did you bring the mirror with you?"

"I did." Elva pulled the glass from her basket and held it up. "But may I ask why you left it behind in your old cottage? Were you ever planning to come back for it?"

The witch's knitting needles slowed a bit. "I had hoped to return at one time."

"But you changed your mind?"

"I was silly and sentimental. But we aren't here to talk about me," Mathilda said abruptly. "I want you to demonstrate your ability with the mirror. Don't call up a specific image. Just use it as you have used water in the past."

Elva's stomach fluttered as she obediently looked into the mirror. It still felt strange to be encouraged to use her ability after years of hiding it, and by two people, no less: Willem, who loved her, and Mathilda, who would help her. In the firelight, she thought her reflection looked more like Mama than ever, with tendrils of bright hair framing her round, pink-cheeked face, and she wondered if the resemblance struck Mathilda, too. She willed her anxious mind to relax, and as soon as it did, a vision appeared: Mathilda herself, walking through the woods.

It was odd, knowing that the person she watched in the mirror was also sitting nearby, watching *her*, but Elva let go of that thought and sharpened her focus.

In the mirror, Mathilda had a bright yellow handkerchief tied over her black hair. She was picking large mushrooms that bloomed against the trunk of a tree, breaking them off tenderly and putting them into her basket. Every so often, she stooped to gather roots and berries.

Suddenly a man spoke in a deep, gentle voice. "Find any good mushrooms?"

The Mathilda in the mirror leaped to her feet, her face pale. "How did you get in?"

The stranger looked to be in his midthirties, with a thick black beard and twinkling eyes. He was tall and broad-shouldered, and wore the checked shirt and overalls of a woodcutter, with an axe tied to his back. The bundle of chopped spruce in his arms shook as he laughed. "What do you mean, how did I get in? This is the North Woods, isn't it? Open to anyone?"

Despite his friendly, kind tone, Mathilda had backed up against a tree, trembling. "Of course," she muttered. "I wasn't paying attention. I stepped out of my own boundary. Stupid..."

"I beg your pardon?"

She hugged her basket tight to her chest. "N-nothing. I bid you good day."

"Please don't be afraid," the woodcutter said gently. "I'll leave you alone if you want me to. It's just... Don't I know you from somewhere?"

Mathilda froze, and Elva could read the thoughts on her face like a book: Perhaps this man had recognized her from one of the notices nailed up all over town.

"I'm sure I've seen your face before. I wouldn't soon forget it, as lovely as it is," the woodcutter added, his cheeks reddening.

The witch blinked. "You are too kind, but I'm sure we have never met."

"Herr Schmidt's Christmas party?" he persisted. "Or maybe the summer fish bake?"

A surprised laugh escaped Mathilda. "I, at a fish bake! On the riverbank with friends and family and neighbors all cooking fish together on a fine June day? Can you possibly mean me?"

"Why not?" he asked cheerfully, as though it were the most natural thing in the world.

For a moment, Mathilda just looked at him, her eyes bright with astonishment. And then the light faded, and her face closed once more.

"If you knew me, you would not say that. Good day," she repeated, and started walking away, her basket pressed to her chest like armor.

"I hope I see you again," the woodcutter called.

"If you knew me, you would not say that," Mathilda said again, under her breath. Her eyes glimmered with tears as she hurried away through the trees.

The vision ended, and Elva saw only her own reflection in the mirror. She looked at Mathilda. The woman had stopped knitting, and her cheeks were flushed and eyes wet.

"Who is he?" Elva asked softly.

Mathilda pushed the cat off her lap, and it gave an offended yelp as it slunk away toward the kitchen. The witch bent over the yarn as though untangling it, but Elva saw her wipe a tear from her cheek. "No one in particular," she said in a low, thick voice.

"He's very handsome," Elva ventured. "When did you meet him?"

The witch looked up sharply. "What you saw happened many years ago, and I don't want to talk about it. If I am to teach you, you are never to ask me personal questions, or I will send you back out to the forest path and close the protective boundary to you. Do you understand?"

"Yes, I'm sorry," Elva said, then quickly changed the subject. "Last time I was here, you told me that all magic-wielders have a special gift. If yours is potions, how can you see my visions?"

When Mathilda spoke, her voice was as calm as before. "People like us can perform many different types of magic, even if one calls to us more strongly than others. You, too, would be able to work with potions, just as I am able to see and hear your visions."

"Do other people's abilities come from broken vows, too?"

"Not all of them. Most are born with magic, as I was, but our gifts diminish if they aren't nurtured. That's why the strength of your ability surprised me, with your lack of training." The witch went back to knitting. "There are two types of magic: grounded and spoken. Grounded magic depends on nature and physical objects."

"And that's the type of magic we can both do?"

"Correct. Your ability requires a reflective surface. My gift of alchemy—the mixing of potions—needs plants that grow from the earth. Other people might have the gift of healing, which requires a body. Or disguise, which works by weaving enchanted cloaks; or the ability to move objects with the mind alone. Those are all examples of grounded magic."

"And what about spoken magic?" Elva asked.

The witch's lips thinned. "Spoken magic, like promises or wishes, is unreliable because it depends on human nature. People change like weathervanes: loving one moment, hateful the next. Easily swayed, easily tricked. Selfish, untrustworthy. As such, spoken magic can produce unpredictable consequences, which can't be stopped or controlled by anyone."

"I see. That's why you can't take away my ability," Elva said. "Because it was a consequence of Mama breaking her promise in exchange for your magic."

Mathilda stopped knitting. "If I *could* take it away, would you want me to?"

"No, because then I wouldn't know about the storm," Elva said at once. "It looked awful—lightning, fences and branches torn up, and more rain than I've ever seen in my life. Our entire farm was destroyed, everything my family has worked for—gone in an instant." She met the witch's eyes. "Is there truly nothing I can do to stop it?"

"Did you see what caused it?"

Elva shook her head. "But I think it's the family curse," she said, and Mathilda looked puzzled. "Every time two good things happen to us, one *bad* thing comes without fail, over and over, as steady as the seasons. Last spring, for example, our cows gave more milk than ever and made us a great deal of money. Papa repaired the stables from those profits alone. That was the first good thing. Next, my brother Rayner noticed a faulty wheel on the plow just in time, before it could hurt him or any of the farmhands."

Mathilda was very still, listening.

"And then a few days later, one of our horses began to act up. It was odd, because she's usually so gentle. Papa went into her stall, and she kicked him right between the ribs, without any warning at all. She broke three of them." Elva shivered, remembering how her father had cried out in pain as the farmhands carried him into the house. "That's why it's the family curse: We can't ever enjoy good fortune, not really. Not knowing that something terrible is about to happen, because it always does. Three is a powerful number."

"I was the one who told your mother that," the witch said, looking pained. "The potion I made for her also dealt with the number three: three active ingredients, three doses, three nights. Perhaps that broken promise had more consequences than we thought."

Elva sat back in her chair, goose bumps rising on her arms and neck. "Then I'm right. The storm will be our next bout of bad luck, all because you helped Mama and she didn't repay you."

"I understand if you blame me," the witch said in a low voice.

"I don't blame you."

"Why not?"

"Because if you hadn't helped Mama, I wouldn't be here." A thought occurred to Elva. "And maybe Rayner and Cay wouldn't, either. There are three of us . . . that number again."

"Do either of them have magic?"

Elva shook her head. "They're both perfectly unmagical. I would eat this mirror if Rayner turned out to have any unnatural powers." She laughed and was surprised to see Mathilda crack a smile, too. "Cay is special, but not in that way. He's brilliant and curious and adventurous, and always on an epic quest. His next mission is to find a wishing well."

"You love him. I can tell by the way you talk about him," Mathilda said wistfully.

"I do. I wish you could meet him, too, though he wouldn't give you a moment's peace. He'd ask you questions about absolutely everything."

"I don't think I'd mind so much." The woman cleared her throat. "Well, I think we've spoken enough for one night, and it's time you went home."

"Already?" Elva asked, disappointed. It was so comfortable sitting there by the fire, finally getting a chance to talk through everything that had worried her for so long.

"You've already been here for two hours," Mathilda said, looking amused. "And besides, I want to see this storm you've foreseen and don't want to overtax your strength by having you call it up tonight. Are you able to come back tomorrow evening at the same time?"

Elva nodded eagerly. "I can't wait."

Again, the corners of Mathilda's mouth turned upward. "I'll see you then."

14

"**Y**ou don't have to keep bringing me offerings, you know," Mathilda huffed, when Elva came back the next night with a basketful of Mama's famous molasses cookies. "I'm not some vengeful goddess you have to appease."

"I just wanted to pay you back for agreeing to teach me."

"One good deed deserves another, then?" the witch asked dryly. "You most certainly got that from your mother. Bring that mirror over and we'll get started. I want to see you call up the vision of the storm."

Elva sat down, fidgeting with the mirror. "The first night I saw it, I had other visions, too: an old well, my parents running through the woods, and strangers in odd clothing. I want to see it all again, but I'm not sure if I can."

"Just try your best. I'll pull you back if you're expending too much energy."

Elva's hands shook as she lifted the mirror. "I'd like to see the storm and the visions that came after, please," she told it. It felt silly to say it out loud with Mathilda watching, but it seemed to do the trick. Her reflection vanished to show the symbol of the willow tree, burning bright, before the roiling dark sky and ravaged farm reappeared in its place. Elva shuddered at the sight of the dead goats and ruined barn but did her best to maintain her focus.

When the tree symbol glowed again, she thought she spotted a strange squarish outline around it, but the next vision came before she could look closely.

Mama and Papa were running through the North Woods, terrified, and then the scene turned into that of Elva herself, kneeling over a body beside the well. She'd had multiple dreams about it but still couldn't get used to the grief and horror on her own face. Mama's voice murmured dreamily from the mirror: "The price of breaking a promise ... the price ..."

The tree symbol appeared once more, and this time Elva was

certain that a shining square surrounded it. It was almost like a door that stood ajar, revealing the bright room that lay beyond. If she could only reach out and open it...

But then the dizzying succession of images came into view: the young man in the odd hat, yelling in a foreign language; the pretty girl looking frightened as candlelight flickered over her face; and the boy and girl, who looked about Elva's age, running through a strange world full of impossibly tall, shiny glass columns.

"That's enough now," Mathilda said curtly. "The visions are taking too much from you."

Elva slumped back in her chair, breathless, as nausea tugged at her stomach. "Thank you," she panted, as drops of sweat glided down her face.

"In the future, you won't need me to pull you back. You'll know your own limits, and you'll develop better endurance." Mathilda frowned. "That is no ordinary storm you saw. The way the lightning tore the sky, the thunder, and the violence suggests some sort of magical involvement. Your family curse indeed seems to be another result of your mother's promise."

"Will it ever end?" Elva asked shakily.

The witch shrugged. "I told you, the consequences of magic are unknowable. The curse may never end, and even if it does, that might be in three years, three decades, or three generations. Who knows?

But I can help you protect yourself and your family, at least. I'll teach you how to move objects with your mind, to start. You'll move smaller things at first, and then build up bit by bit, until you can stop a branch from smashing your house or a piece of that barn roof from crushing your animals. And it wouldn't hurt to tell your family what you've seen, if they'll believe you," she added. "Perhaps they can reinforce the barns and bring the animals somewhere safe at the first sign of trouble."

"Who do you think those strangers could be? And what language was the man speaking?"

"English," the witch said with certainty. "But not the English of Britain. That young man was from the New World, as were all of the others. You saw far, far into the future."

Elva shook her head in disbelief. "Why am I seeing people from the New World?"

"Didn't you notice anything familiar about them?"

Frowning, Elva thought of the strangers' faces. It *did* feel as though she knew them from somewhere, and she'd had the same sensation the first time they had appeared in the mirror.

"That young, English-speaking man looked a great deal like your father, Oskar, didn't he? He had the same nose and chin," Mathilda said. "The pretty, olive-skinned girl had eyes not unlike yours, and those young people running through the city . . ."

"That was a city?" Elva asked, taken aback. "What were all those tall glass columns?"

"Buildings of the future, I expect," the witch said calmly, and Elva gaped at her. "But didn't you notice how those people who were running had dark skin, yet resembled your mother in face? I believe they are all your family. Or at least, they *will* be your family someday."

"My descendants?" Elva stared at her in wonder. She let out a breath, gripping the edge of the mirror. "My descendants will go to the New World one day? So far from Germany?"

"It seems that way."

Elva felt a smile blossom across her face. Those strangers were not strangers at all, but perhaps the grandchildren or great-grandchildren she and Willem would share. She imagined sailing with him to the New World, hand in hand, surrounded by everyone they loved. But her smile slipped away at once. "None of them were safe or happy," she said softly. "The man in the hat sounded scared and angry. That girl looked frightened, too. And those two people were running away from someone. Do you suppose the curse will continue on all that time?"

"I don't know," Mathilda said, not unkindly. "For your sake and theirs, I hope not."

Elva got up and paced before the fire. The cat, which lay nearby, eyed her with sympathy. "But if it is the curse, there must be *some* way to stop it. Some magic I can perform, something to right Mama's wrongs and bring back that balance you talked about." She looked desperately at Mathilda, who regarded her with the same pity as the cat. "What do you think is behind that symbol of the willow tree? It looked like a door, didn't it?"

Mathilda tilted her head. "What?"

"The willow tree. The one that looks like that carving on the floor of your old cottage and appears between every image. Didn't you see the square around it?"

"What are you talking about? What tree?"

"You didn't see it?" Elva demanded. "What did you see between the visions, then?"

"Nothing. One image blended into another. I saw no tree," Mathilda said, and they looked at each other for a moment, puzzled. "Perhaps this is some element of your gift of foresight that I don't have. Did you try to open the door?"

"No, I didn't have time to."

"Good. Don't try yet, not until we find out more about it." The witch rose. "Put on your cloak and come out into the garden. I'd like to show you a few things before you go home."

Outside, the North Woods was eerily silent. Not a single cricket chirped or owl hooted, and it made Elva shiver. The witch's cottage seemed to exist in a cold, lonely world all its own, without any other living thing. "What did you mean earlier about your boundary?"

"The boundary is a protective, invisible wall surrounding my home," Mathilda said. "I can get out of it anywhere, but the only way back in is through the tree landmarks. To a person who wields magic, it would feel like a veil or curtain, blocking their way in, and those without magic would pass from one side to the other without ever knowing it or disturbing my privacy."

"What about fairy rings?" Elva asked, half-jokingly.

"Not even I can stop the occasional fairy ring cropping up, but they don't disturb me and I don't disturb them. Unless a clumsy, distracted girl falls into their clutches," the witch added, her mouth quirking. "Otherwise, magic respects magic. There are many doors and secrets and ancient beings in these woods that I don't know about. I wouldn't be surprised if a wishing well *did* exist, though I've never seen one. The forest is a place of deep-rooted sorcery and pockets of enchantment, built up over the years from those who were forced into hiding here."

"People with magic?"

"People with magic," Mathilda agreed, stooping next to a row of plants. She pointed at each one. "Heartsbane, wife root, moon lettuce, and rosemary. They are stronger when planted close together. And the next row is widow's wish, sage, blue clover, and dragonfoot. Those need to be hidden from direct moonlight and sunlight in order to be more potent in tonics." She looked up at Elva, eyebrows raised. "Are you paying attention? I'm going to test you on these."

"B-but my strength isn't potions," Elva stammered. "I'm here to learn about my visions."

"You're here to learn about *magic*. You must understand and respect every type, even if you never use them all. Now, name these plants." The witch pointed at each and rolled her eyes as Elva stumbled over the names. "We're coming out here every night until you get them right."

They wandered over to a bush blooming with strange, beautiful roses Elva had never seen before. Each flower ranged in color from crimson red to sunset orange to butter yellow, all melding together like a magnificent watercolor painting and smelling like smoke and embers. Looking at them was like gazing at a midsummer bonfire.

"These are flame-roses." Mathilda knelt and pulled a pair of garden shears from her pocket, snipping off a dozen and wrapping the thorny stems in frost-blue ribbon. "I cultivated them myself. The petals, when dried and pressed, make a delicious tea. Hold out your hands."

Elva obeyed, expecting the witch to give her the bouquet, but instead the woman laid the flowers on the ground and closed her eyes.

"I am imagining myself in an empty, quiet room," Mathilda said softly. "I do this before performing any spell. I clear my mind of the world until there is only me and my intent. Magic can sense when you are troubled, and if you act upon it in an unhealthy state of mind, that, too, can bring on unwanted consequences. In this peaceful space, I envision myself reaching out to the roses. I let my energy seep from my bones and hold it fiercely in my mind, like a dream that might slip through the cracks of memory at any moment. And then..."

Though the woman did not move an inch, the bouquet began to lift slowly off the ground. Elva watched in astonishment as the roses floated up into her hands. The smoky, sweet smell filled her nostrils, and she felt the edges of the huge, sharp thorns through the ribbon. "That was wonderful," she breathed, looking at the exquisite flowers. "I'm going to learn how to do that?"

"Among other things, yes. You need to learn how to clear your mind first. I'm sure you've noticed that the visions come more easily when your mind is relaxed?" Mathilda asked, rising to her feet, and Elva nodded. "It's the same with every other spell or enchantment. Each feat of magic has a price and takes something from you, like energy."

"And that's why my visions make me feel sick?"

"Correct. And as you build up your skill, you will use less energy. As simple as that spell was, it did take a bit from me, but you wouldn't know it because of my experience. If *you* were to try that right away, it would be exhausting and you likely wouldn't be successful."

"Is the price of magic always energy?" Elva asked.

"Not always. Sometimes it is a memory, a fear, or a secret. And still more complex magic demands youth, beauty, health, sanity...things you may be reluctant to give up, so it's wise to learn your limits. Magic is about give-and-take, and drawing power from different sources: For me, it is the earth; for a healer, a person's broken bone or illness; and for you, reflective surfaces." She fixed Elva with a penetrating stare. "You seem to be a sort of mirror yourself, echoing what you look into. But instead of showing the here and now, you reveal the past and the future. And in doing so, you take the energy from the mirror and expend a bit of your own."

Elva considered this as they went back inside. "What would have happened if I had kept going just now? And you weren't there to stop me?"

"It's hard to say. Overtaxing oneself never has good consequences; indeed, I've heard of people dying or going mad, or even giving up their souls entirely." Mathilda gave Elva another stern glance. "Now do you understand why I warned you against playing with time? That's a powerful, complex bit of magic that would cost far more than it is worth."

"I do," Elva admitted, handing the bouquet to the witch.

"It's the reason the North Woods is full of magic. All of that energy spent lingers here," Mathilda said, cupping a bloodred rose. As Elva watched, the crimson petals slowly unfurled against her fingers and turned a brilliant deep pink edged with gold, like the first flush of sunrise at dawn. "Unfortunately, it tends to attract nonmagic people.

That's why so many children are drawn to this forest. Their minds are open to possibility and they follow it blindly, entranced."

Elva's heart sank at the memory of the crumpled body in her vision. She hadn't seen who it was, but there were few people over whom she would grieve like that—and only one she knew who longed to wander in the forest. "My brother Cay is obsessed with finding a wishing well here, and I'm so afraid he'll get lost."

"It wouldn't be the first time that happened to a child. If I ever catch him wandering nearby, I'll send him back out of the woods for you," Mathilda added gruffly.

"Oh, would you?" Elva cried.

The witch scowled. "I'm not promising anything, mind you. I have enough to worry about without patrolling the forest for lost children. I've a solid reputation for kidnapping and it would be ruined forever if the town saw me saving a little boy."

Amused, Elva said no more, but she thought she could understand what Mama had seen in this prickly woman, with a heart like a rose behind her wall of briars. She watched as the pink-and-gold flower in Mathilda's hand opened and closed its petals, turning a rich royal purple and sprouting two plum-colored buds on its stem. "It's beautiful, what you can do with magic. I wish more people could see this," she said, as Mathilda placed the roses in a stone jar full of water.

"If they could, I'd likely be killed on sight. But thank you."

Elva thought of Willem calling her ability a gift, the same word Mathilda often used. If he could accept powers he didn't fully understand, surely there were other people, too, who might appreciate what she and Mathilda could do instead of fearing it—others who could recognize the usefulness of knowing the future and the beauty of making roses bloom before their very eyes. Maybe someday, there would be a chance to change Hanau's general opinion of the witch and of magic in general. "You said one branch of magic was disguise," Elva ventured. "Could you disguise yourself somehow and walk around the village, if you ever wanted to?"

"Why would I want to do that?" Mathilda snapped.

Elva shrugged. "I just thought if you ever got tired of being alone, or..."

"Let's be clear on two points." The witch set the jar of flowers on the table with a loud clunk. "I *choose* to be alone. I chose it a long time ago. And as for disguising myself, I'm not ashamed of who I am. I won't walk around this town that hates me unless I get to be myself."

"I understand that, but—"

"And I'm not lonely. I don't need people."

"Everyone needs someone," Elva said quietly.

"Not me. And this conversation is over. It's time for you to get home." Mathilda pointed ungraciously at the door, and with a sigh, Elva gathered her basket and slipped the hood of her cloak back over her hair. No matter what the woman claimed, she could never hide her pleasure whenever Elva came back or her wistfulness when Elva spoke about Cay. Nor could Elva forget the vision of the woodcutter and the longing in Mathilda's eyes.

It was true: Hanau didn't have a tolerant reputation where magic was involved, not when women had been suspected and driven out of town for all sorts of reasons. But it *was* 1865, and times were changing, and Elva longed to see Mathilda step out of her self-imposed prison.

Not only to prove to the witch that people could be kind and understanding, but to herself, too, for every lesson with Mathilda made her more sure that she wanted to keep honing her magic, even if she would never be considered *normal*.

If her ability could help her protect the people she loved, if it could potentially quell the family curse, then it was not shameful or evil, as she had been taught to think. It was not a burden. Elva felt more certain than ever that magic could be both beautiful and useful, however frightening the world found it to be.

It was a blessing . . . a *gift*.

15

"Elva. Elva!"

Elva jerked awake. "What is it?"

"You're spilling milk *everywhere*!" Cay said crossly, hurrying to right an upturned bucket at his sister's feet. "And Pearl is this close to kicking you for leaning on her like that."

"Oh, poor girl, I'm sorry." Elva rubbed the agitated cow's side. She had been sitting on a stool and leaning almost all of her weight against the animal's flank when she had fallen asleep. She took the bucket of milk sheepishly and repositioned it under the udders.

"What is the matter with you?" Cay demanded. "You're always so tired these days. Mama almost sent out a search party when you were napping in the cornfield yesterday."

Elva struggled to stifle a yawn. "I haven't been sleeping enough," she said, blinking her watering eyes. Every night for over a week, she'd had to wait until her family had gone to bed before sneaking out to Mathilda's cottage in the red shoes. Returning only a few hours before dawn never gave her much time to sleep before the day's work on the farm began.

Cay folded his arms across his chest. "Also, why did you tell Mama I was planning an expedition to the North Woods? Now she barely lets me off the farm."

"I was worried. I don't want you going off into the forest by yourself."

"I'm *eleven*, Elva. I'm not a baby. I think you can trust me to find my way back home."

"I know you can; it's just that the North Woods is a dangerous place, even according to Mat—" Elva stopped herself just in time, but Cay's frown got deeper.

"You've never kept secrets from me before, or gone behind my back and told Mama things I wanted only you to know." He glowered at her. "I'm starting to think you might be like Papa and Rayner, after all. Maybe you think I'm silly like they do, studying fairy tales and going on quests. You don't believe in me either, do you?"

"Cay!" Elva cried, hurt, as he stormed off to feed the chickens.

She let out a sigh and finished milking Pearl. She placed the milk in the barn to keep cool, then went to find Cay. He was kneeling by the chicken coop, aggressively plucking eggs from underneath the squawking hens. "Listen," she said. "I'm sorry I told Mama about the quest. I know you're going to find your magical well, and I'll come with you so I can make a wish, too. Mama won't make a fuss if you and I go together."

He narrowed his eyes at her. "Are you just saying that?"

"No, I'm not. I'll talk to Mama, I swear it." Elva held out her hand, and after a moment, he shook it, his face a bit less stormy. "After all, I'm going to be the squire to your adventuring knight, remember? When we travel all over and collect folktales together like the Grimms?"

The corners of his mouth lifted. "I want to explore the entire world. Go east and find some old valley where the monsters roam. Are you sure you want to come all that way?"

Elva grinned. "Only if we visit a haunted monastery, too. Or an island where a legendary sea creature only shows itself every full moon."

Cay chuckled, looking down at the eggs in his basket. "I'm sorry

I said that about you being like Papa and Rayner. I know you don't think I'm odd the way they do."

"I think you're perfect." She squeezed his shoulder. "You're going to be a famous explorer someday, and I'll be there to see it all. I just need more sleep first. All right?"

For the rest of the day, they chatted together as they did the chores. The subject of Mathilda—and her decision to let Elva try to practice moving objects with her mind—was on the tip of Elva's tongue, but she held back from telling Cay. The fewer people who knew about these lessons, the better, even if the secret drove a wedge between her and Cay and lingered in her mouth like a bad taste.

Still, the guilt ate away at her long after everyone had gone to bed, and she dropped from her window, landing noiselessly on the grass in her slippers. Her heart stopped when she thought she glimpsed movement at one of the other windows, but it was only the shadow of tree branches.

When Elva arrived at the cottage, she was stunned to hear voices coming from inside.

"But how did you get here?" Mathilda was asking somebody, exasperated. "And when?"

"I don't remember," answered a small voice.

"How can you not remember? Was it today? Yesterday?"

"I don't remember," the voice said again, and then it began to cry.

Elva pushed open the door to see Mathilda crouching beside a girl of about five or six. The child had dark brown hair and a round, wide-eyed face smudged with dirt.

"Thank goodness," the witch said, sighing with relief at the sight of Elva. "Maybe you can help me figure out where this creature came from. I found her outside my boundary, and the sniffling and wailing was driving me mad. I had no choice but to take her in."

"Don't be afraid," Elva told the child kindly, kneeling down. She noticed that the girl was wrapped warmly in one of Mathilda's blankets and was holding a fistful of cake, and her skinned knee, too, had been carefully cleaned and bandaged. Elva glanced at the witch with a raised eyebrow.

"What? I only did it to try to stop her crying," Mathilda said defensively.

"What's your name?" Elva asked the child.

"Hannah. I don't know where my mama is. And it got dark and I couldn't find her."

Elva patted her shoulder. "I'm sure she's looking for you, too, and we'll make sure you get back to her safely. Did you sleep in the forest?" she asked, and Hannah shook her head. "Was it still bright out when you lost your mama? Yes? Then it sounds like it just happened today."

"We were having a picnic near the stone frog," the little girl said, encouraged by Elva's soft manner. "But then I saw a *real* frog hop in here and followed it. And then it got dark and I fell, and that lady got mad at me." Her wide brown eyes moved to Mathilda.

"I wasn't mad! I only wanted you to stop that infernal crying. Yes, *that*, exactly," the witch added dryly, for at the sound of her voice, the child had begun to cry again. "Well, at least now we know where she got separated from her mother. Can you take her by yourself?"

Elva bit her lip. "I don't know where the stone frog is. Would you mind taking us?"

Mathilda sighed and slipped on her cloak, covering her hair and face with the deep hood. "It's a statue at the north end of the river. Come along," she said, as Elva and the little girl followed the witch out of the cottage, hand in hand. Instead of taking the path Elva used every night to get there and home, Mathilda veered off in a different direction.

"Are you tired?" Elva asked, and Hannah nodded, so she hoisted the child up and carried her after the witch, glad for her comforting weight. At night, in this unfamiliar part of the forest, the North Woods looked every inch the place of secrets and sorcery Mathilda had said it was. The trees seemed to glow with a pale light, leaves rustling like voices conversing in the still air. Bright rings of fireflies danced around them as Mathilda led them past a row of spruce trees.

"Here's the boundary," the witch warned, and as she spoke, Elva felt something invisible brush her face. Mathilda made a motion like lifting a curtain, and the sensation disappeared.

"I've never been this far north down the river," Elva said.

After several minutes, they emerged from the trees near a section of the Main. Voices sounded out and footsteps hurried toward them as a frantic woman and a group of exhausted-looking people came into sight, carrying torches. The minute the woman saw Hannah, she burst into noisy tears and snatched her from Elva, hugging her tight as they both cried their hearts out.

"You found my baby! Oh, thank you!" the woman sobbed to Elva.

"I'm not the one who found your daughter," Elva told her, seizing Mathilda's arm to keep her from melting back into the forest. "My companion is."

Though the hood covered her face completely, Mathilda still flinched when the woman's eyes turned to her. "Thank you for everything," the mother said, looking at her child's sticky fist. "And how good you are to give her something to eat. Let me return your blanket..."

"No, please keep it. And good night," Mathilda said quickly, freeing herself from Elva's grip and hurrying back toward the woods.

"May I at least know your name? Or where you live?" the mother persisted, following the witch. "I'd like to send you a little gift as a thank-you for keeping my Hannah safe."

"There's no need. Good-bye," Mathilda said, and disappeared into the trees.

"But . . ."

"Good night. And good-bye, Hannah," Elva said, smiling at the stunned mother and child. She hurried after the witch. "You should have let her send you something as a thank-you."

Mathilda snorted. "Taking that screaming creature back is enough of a gift, trust me."

"She just wanted to show you her gratitude. Maybe you could have made a new friend."

"Yes, wouldn't that be lovely? And then I could hear her shriek *devil-woman* and *sorceress* at me when she found out who I was, like all the rest. I just don't know *why* I'm not putting myself through that wondrous experience again."

"You don't know that," Elva pointed out. "There might be decent people out there who would accept you. You shouldn't spend your life hiding."

"So you're saying I should leave my safe cottage and plunge into that Hanau out there? I should risk everything for the slim chance of making a friend I don't need?"

"All I'm saying," Elva said gently, "is that not *everyone* is hateful. And if they knew how good and kind you are, they would want to give you a chance."

The witch cackled. "You think I'm good and kind? You know what I've done."

"That was years ago! I wouldn't be here if I thought you were evil. And you agreed to help me when you could have turned me away. That's kindness."

"I told you, that's only because—"

"You also offered to protect Cay if you found him in the woods, *and* you took good care of Hannah just now," Elva added, as they walked alongside a quiet stream running through the forest. "Deep down, you are decent and there are people who will see that. Like me . . . and that woodcutter." She knew she was treading on dangerous ground by mentioning him, and as expected, Mathilda stopped in her tracks.

"What do *you* know? Nothing. You don't know that meeting Alfred was what convinced me I would be killed on sight if I ever left my sanctuary. You think he saw the goodness in my soul?" Elva had never heard a sound more bitter than Mathilda's laugh. "The vision you saw was the first time I met him, but not the last. From then on, whenever I went out, I made sure to stray just along the edge of my boundary so he could find me. We spoke more and more, but I never told him who I was. Someone else did."

"Who?"

Beneath her hood, the witch's eyes glinted with tears. "His brother caught us talking and recognized me as the witch of the North Woods.

The way Alfred looked at me when he found out...the horror in his eyes...oh, Elva, I could take any other cruelty in the world, any other insult or injustice but that. I had let myself hope that Alfred would not turn me away if he knew what I was, but I learned the truth that day."

Elva's heart ached at the thought that Willem could have been so cruel toward *her*. Instead, he had shown compassion where Alfred had not.

"I saw Alfred one last time. I went to find him and explain that I hadn't meant to deceive him, but he wasn't alone. He was with men he had gathered to hunt me down and have me executed. He accused me of using magic to make him unable to think of any other woman. That was how I found out he had fallen in love with me." Mathilda looked at her tearfully in the eyes. "You don't know how much I hunger for what you have, for people who care about me."

"You can have that," Elva said fiercely. "I will help you. My family will help you. Mama and Papa are respected in Hanau, and I'll explain. I'll tell them..."

But the witch shook her head. "I can't risk my heart again. I thought happiness was within reach once, but no more. Every time I opened up—to your mother, to Alfred, to others before them—all I ever got was pain and betrayal. I've hurt enough, Elva."

"You have me. And just as you have been teaching me, I am going to teach *you*," Elva told her. "I am going to help you be so charming and delightful that people can't help but like you—please don't snort, it isn't polite—and you will live among us in peace. Then, when you reveal your magic, everyone will already respect you and perhaps be more accepting of it."

The witch gave a weak laugh, wiping her eyes. "You really are your mother's daughter. Ever the optimist. But I'll say this for you, you're a lot more reliable than Agnes. You've already come to my house more than she ever did."

"And I will keep coming as long as I'm welcome. You have my word."

Mathilda pursed her lips. "You know how I feel about promises."

An idea occurred to Elva. She knelt beside the stream. "Can you give me some light?"

"What are you doing?" the witch demanded, but waved her hand obligingly at some fireflies. They gathered in a spiraling halo around Elva's head, illuminating the surface of the water so that she could see her reflection. She slowed her breaths and envisioned an empty room, just as Mathilda had been teaching her all week. The fireflies seemed to fade, and then there was only her and the water. She turned her thoughts toward her family sleeping peacefully at home, and the vision emerged clear and bright in the darkness.

It was of her family, gathered around the dinner table. Mama set a roast ham in front of Papa, who kissed her, eliciting groans of protest from Cay and Rayner that made them all laugh. Elva thought she could watch the happy scene forever, but she hadn't yet learned how to hold one vision steady in the water, and it flickered away to reveal the willow tree symbol once more. A shining square surrounded it like a door held ajar, and Elva reached out without thinking. But as soon as her fingers touched it, a sharp ache formed in her temples and she withdrew her hand with a cry.

She heard Mathilda say something, but her voice was muted and Elva wanted to keep going. She felt the pain subside as she cleared her mind and turned all of her focus toward the people of Hanau. The vision of a bright, sunny day in town appeared, and Elva saw herself with Frau Bauer and Freida as the baker and his wife passed by with a warm greeting. Willem was there, too, and Elva's heart tugged at the way he held her eyes in the vision.

The willow tree symbol shimmered again. Instinctively, Elva reached for it.

"Stop it!" Mathilda cried.

And then the trance was over. Elva was back in the North Woods again, on her back looking up at the trees, realizing that Mathilda had yanked her away from the stream. She winced as the sharp pain throbbed in her temples. "Did you see everything?" she asked breathlessly.

"Not everything, I suspect. Were you reaching for that door again? Didn't I tell you not to try until we learned more about it?"

"I wanted to see what was behind it," Elva said. Her legs shook so much when she stood up that the witch had to support her as they moved through the woods.

"It cost you more energy than it was worth," Mathilda said crossly. "Careless girl! How many times have I warned you not to overextend yourself?"

"I wanted to show you what your life could be like, living near us and being a part of our town," Elva explained. "Eating supper, greeting neighbors, shopping at market."

"Careless girl," Mathilda said again, but not as forcefully. She waved her hands at the fireflies still following Elva, and they transformed into many-petaled white flowers that shone like stars plucked from the sky. Elva gasped at the beauty of the enchantment: the graceful movement of the witch's hands, the light of the fireflies intensifying just before they changed, and the musical sound of the flowers bursting from the air where none had been before.

"See what I mean?" Elva said weakly. "You'd be the most popular woman at all of the fish bakes."

"Oh, do be quiet," Mathilda told her, stuffing the flowers into Elva's hands. But on her lips was the barest hint of a smile, and her eyes held something even more precious: hope.

Elva strolled home from market on a perfect June day, hot and bright. She had gotten two full nights of sleep for the first time in a month and a half of magic lessons, and she felt as cheery as the weather. Mathilda had asked her not to come for a few days, saying she had business to attend to. "But I expect you to practice everything we've been working on. Please," she had added, after a pause, and Elva had grinned in approval. They had been working on improving

Mathilda's manners, which were a bit rusty after so many years alone in the North Woods.

"So you *are* alive after all!" Freida Bauer exclaimed, passing Elva on the bridge. The girls hugged. "I've hardly seen you since the Easter party."

Elva lifted her basket apologetically. "It's been busy on the farm and I've only just gotten a chance to get away. Mama needed some things in town."

"And *you* needed to see Willem, I'm sure," Freida teased. "He's by the old tree. I have to run to market myself, but come see me next week?"

"I will." Elva hugged her again before heading to the riverbank with renewed excitement. As Freida had said, Willem was sitting against the willow tree, the remains of his lunch scattered around him. Elva's heart picked up at the sight of him, his hair shining in the sun and his eyes fixed dreamily on the river. She snuck up behind him and covered his eyes with her hands.

"Freida, you'd better go before Elva sees us together," Willem said, without missing a beat. He burst into laughter as Elva gave his shoulder a playful swat. "You got my note, then?"

"I did. I'm sorry it's been so long since we've seen each other." Elva leaned into his kiss as he wrapped his arms around her. She felt safe and comfortable with him, and someday they would be together like this forever. She wanted him to know everything about her, the way Papa did about Mama. *Well, almost everything*, she thought. It didn't feel right to talk about Mathilda yet, but it didn't feel right to keep such a secret from him, either. "I made a new friend. A woman about Mama's age," she added hesitantly.

"Who is she?"

"You wouldn't know her. She keeps to herself and doesn't have anyone to care for her."

"It's just like you to be kind. Have you invited her over for supper? I'd like to meet her."

"Well, no." Elva bit her lip. "She hasn't been out in society for a long time, and she's very shy. But I wish you could meet her. She knows so much about everything, and she bakes delicious cakes and knits the warmest blankets. You're the only one I've told about her. I don't think Mama and Papa would approve."

"Why not?" he asked. "They wouldn't disapprove of you befriending a lonely woman."

They would if she was a witch, Elva thought. "I guess they might think it was odd that she's all alone. But she's wonderful." She laughed, thinking of Mathilda's jokes and sarcastic quips. She had been looking forward to seeing the witch again all day.

"What else have you been doing? Have you had any more visions?"

"Nothing new, though I've been practicing," she told him. "I'm stronger and I don't get sick or tired as quickly. Would you like me to see how many calves Herr Bauer will have soon?" Papa had told her that the Bauers' cows were all expecting babies in early June.

"Yes, please," Willem said, delighted. "I have a cup of water."

Elva took it from him. After so much practice with Mathilda, it was simple now to clear her mind. She turned her thoughts toward Herr Bauer's farm, smiling when an image appeared of Willem filling the cows' water buckets. "You did well, Rosie," he told one of them kindly. "And you, too, Marigold. Three new babies! Herr Bauer will be pleased to have another bull in a couple of years." The animals blinked their gentle, trusting eyes at him as he spoke. In the background, a farmhand tripped over a rake someone had carelessly left on the ground.

Then the willow tree flashed, and the square around it glowed more clearly than ever. Elva hesitated, thinking of Mathilda's warning. And then her fingers darted forward and gripped the edge of the square, pulling it open like a swinging door. She *had* to know what was behind it. It was a place not even the witch could go, and perhaps Elva was the one meant to open it.

She held her breath, waiting to see what would happen. But then the image of Willem filling the water buckets appeared again, exactly as she had seen it. Again, she heard him tell the cows, "You did well, Rosie. And you, too, Marigold..."

Elva shook her head, confused. The door had only made the vision replay. As the cows blinked gently at Willem, her eyes moved to the farmhand in the background, knowing he was about to trip on the rake. She wished she could move the rake and prop it against the wall.

And suddenly there it was. The rake leaned against the wall of the stables, and the farmhand who had tripped in the earlier vision went about his business, whistling.

"Elva?" Willem asked, and she came out of her trance to find him looking at her, worried.

"I'm fine," she said, forcing a smile, as a pounding headache pricked at her temples. "The cows will have three calves. One of them will be a bull."

"Here, lean against the tree." Willem scrambled to his feet and helped prop her against the tree trunk. He wet his handkerchief in the river and pressed the cool cloth against her face. "You look so pale. Should I get a horse to bring you home?"

"I'll be all right," she reassured him, closing her eyes. "I just need to sit quietly."

She had opened the willow tree door in her mind, but for what?

Sometimes, in her more vivid dreams, she could control what happened, whether it was making horses fly or imagining herself in elaborate gowns. She must have done that just now, except she was wide awake. She had known the farmhand would trip and had pictured moving the rake—that was all. Changing the future was impossible, as Mathilda had told her over and over. Wasn't it?

"Klaus!" Willem called to a man who came jogging over. "What are you doing out here?"

"The cows are about to give birth. You told me to get you when that happened," the man said, his light gray eyes darting to Elva. He was short and strongly built, with thick black hair and a sharp, clever face—a familiar one at that, given that she had seen a vision of him talking to Willem about Berlin. "Is she all right? Should I get help?"

"I feel a little better," she said, looking up at the newcomer. "I'm Elva Heinrich."

"I know who you are." His shrewd, pale gaze took in her whole face. "Willem talks of nothing else. I'm Klaus Eibner. Pleased to meet you at last."

"And you. I think the sun must have gotten to me," Elva added. "It's so hot today."

Klaus's eyes moved slowly to the cup Elva had dropped, now lying empty beside her. "Perhaps you haven't drunk enough water yet," he suggested.

"Perhaps not," she said, feeling a bit uneasy under his perceptive stare.

Willem helped her to her feet. "Are you sure you're all right? Would you rather go home or come with us and see the baby cows?"

That made Elva pause. If she went to the Bauers' barn, she would not be looking at the cows, but at the farmhand and the rake. She knew deep in her heart that Mathilda was right—that no one could play with time without devastating consequences—and yet a small voice of doubt sang at the back of her mind. "I'll come with you," she said. "It's on my way home."

"Here, take this," Klaus said, handing over his wide-brimmed straw hat. "That should help keep the sun off your head. And let me carry your basket."

She smiled and put on the hat, shaking off her uneasiness about him; she knew it had only been fear of discovery. "Thank you," she said, taking Willem's arm on the walk back. When they got to the Bauers' farm, Herr Vogel, the animal physician, was coming out of the barn. He was a tall, gray-haired man who had always brought candy for Elva and her brothers when they were smaller on his visits to Papa's farm. He greeted her warmly, then turned to Willem.

"You're too late," he said merrily. "Your favorite, Rosie, struggled on for a while, but she and Marigold and all *three* of their calves are fine and healthy. It's a shame Bauer wasn't here to see, but he'll have two new cows and a new bull in a few years."

Willem gave a decent impression of being pleased and surprised, though his glance at Elva was full of amusement. "Let's go see them," he said, leading her into the barn.

The cows stood in their clean stalls, with their newborn calves beside them. Willem grabbed a large tub of water and filled the animals' buckets. "You did well, Rosie," he told the bigger cow affectionately. "And you, too, Marigold. Three new babies!"

Elva held her breath, her eyes not on him or the calves, but on the space beyond them. A farmhand was whistling as he walked across the barn, carrying a bale of hay. He took one step after the other, straight-backed and busy, as she watched him in shock. He hadn't tripped, and there was no rake in the straw. She *had* changed the future!

But then he gave a shout and the hay went flying as his foot rolled over something: the rake, lying in the straw after all. It had taken him longer to fall, but there he was, sprawled out.

"Haven't you learned how to walk by now?" someone yelled from the back.

"If that was your rake, I'm going to pummel the life out of you!" the farmhand shouted. He got up, unhurt, and propped the rake against the wall where Elva had reimagined it to be. He picked up his bale of hay, shaking his head. "Blast these new hired hands."

Elva let out a breath, both relieved and disappointed. It seemed that the willow tree door served no purpose, aside from allowing her to delay what would inevitably happen . . . yet why was it there? And why could she see it when Mathilda could not? Her head throbbed, though the pain was duller. "I should go home now," she told Willem. "I'll let you get back to your work."

"Will I see you again soon?" he asked softly.

"Very soon," she said, and turned to Klaus. "It was nice to meet you."

"And you," he said, his pale eyes never leaving her as she walked back out into the sun.

"Of *course* you didn't change the future. Haven't you listened to a word I've said?" Mathilda exclaimed when Elva told her about it that night. They sat by the hearth, where a fire always roared even on warm nights, sipping flame-rose tea and eating the molasses cookies Elva had brought. "Your imagination just needs an outlet. That must be what the door is all about."

"I think there's more to it than that," Elva argued. "I just haven't found out what yet. I *know* it took longer for that farmhand to fall. Anyway, you can't blame me for hoping that I can do something to stop that storm." All day, she had envisioned herself opening the willow tree door and somehow changing everything she had seen about the coming disaster: make the sun shine, make the wind die down, make the barn stand strong and intact.

"Well, it's a foolish hope. But I think what happened shows how strong you're getting. Willem isn't frightened by what you can do?"

"He thinks of it as a gift, like the intuition someone has for their loved ones," Elva said proudly. "If he understands that much, others in Hanau might, as well, if we gave them a chance."

"He must love you very much. I'm glad you have someone who accepts you as you are."

"You deserve that, too, you know. Just as much as anyone else," Elva said gently. "Have you ever had any family? Who taught you magic?" She expected Mathilda to bark at her about privacy, but to her surprise, a sweet smile crossed the witch's face.

"Josefine. She was a big, beautiful woman with a voice like thunder and eyes like the winter sky. She took up two chairs sitting down and moved with the grace of a dancer. She was formidable and sharp and hotheaded, and I loved her more than I ever loved my own mother."

"Did she raise you?"

"Yes, with my aunt Louisa." Mathilda was silent for a moment, as though weighing something. "They were deeply and irrevocably in love. They had met as children and from the start, it was like two halves of a soul coming together. They were forbidden to marry as adults, but still, they pledged the whole of their lives to each other. Does that shock you?"

"It might shock my parents," Elva said slowly. "And many others in town. But I don't think love will ever distress me."

"I wish more people felt that way. Josefine's and Louisa's families did not, so they were disowned and driven out of their village. They built a cottage on a hill outside Hanau and were two of the happiest people I ever knew. They wanted nothing but each other, yet I imagine there is something missing when the world is denied to you, both for loving someone people think you shouldn't . . . and having powers people consider unnatural." Mathilda gazed into the fire with an uncharacteristic softness on her face. "I knew from a young age that I wanted to become a great witch, like Josefine. But I also knew that if I did, I would have to give up the world."

Elva listened, thinking of all that had passed. No matter how much she wanted to bring Mathilda back into society, there would always be people who hated the witch for what she was. People who would hate Elva, too. "What was Josefine's gift?"

A smile touched the witch's lips. "Speaking to animals. Deer would burst from the woods at one word from her, flocks of birds would circle the cottage, and fish would dance in the creek whenever she was happy. I felt lucky to know her and be her adopted niece. Though I didn't always think that way." Her smile slipped. "When I was ten, my father told me he was giving me to Josefine and Louisa. My parents had always hated my strangeness and couldn't wait to get rid of me. I was taking up room and food they wanted to give to their *normal* children."

"I'm sorry," Elva murmured.

"I don't want your pity," Mathilda said sternly. "I'm telling you this because I want you to understand that everything has a purpose. Going to live with Josefine changed my life, for better *and* for worse. It helped me come into my powers, but it also marked me forever as an outcast like her. Those ten years with her and Louisa were the only happy ones I've ever had. When they died of old age, I grew ever more isolated, because loneliness is another cost of magic. But Josefine told me something that has always stayed with me: Our abilities die with us when we pass, so we might as well teach others while we can."

"And that's why you decided to help me?"

Mathilda hesitated. "Yes, and also because you remind me of your mother. I remember Agnes's betrayal, but I also remember her kindness when no one else in the world cared for me. She made me feel like I was somebody. Like I was worthwhile."

"You *are* somebody," Elva said, angry that people had made Mathilda feel like anything less. It wasn't fair. "You're one of the only people who has ever seen *me* as I am, and not as I pretend to be."

"But the things I've done in my past—" the witch began, her voice frayed at the edges.

"No one knows what it's like to be you. To be *us*. They don't know what that can do to a person, and what that person might have to do to survive. The things that happened to you could have happened to anyone, and still could to me." Elva clenched her jaw. "So I am going to do whatever I can to convince Hanau to accept you. I need to do it for you, and I need it to do it for me, too. I need to know that my family and friends won't turn me away."

Mathilda stared at her in silent astonishment.

"Josefine and Louisa may have had to hide from the world for the rest of their lives," Elva went on. "But that will not be the case for us. I won't let it be. I'm going to fight for you."

The witch's lips trembled. "I've never had anyone fight for me before."

"Well, you've got me now. And I want to help you the way you've helped me." Elva shrugged, feeling shy. "I . . . I want to be to you what you were to Josefine."

"A nuisance?" Mathilda asked wryly, though her voice shook, betraying her emotion.

"No. An adopted niece." Elva looked down at her folded hands. "I can talk to you freely about my secret. You're the only one. And I'd like to think of you as someone I could go and talk to whenever I needed it, like . . . like an aunt who had taken me in. An aunt whom I loved and respected the way you did with Josefine."

There was a long silence.

"Would that be all right with you?" Elva asked nervously.

It was as though she had broken down a wall between them. The witch sank to her knees on the rug and wept, her face in her hands and her shoulders shaking. It was a violent, cathartic outburst, and Elva's instinct told her to be still and silent, even as she longed to hug the poor woman. She sensed that Mathilda had not let herself cry for a very long time.

Elva closed her eyes and found that quiet space in her mind, where there was no roaring fire or sobbing witch. Only emptiness. She pictured the mirror on Mathilda's table and held the image behind her eyelids until it was as solid and sure as though she was looking right at it. And now came the tricky part she had struggled with in their lessons: maintaining that calmness and peace while reaching for the mirror with her mind. She breathed slowly as Mathilda had taught her to do and imagined her arm stretching across the space to the mirror.

She felt its edges, cool as marble, in her hand. Its weight settled against her fingers, and when she opened her eyes, the mirror had flown across the room from Mathilda's table into her hand. She had not moved an inch.

In her shock, Mathilda had stopped crying. They stared at each other as Elva clutched the mirror in disbelief, and then the witch said, "I guess you *have* been practicing like I told you to."

A laugh bubbled up in Elva's chest, answered by a great chuckle from Mathilda, and then they gave in to their laughter until tears ran down their faces once more—happy ones, this time.

"Here," Elva said, wiping her eyes. "Let me show you something."

It was harder, this time, to clear her mind. She was a storm of emotions, of tenderness and hope and fear for what she hoped to do for her new friend. But it was a testament to the witch's teachings that Elva managed to summon the vision. The mirror showed her family once more: Papa, smoking his pipe by the fire; Mama in her rocking chair, listening to Cay read fairy tales to her; and Rayner on the rug, scratching the dog's ears. Elva saw herself, too, chatting with Papa. It was an image of such warmth and comfort that she felt sure Mathilda would be moved by it.

This time, when she saw the willow tree symbol, Elva did not hesitate. She pulled it open, even as her head throbbed with pain. The vision began again, and this time, she bent her focus on Mathilda walking into the room. At once, the witch appeared, blushing as Mama got up and greeted her with a hug and Papa and Rayner shook her hand.

Cay talked to her about wishing wells and magic as she was drawn into their circle by the fire and given a comfortable seat.

Everything Elva imagined came to life in the vision. She decided they would play games, and there was Rayner putting the board in front of Mathilda so she could reach it easily. She thought of Mama's delicious cooking, and trays of cookies and cakes appeared beside the witch. The Mathilda in the vision laughed and chatted, looking every bit like a member of the family.

The ache in Elva's head intensified, so she looked away from the glass and ended the vision. "This is what I want for you," she told Mathilda, whose eyes had filled with tears once more. The witch folded her hands over her chest, as though protecting her yearning heart. "And I'm going to do everything I can to make it happen."

Mathilda swallowed hard. "There was a part of me that thought you might be good for me, Elva Heinrich, the first day you came to my cottage. I silenced it because I knew better than to hope, but I should have listened instead."

"You should have," Elva agreed, smiling.

"I suppose," the witch said, with an attempt at her usual tartness, "I have a new niece now, whether I want her or not."

"And you'll have her for life." Elva held out her hand, and Mathilda took it and squeezed.

17

"Oh, Elva, I don't know about this." Mathilda hesitated as she looked out into the forest. Anyone might think she was admiring the sun-dappled wood on this lovely June morning, but Elva knew she was looking at the invisible boundary that curtained her off from the world.

"We won't go far," Elva reassured her. The boundary felt like a veil of cobwebs over her face, tickling her skin as Mathilda reluctantly lifted it over the two of them. "We're going to gather herbs and mushrooms, just as you wanted to do today. Only we'll do it on the other side."

"This whole plan is madness," the witch grumbled.

It had taken a week for Elva to convince her about the plan to reintegrate her into Hanau. Getting the witch to step outside the boundary in daylight, she decided, was progress. "You're doing wonderfully. And if we run into anyone, what did we agree you would do?" she prompted.

Mathilda sighed. "Smile and make cheerful conversation."

"And if there are children?"

"I can't stare at them long, speak in a loud voice, or show frustration, even if they cry."

Elva laughed at the witch's despairing expression. "This will be good practice, and you'll get used to talking to people again. Then, later on, I can reintroduce you to Mama and Papa."

"I know Oskar will *love* that."

Elva chuckled at her sarcasm, but in truth, she *was* worried about how her parents would react. Not only had she read Mama's private letters and sought out the witch, but she had also been strengthening her magic instead of suppressing it. Cay, too, would be furious that she had kept this secret from him. *They'll all understand when I tell them about the storm*, she tried to reassure herself.

"If people see you as Mama and Papa's friend, they'll be more willing to welcome you," Elva explained. "Papa will speak to the town council about setting up a vote to protect you as long as you're here in Hanau. And then no one, not even the most closed-minded people, can do anything about it. You'll be free to live among us like anyone else."

"Do you really think it will work?" Mathilda asked. "Some of these people won't ever leave me in peace, whether or not the council decrees it. And I'm not sure I want some sort of trial where strangers decide whether I get to exist or not."

"We have to try, and if a decree is passed, anyone who bothers you will be punished." Elva put her hands on the witch's shoulders. "I won't let anything happen to you, and I'll be with you in front of the council, pleading your case. You won't be alone. That's a promise."

Mathilda's eyes on her were steady, even as her chin trembled with emotion. "I don't like it . . . but I accept, because I know you keep your word," she said, with a shaky laugh. "It was always going to be an uphill battle for me. Though I *am* tired of living like this."

"We're going to fix that. But first, we'll enjoy today," Elva said brightly. "Don't worry about anyone recognizing you from those awful posters. The drawings don't even look like you. And if they do, you'll have that spell ready to make them forget they saw us."

Mathilda opened her mouth to reply, but suddenly went tense and still.

Footsteps sounded nearby and a family appeared, combed and dressed in their best: a father, mother, four children, and another man.

Elva felt thankful not to recognize them, though there weren't many people this far in the North Woods who would know Mama and Papa and tell them Elva was in the forest when she was supposed to be running errands.

The men doffed their caps politely. "Good day, ladies," the father said. The small boy riding on his shoulders waved at Mathilda, who waved back timidly when Elva nudged her.

"Good day. It looks like you're headed to the river for a picnic," Elva said cheerfully. She elbowed Mathilda again, urging her to speak, and got a glare for her troubles.

"Are ... are you going for a swim?" the witch ventured.

"Mama doesn't think the water's warm enough yet," said the little boy, glancing at the other man, "but Uncle Frank doesn't agree."

The man laughed, shifting the heavy picnic basket in his arms. "I think it will be a nice outing, with or without swimming," he said, with an admiring glance at Mathilda. "Do you and your friend live hereabouts? I don't think I've ever seen either one of you around."

Mathilda looked helplessly at Elva. "We live ... uh, over that way. And you?"

"We live back that way," Frank answered, pointing in the opposite direction.

"That's a lovely shawl you're wearing," said the mother, studying the frost-blue knitting draped over Mathilda's shoulders. She turned to her three daughters. "Isn't it nice, girls? That's the kind of needlework you're practicing right now. Someday you'll be as skilled as this lady."

"Th-thank you," the witch stammered. "Did you girls make those?" She pointed at the uneven crochet on their baskets, and the children nodded, blushing. "You're all very good."

"Thank you," the girls chorused, and one of them gave Mathilda a big white daisy from her basket. The witch looked as stunned as though she were being offered a rock, not a flower.

The parents said good-bye and moved along, but Frank lingered. "My sister always packs too much food," he told Mathilda, glancing at the basket she carried. "If you and your friend finish mushrooming early, we'll be sitting by the stone frog. We'd be glad to have you join us, if you want."

"Will you make us swim?" the witch asked, and Frank's eyes twinkled at her.

"Only if you want to. But please do think about joining us."

"I'd like that," Mathilda said shyly, and he walked away with one final admiring glance.

"Well done, you!" Elva teased her, when he was out of earshot. "A suitor already."

"Oh, hush," the witch told her, but her eyes shone. "If he only knew who I was . . ."

Elva shook her head. "Don't think like that. The more people see you around town like any other citizen, the more friends you'll have . . . and admirers," she added, laughing as her companion blushed. For the next hour, they filled their baskets and chatted with everyone they met, all of whom were perfectly cordial to Mathilda. Watching the witch open up was like witnessing a shy turtle emerge from its shell, Elva decided, pleased.

"Should we go back? Your parents will wonder where you are," Mathilda said at last.

"I suppose so. I wish I could stay with you longer, though."

The witch slipped an arm through hers. "I haven't had such a pleasant day in a long time. Thank you." She hesitated, then added, "Will you be telling Agnes and Oskar tonight?"

"No time like the present," Elva said confidently, though her stomach swooped with nerves. "Maybe I'll even show them *this*." She closed her eyes and pictured the heavy branch lying in their path. She thought of her energy as a stream, flowing outward, and envisioned herself picking the branch up and flinging it aside. When she opened her eyes, the branch floated up from the ground and threw itself into the woods.

"That took you no time at all!" Mathilda praised her. "And when you get even better, you won't need to close your eyes or . . ." She trailed off, her face troubled.

"What is it?"

"There's someone outside my boundary. The magic lets me sense when they're near. They'll pass through to the other side, but it's happened too often lately. First that little girl, Hannah, and now a boy I've seen twice this week alone. I wish magic wasn't so attractive to children. They're drawn to it even if they don't know what it is. What's wrong?"

"What did the boy look like?" Elva asked, going cold all over.

"He had pale blond hair and was about this tall. His back was turned to me both times, but I did find a few spools of thread where he was standing." Mathilda frowned thoughtfully. "There was a trail of them for a short distance, leading back the way he had come."

"Bread crumbs," Elva muttered.

"What's wrong? Do you think it was your brother Cay?"

"I certainly hope not, after I told him not to come here without me." But even as she spoke, Elva knew in her bones that it *had* been Cay. He had ignored her warning.

"Don't worry," Mathilda said. "I'll look out for him, and anyway, there aren't any wells around here that I know of." She led Elva toward the tree landmarks but then stopped again. "I can still sense the people there. I should go and make sure ... You run home...."

"No, I'll come with you," Elva said, pointing at her red shoes. "I won't make a sound."

Even without enchanted shoes, the witch moved like silent mist as they skirted the perimeter of the boundary, her hand on the invisible curtain. They hid behind an oak tree when they heard men's voices, and Elva's heart leaped when she recognized Willem and Klaus in the group of four.

"Didn't I tell you the best spruce is found in witch territory?" asked one of the farmhands, his voice loud and boastful. He had an axe strapped to his back. "Magic makes the trees grow taller around her, so no one can find her."

"How is that supposed to hide her?" scoffed another farmhand in a red work shirt.

The first man gave him a withering look. "Oh, Jonas, you don't know anything about it. You've never gone on a witch hunt with us. Has he, Willem?"

Elva frowned at the offensive remark, knowing Willem would never go along with such nonsense. But her heart stopped when she heard his familiar laugh.

"We'll take Jonas on our next hunt," Klaus suggested. "He could learn a thing or two."

"I'm sure I know more than you, at any rate," Jonas told him. "You're the newest."

The farmhand with the axe clapped Klaus on the shoulder. "He catches on quickly."

"All I need to do is bring a child with me," Klaus said, with a cold smile, "and the witch will come right out, isn't that so? They *are* what she eats, aren't they?"

Everyone laughed, including Willem, who said not one word to defend the woman or even change the subject. Elva leaned against the trunk, heartsick. She didn't want to hear any more of the conversation, but they couldn't move without risking the men seeing them. She thought of the Easter party, when Willem had promised her never to repeat gossip. And here he was, chuckling along.

A rapping sound rang out in the forest. Klaus had taken one of the heavy spruce logs and hit it against an oak. "So it's true that she lives here, then? Why won't she come out?" he asked. "I'm sure she could make a deal with the town. Make some money for her poisons and such."

Mathilda stiffened.

"I've wondered the same thing," said the farmhand with the axe. "If I could do magic, I'd try to get rich off it instead of sulking in the woods."

"That seems practical," Willem agreed, and the roaring in Elva's ears grew louder.

"And if anyone caught me, I would move from town to town, changing my name and my appearance," the farmhand continued. "It seems like it would be a simple thing to do."

"But you'd always have to be on the run," Jonas argued. "That's no way to live."

The farmhand scoffed. "Oh, shut up. You'd be stupid not to try to make a profit. Too bad she's a coward."

Klaus turned, his gray eyes glittering. "Maybe we could be the ones to find her and get her out of hiding. We could strike a deal with her and get a portion of the money she'll make. Or," he added, studying his nails, "we could always kill her and get reward money for it."

Everyone laughed again, and Willem leaned casually against a tree. Even the physical stance he adopted around his peers looked unfamiliar to Elva. "Who has time for that?" he asked. "We might not be staying around Hanau, anyway. Klaus and I have more promising horizons."

"What? You're leaving Herr Bauer?" Jonas asked. "What about your girl?"

Elva's nails dug into the tree. This was something Willem had never shared with her.

Klaus put up his hands. "We've already said too much. But this is a small town, and our sights are set on something bigger. And as for Willem's girl, she'll come with him, of course. She's going to be his wife, isn't she? She'll have to go, too."

The vision of her descendants came flooding back into Elva's mind. In the future, their family would go to the New World, but she had imagined a happy sea voyage, hand in hand with Willem, everything honest and clear between them. Not a journey he had decided on with Klaus and not her.

Thankfully, the men seemed ready to get back to the farm. They carried off their loads of lumber, voices and footsteps fading until silence returned to the North Woods.

Still sick with shame and disappointment at Willem, Elva looked at Mathilda's pale face. "I'm so sorry," she said, her heart aching. The experiment with getting her friend back out into the world had gone so well until now. Surely the witch would not want to continue, not after this.

But when Mathilda spoke, her voice was low and determined. "They think I'm a coward. They think I want to hide forever. Well, maybe I did once, but I'm going to show them and all of Hanau. I deserve to live in the open, just like everyone else."

"Then you still want to go on with this?"

"If you can get your parents' support and ask the council for a meeting, that's all we can do," the witch answered, and Elva hugged her impulsively. "And you? Are you all right?"

"Willem . . ." Elva swallowed hard, trying not to cry. It was difficult even to just say his name. "I can't believe he just stood there and laughed along with them. But there's no time to think about that now. I need to go home. If you still want to go through with this, then I will tell my family everything tonight."

The witch's face was still pale, but her gaze was steady. "I'll be ready for whatever comes. As long as you are there."

"And there I will be," Elva said.

18

The room was silent. Mama's and Papa's faces were frozen, Rayner looked bewildered, and Cay gazed fixedly at the floor. Elva wrung her hands, waiting for someone, anyone, to speak.

"This can't be real," her mother said at last. "You must be joking."

"It's the truth, Mama," Elva said. "I found your letters by accident and I'm sorry Papa had to find out about them this way. But it's like what you always say: Everything happens for a reason. Now that we know the storm is coming for us, we can prepare."

"All these years, you've avoided using that cursed ability of yours. Why did you have to have a vision now?" Mama demanded. "Why did you ever look into your water basin?"

"It's not cursed if it will keep us safe. If I can see the future, why not use it? Why not be aware of what's coming?" Elva asked, looking to Cay for help, but he refused to meet her eyes.

"I cannot believe you invaded my privacy and went behind our backs."

"But I needed Mathilda's help, Mama...."

"And instead of going to her to get rid of your powers, which I might have understood," her mother ranted, "you went and asked her to help you use them!"

Elva pressed her lips together, trying to stay calm. "I don't want to get rid of them. How could I ask her to take away something so valuable? Something that could protect all of you?"

"Valuable, you call it!" Mama threw up her hands. "It might get you killed!"

"This storm is coming because of the family curse, don't you see? It's a consequence of your broken promise, just like my visions. This is going to be our worst bout of bad luck yet."

There was a silence, thick with the tension of long-kept secrets spilled out into the open. And then Papa spoke at last, his voice ringing out. "Does anyone else know about all this?"

Elva swallowed hard, unable to tell them about Willem yet. "No one else knows about Mathilda. Please, Papa, I know you've never liked her. But she is good and she's helped me."

"But how can you trust her? What if she plans to use you against Mama and me?"

"She won't," Elva said wearily. "I love all of you above anything, and I don't want to see you or our farm hurt. I'm sorry I lied to you, but I wanted to help. I had no one else to turn to."

"How can you be sure this storm will come?" Papa persisted. "How do you know the vision wasn't just a dream, or your imagination?"

Mama sighed. "I think you know the answer to that, Oskar. You know that if Elva saw a storm, it will come. And we're due for our next round of bad luck."

Papa rubbed his forehead. "I don't like it," he muttered, sighing. "I don't like witchcraft dictating what we should and shouldn't do. But it can't be helped now. I suppose it wouldn't hurt to reinforce the barns and dig shelters for the animals, and we could find someplace to store the crops, though I don't know *what* the farmhands will think when I tell them to do it."

"I don't suppose you saw *when* the storm will come?" Mama asked Elva.

"No, but Papa's ideas are good ones," Elva said, her spirits rising slightly. Her parents might be willing to believe her about the storm, at least, which meant they could prepare for it. "Mathilda has been teaching me other things I can do to help protect us, too. Oh, please, will you speak to the council?"

Her father shook his head. "The storm is one thing, but this trial you're suggesting is an entirely different matter. What will people think if it looks like I'm supporting the witch?"

"It doesn't matter what they think! It matters what's right!" Elva knelt in front of his chair. "*Please*, Papa. She's been hated and feared and forced to live alone because of something she can't help. Would you want something like that to happen to me?"

"Of course not! But you're nothing like her."

"But I *am* like her. I didn't want or ask for my ability. How does that make me different from Mathilda? That could be me living alone in the woods." Elva turned, appealing to her mother. "Mama, you knew her well once. Surely you saw how good she is and how much she has struggled to be happy. You *know* it's wrong that she's been persecuted like this."

Mama covered her face with one hand.

"I know some people won't like the idea of a trial. They want to hate anyone who's different." Elva's throat went dry, recalling the awful things the farmhands had said in the woods, and Willem laughing with them. "But Mathilda deserves a full life. I know you're scared for me and worried that bad things will happen, but there is also an opportunity for good."

"Elva..." Papa began, but she surged on.

"Yes, there is prejudice against her. But others might see the good in her, like Mama and me. Just think if those voices spoke out together at the trial." Elva took her father's hand. "All these years, she's lived a quiet life. She hasn't harmed or disturbed anyone, and if she could be allowed to live freely, she would be as peaceful a neighbor as anyone could wish."

A halfhearted chuckle escaped Mama. "You speak so feelingly for her, like a young lawyer fresh from university. Do you care for Mathilda so much?"

"You taught me to be kind," Elva said softly. "And this is the best way I know how. She helped me to think of my powers as a gift, and to take pride in what I can do. I never thought I would find a friend like that."

Papa shook his head again. "I didn't want us associating with the witch years ago, and I don't want it now. I believe you," he added quickly, seeing Elva start to argue. "There must be something to this woman if she can win both you and your mother over. But there is too much at stake, and I won't risk our good name and reputation. I'm sorry, Elva."

"Papa..."

"I'm sorry, Elva," he said again, more firmly. "I'm not going to do this."

Elva stood up, trembling. "Then I will. I will go to the council myself if I have to."

Her father stared at her in disbelief. "You've never gone against my word in all your life. Why now? It might not be a kindness, what you're doing for her, you know. Why do you insist on bringing this woman back into a society that doesn't want her?"

"Because I need to believe that there can be justice for Mathilda . . . and for me," Elva said passionately. "She and I are the same, no matter what you say, and anyone who wants to hurt her would want to hurt *me*, too, if they knew about my gift."

Papa took in a deep, shuddering breath, and Elva's desperate eyes met her mother's.

"Oskar," Mama said slowly, "you once agreed that if Mathilda's path and mine should ever cross, you would support me in seeking her help to make Elva normal."

Cay looked up from the floor at last.

"This could be our chance." Mama looked at Elva, her eyes pleading. "You could live a normal life, unburdened by any visions of the future. No fear of water. Nothing to hide."

Elva's chest tightened. "What are you saying?"

"Papa will go to the council and ask for a trial for Mathilda,"

Mama said, and Papa's head swiveled to her. "He could say that she begged for one from our kind, good-hearted daughter, who caught her eye one day, and she was so pitiful that Elva could not refuse. That would keep the woman at a distance, and it wouldn't look like we were outright supporting her."

"I understand," Papa said slowly. "I would go to the council on the condition that Elva agrees to have the witch strip her of her ability. For good."

Grief burned Elva's insides like acid. Her parents would never see the beauty of her gift or even appreciate that she might have helped them avert disaster. Her magic was as much a part of her as her arms or her legs or her heart, but they would never accept that. All they could see was that she wasn't *normal*, like other girls, and not the perfect daughter they wanted.

She clenched her fists, not looking at any of her family. Mathilda had said herself that she couldn't take away Elva's powers even if she wanted to. Instead of being hurt and angry, Elva could be smart. She could tell Mama and Papa what they wanted to hear and pretend to agree to the stripping of her magic to give Mathilda a trial. They didn't have to know it wasn't possible.

"Elva, what we're proposing makes sense," Mama coaxed. "Years ago, I saw what a toll Mathilda's loneliness took on her. I want a full life for you, just like you want for her."

"I could tell them the witch begged for a trial on bended knee," Papa muttered, pacing the room. "And I was afraid of what she would do to my family, so I agreed to help her."

"Papa and I just want you to be happy," Mama went on.

Elva's mind raced. Lying would mean having to hide her gift for the rest of her life. To pretend she was *normal* like her parents wanted her to be. But for Mathilda—for what they were trying to achieve—it would be worth it.

"Well?" Papa asked. "Do you agree to these conditions, Elva?"

Elva took a deep breath, aware that the next words she spoke would change the course of her future. "Yes, Papa. I agree to your conditions."

They will never need to know, she thought.

Her father pressed a kiss against her forehead. "I'll talk to Bauer tomorrow. We'll set up a council meeting and put the trial to a vote," he said. "I have to tell you, though, Elva, that even if they agree to give the witch a chance, odds are high that the trial won't be successful."

"But we have to try."

"But we have to try," he echoed with a sigh, before leaving with Mama. Rayner followed close behind them, still silent and bewildered, leaving Elva and Cay alone in the room.

"Do you think I did the right thing?" Elva asked him timidly.

"I don't know," her brother said, his brow furrowed. "You don't tell me much about anything anymore, so I can't say. But it sounds like you're doing what you believe in."

"I'm sorry I didn't tell you. I was afraid of burdening you with all of this," she said, sinking into the chair Mama had vacated. "My magic, and Mathilda, and the storm that's coming. At least they seemed to believe me about that."

Cay studied her. "Can she really take away your magic?"

Elva looked up. His eyes were clear and sharp, and for some reason, lying to him seemed worse than doing it to her parents. Her jaw worked as she struggled for a response.

"I saw you leave, you know," he said. "Every night. I watched you from my window, jumping onto the kitchen roof with a basket over your arm. You looked so happy to be going to her, you were practically running over the bridge and into the forest."

"Have you been following me?" Elva asked, shocked.

"I tried, but I always lost you. You moved too fast and it was too dark. I came back during the day and tried to look for your tracks, to see exactly where in the woods you were going every night, but I could never find any."

Images flitted before Elva's eyes: trees, whispering in the wind. An old stone well. And on the ground, a crumpled, motionless body over which she wept. "I told you *never* to go to the North Woods without me!" she cried, fear scalding her throat. "Haven't you listened to a word I've said? How many times have you done that?"

"I'm not sure it's any of your business. You're not the only one who can keep secrets."

"'Cay, please!" Elva begged. "I saw a vision of someone hurt or . . . maybe worse . . . in the woods. I can't be sure it was you, but I don't want to take any chances."

"Well, I *do* want to take a chance. You're also not the only one who wants to help our family and get rid of the curse, so stop treating me like I'm a helpless infant," Cay said, his face red with anger. "I'm going to find something that can help us, and that's that."

And he left the room before Elva could say another word.

19

A few nights later, Elva flung open the door of Mathilda's cottage. "I have news!"

The cat yowled in surprise and the witch, who had been chopping turnip roots, dropped her knife on the floor with a cry. "For goodness' sake, Elva," she said irritably, bending to pick it up. "I could have cut off a finger."

"Never mind that!" Elva leaned against the kitchen table, trying to catch her breath. "I ran all the way here to tell you the council's agreed to a trial!"

Mathilda's knife clattered to the floor again. "What?"

"They were reluctant, but after Papa and Herr Bauer pleaded your case, the men put it to a vote and most were in your favor."

"Probably out of morbid curiosity, and not generosity of spirit," the witch said dryly.

"Oh, it doesn't matter *why* they voted! You're going to have a trial!" Elva grabbed the woman's hands and swung her around in circles as the cat looked askance at them. "You're going to have a chance to be a citizen, and to live freely and out in the open like everyone else."

"I don't know what to say," Mathilda said, her face flushed. "I didn't believe it would work, and now it has, thanks to you. But when is the trial? And what will happen?"

Elva collapsed into a chair. "It's set for one week from tomorrow, at noon in the town hall. The thirteen councilmen will be present, along with any other townspeople who want to attend. Papa's sure it's going to be crowded. The council will ask you questions to determine your suitability as a citizen, and they'll call forward witnesses to support your case."

"Witnesses?" the witch echoed.

"Like me," Elva said, smiling. "And maybe even Mama."

"Now *that* I cannot believe," Mathilda said, pouring Elva a cup of cool water.

"She suggested it to me herself. When Papa wasn't in the room, of course." Elva drank the water gratefully. "She's never felt right about the way things ended between you. And she thinks of you as a peaceful neighbor. She's willing to show the letters you exchanged if it might help persuade the council. So we'll both be by your side."

The witch sat down, her hands fluttering from her forehead to the table to her lap. "I don't know what to say," she repeated. "This is more than I ever dared hope. Thank you, Elva."

"Papa says not to hope for too much," Elva warned. "He thinks the council might issue a warrant of protection for you, if you want to move closer to town and go to market and so on. He told me not to expect overnight popularity . . . though that was never your aim."

"No," Mathilda agreed. "What will happen if the council decides against me?"

Elva bit her lip. "We'll worry about that later."

"What will happen?" the witch pressed her.

After a long moment, Elva said, "They're repairing the old gallows behind the town hall. Some of the men insisted on it, the ones who were against you having a trial at all." Even saying the word *gallows* made her feel ill. The day before, she had passed by the town hall and seen the platform with its steep, crooked stairs, dangling loops of thick rope, and the square of wood cut into the center. The image of that square opening and feet plunging helplessly downward had appeared in her mind, and she'd had to run home, almost sick to her stomach.

But if anything, this information seemed to make Mathilda calmer. Her eyes twinkled and she laid a hand, cool and steady, on Elva's. "Don't worry. It won't come to that. And even if it does, do you really think a bunch of farmers and some rope can hold me?"

Elva tried but couldn't keep the smile on her face. "I'm happy we've gotten this far, but I'm scared for you. I wish I could be sure I've done the right thing. There's so much hatred from people who don't even know you. Papa said they brought up Frau Bergmann and her toads and snakes again, and the rat poison and missing children, even though they have no evidence...."

"They don't need evidence when they have prejudice," the witch said placidly. "That's the way it has always been. What will be, will be. If they accept me, wonderful. If they don't, well, then nothing has changed. Don't fret. You know I can protect myself, and it means the world that you've gotten me this chance at all." She crossed her arms, looking thoughtful. "I have to admit I'm surprised Oskar spoke to the council for me. How did you convince him?"

"I, um, asked him nicely?"

Mathilda raised her eyebrows, waiting.

"And ... I agreed to his condition to have you strip my magic away, even though you can't. I know it was wrong to lie to my parents," Elva added hastily, "but I had to."

"I never thought I would live to see the day you lied to anyone," the witch said, laughing. "And lied for me, no less. Well, what Oskar and Agnes don't know won't hurt them."

Elva took the mirror out of her basket. "All day I've been too afraid to call up a vision of the trial. I want to know what happens, but I don't at the same time."

"Do it, if it will make you feel better."

She unwrapped the looking glass from its velvet covering, her stomach clenching with anxiety. "I'm not going to ask it to show me anything. I'm just going to see what I see."

It took Elva much longer to get to the state of mind she needed. For several minutes, all she could see was her own worried reflection, but at last, a vision appeared in the mirror. It was the storm raging once more, tearing up the fields and ripping branches from the trees. But there was something different this time: The barn shook in the gale, but it stayed whole. Extra boards had been nailed over all the windows, and Elva saw new wood gleaming on the roof. *They listened to me*, she thought, scarcely daring to take a breath. *They reinforced the buildings*. The fields, too, were empty of full-grown crops, and there were no dead animals lying on the grass this time. This was the future as it stood now, after she had told her family about the storm.

The vision faded as her concentration slipped, and she forced herself to focus harder. The willow tree symbol preceded the scene Elva both hoped for and dreaded: Mathilda's trial. Every spot on the benches inside the town hall was occupied, and in the center of the room, the witch stood straight-backed and proud, facing a half circle of men, their faces grim and stern.

"Is that the truth?" asked Herr Werner, the head of the council.

"It is," said the Mathilda in the vision, and before Elva could see or hear any more, the willow tree flashed again. She almost cried out in her disappointment, but her voice died in her throat when the next image appeared in the looking glass.

It was of Elva herself, sleeping in the forest. Her long golden hair streamed out around her head, dotted with pure white starflowers, and she wore a white lace dress she had never seen before. Her eyes were closed and her face was peaceful. Her arms were crossed over her chest, pressing a bouquet of pink and yellow wildflowers against her. The ferns and grass around her swayed gently in the breeze, and at her head were the spreading roots of a great tree.

There was something strange about the image of her own face, like it was frosted somehow. As though she wasn't sleeping on the ground outside, but beneath a sheet of glass . . .

The mirror went blank. Elva blinked and sat back. "I couldn't concentrate. I had to let go," she gasped to Mathilda. "What does it mean?"

"I don't know. But that last image frightens me more than the trial." Mathilda frowned. "You must be careful. You're getting stronger and better at magic, but you are by no means experienced yet. Don't get so overconfident that you lose yourself in a vision, or expend too much energy."

"I won't." Elva gulped in a few deep breaths. "Did you see the changes to our farm?"

Mathilda nodded. "It seems your family will take your warning seriously."

"That means I changed the future, doesn't it?" Elva asked, and the witch looked at her in silence. "We can't prevent the storm from coming, but we can arm ourselves against it. I affected the course of events by telling my family what would happen. That means that some aspects of the future I see in the mirror *can* be changed."

"What are you getting at?"

"Nothing. I just thought it was interesting, that's all," Elva said hastily. She got up from the table. "I should be getting home. I don't want Papa to worry, now that he knows where I've been going. But I'll come back to you tomorrow night."

"Promise?" Mathilda asked, with a slight smile.

"I promise."

The witch patted her shoulder. "Go on, then. I've think we set more in motion than we realize, but I'm glad I'll be weathering it all with you."

The next day, Willem came into the stables while Elva was feeding the horses. Her stomach dropped when she saw him smiling at her with a bunch of white daisies in his hand. She had been doing her best to avoid him, but now the dreaded moment had arrived.

"These are for you," he said, giving her the flowers. "I haven't seen you in a while."

Elva wished she didn't have hay in her hair and dirt on her apron. "I've been busy."

"Helping your parents reinforce the barn and harvest crops early, even though the almanac predicts dry weather? Is there something you know that no one else does?" he asked, but his twinkling dark eyes didn't give her the fluttery feeling they usually did.

She turned her back on him. "You never know what might come," she said lightly.

"You've probably been busy preparing for the witch's trial, too."

Elva stiffened. "Yes, I'm sure you've heard all about it from Herr Bauer."

"But why didn't I hear about it from you?" Willem asked, leaning against the stall door. "You could have trusted me with that, Elva. I should have known the night of the Easter party, when you were angry with me for speaking against her, that you were friends with her."

"We weren't friends then. I was angry with you because you were spreading evil talk."

Willem blinked at her tone. "Have I done something to upset you, love?"

The term of endearment would have thrilled Elva a week ago. Now it only grated on her nerves. She turned to face him. "I heard you laughing along with what your companions said in the forest, Willem. I was there for the whole discussion. Mathilda eats children, does she?"

Willem let out a laugh of disbelief. "They were joking! You shouldn't be so serious all the time. That's just the way Herr Bauer's farmhands talk amongst ourselves."

"A joke and a vicious lie about my friend are not the same thing," she said evenly.

"I didn't know she was your friend! You wouldn't tell me!"

Two of Papa's farmhands came in with fresh bales of hay, but when they saw Willem and Elva facing off, they quickly and silently went back out.

"You come in here acting hurt that I didn't tell you about Mathilda," Elva exclaimed, her breath coming out in short, furious gasps, "yet you didn't tell me you had gone *hunting* for her! As though she were an animal! Do you think I'm an animal, too? Would you hunt *me*, Willem?"

"Please, Elva, you're overreacting...."

"How could you take part in all that hate?" Elva's eyes stung and her chest felt so tight, it hurt to breathe. "I was so happy with you. I thought you were the sweetest, kindest person. You loved me for who I was and wanted to marry me, even knowing my secret."

"Don't speak as though that's in the past. I *love* you and I *want* to marry you," Willem said fiercely. "Your secret makes no difference to me. I accept it. What the others said about the witch was wrong, perhaps, but I don't think of you the way I do of her!"

"But she and I are the same! Why can't any of you understand that?" Elva cried.

"Listen to me. I'm sorry they joked about her that way. I didn't know you cared about her, or I would have spoken up. None of us believed we would ever find her, let alone harm her! They were just boasting about impossible things and I wanted to play along." Willem reached for her and she relented, letting him take her hands. "But I came here with happy news that you'll be glad to hear. We can be married right away. We don't have to wait! Do you remember Klaus?"

"Yes, and every cruel thing he said about Mathilda in the woods."

Willem squeezed her hands. "Klaus is leaving Herr Bauer soon for a new position. There's a traveling circus coming to Berlin in two weeks, and he's going to find work with them. He's up for anything: feeding animals, sweeping up, cleaning trash. The circus is well-known and it goes all over the world, and Klaus says it pays well. Now," he added, looking a bit hesitant, "I know you'll be a little angry with me when I tell you this, but please hear me out."

"I heard what he said. You're taking me with you, and as your wife, I have no choice."

"It was wrong of him to say that," Willem said soothingly. "Of course you have a choice. And I'm sorry I discussed the plan with him first. But there's something else." He looked down at their joined hands, avoiding Elva's eyes. "I ... I told Klaus about your visions."

Elva let go of him and fell back against the door of the adjoining stall. Her side hit the wood, hard, but she barely felt the pain. "You did *what*?" she shrieked.

"He's the only one I told." Willem's words came tumbling out in an eager rush. "And he swore on his mother's grave that he would tell no one else. He doesn't want Herr Bauer to hear about the circus and mock him for wanting to work with monkeys and clowns, anyway. But I told Klaus about you because he said the circus was hiring. They're looking for performers, Elva. That's why they travel so much—to find new audiences but also to seek talent from all over."

"I sincerely hope," Elva said, as the blood drained from her face, "that you're telling me all this because you're getting a job as a tight-rope walker."

"*You* could be that talent!" Willem cried, moving closer to her. "Just think: You'd have a beautiful tent and lovely clothes, and tell people what's coming in the future. It doesn't have to be serious! It could be something silly, like what they'll eat the next day, or the next time they'll see their true love, or what color eyes their baby will have. This circus pays more than any farmhand would see in his *lifetime*. How rich and successful you would be!"

Elva stared at him in speechless horror. The whole conversation felt unreal. Even the visions in her mirror had been more real than this. This was only a nightmare, a torturously bad dream, and any minute now she would awaken and it would be over.

Willem was still talking eagerly. His voice sounded like it was coming from an opposite shore. Elva looked at him and saw a complete stranger, not the boy she had fallen for. Once, she had thought he understood how her magic was a special, private corner of her heart, but now she knew the truth. He would never see her or Mathilda as people, but as tools, as *creatures* to be hunted or feared or used. Her loving, understanding Willem, who had kissed her and made her laugh and stolen her heart, had been imagining, all this time, how to make money off her.

"And of course I would work hard, too," he said quickly, misunderstanding her silence. "We could save for a house, and in a few years, we could settle and raise our family."

"You want me to perform?" Elva asked quietly. "You want your wife to stand beside the dancing monkeys and clapping bears? Will people throw money at me, too, Willem? Will they shout how clever I am, as I tuck their coins into my hat? Will I also dance and clap for them?"

His face had gone stark white. "I thought you would be happy and excited for our life together," he said in a strained voice. "I was thinking of you the whole time, of how to turn your gift into something useful, and to protect you, too. If people need you, they wouldn't be so afraid of you, don't you see? They wouldn't hate you the way they hate that hag in the woods."

"So because I have magic that I didn't ask for, I should bow to people's whims and be paraded around a circus like a show pony? I should be happy to sell myself for money?"

"You wouldn't be selling yourself!" Willem cried. "You'd be selling your visions!"

"Which are *me*. They are a part of me." Elva longed to take him by the ears and shake some sense into him. "I want to use them to help my family, not turn a profit."

"You *would* be helping your family," he argued. "You could send money home to your parents. Cay is a brilliant boy and he's going to go places. I could see him doing great things at university someday, and you could help pay for his education."

Elva shook her head slowly, unable to speak.

"Elva, your gift is a blessing," Willem told her. "Imagine all of the people you'll help!"

"By telling them what they'll eat the next day?"

He was silent for a long moment. "I came to you with good intentions. A plan to protect you and ensure that you have a happy life. And all you've done is put down my ideas."

"I don't want to hear any more."

"I'm not finished."

"I want you to leave, please," Elva said firmly.

"I am not finished," he repeated. "You have well-off parents. You've never known a day of hunger in your life, but I have. I know what it's like to be dirt poor and to watch my own mother suffer without the medication she needed. Do you think I would miss a chance to avoid that fate? To become rich beyond my wildest dreams and see my wife and children happy and well-fed? We can have all of that together, Elva."

"I'm sorry for your suffering," Elva told him. "I truly am. But I won't have any part in these plans. I won't be used. And you had no right to tell anyone about my ability. You can run along and find another dancing monkey to make you rich."

He gaped at her. "What are you saying?"

"I'm saying that you're not who I thought you were." Elva wished she could cry and rage at him and unleash this unbearable anger like a great storm tearing through her mind. But all she felt was numb and sick. "I was wrong about you. I don't want to be your wife anymore."

Willem took a step back, and then another. His face had completely drained of color. "You really mean it," he whispered.

"I do."

He stared at her for a moment longer, then ran a hand over his eyes and laughed. "You're jilting me. You agreed to marry me, and now you're taking it back, just like that. You've played me for a fool." The color returned to his cheeks, a dark, furious red. "What will Herr Bauer say? What will I tell the other farmhands? What will everyone in Hanau think? This is going to make me look ridiculous. Don't you care what a huge embarrassment this will be for me?"

"No, I don't," Elva said in disbelief. "I made the right decision if the only thing that concerns you is what others will think."

Willem clenched his jaw. "I think you should start caring about what others think, too. What's going to happen when I tell more people about you, Elva?" he asked, his eyes cold on her. "I know your deepest, darkest secret now. Shall I tell all of Hanau about your little visions? Shall I tell them how I barely escaped marrying a witch?"

Elva's stomach lurched. "You wouldn't do that to me."

"Who else is going to marry you after this? Do you think anyone would be as caring and understanding as I am? Would anyone else think of ways to keep you safe and make us money at the same time?" He shook his head. "I don't think you meant what you said about ending our betrothal. I think you're still going to be my wife, and you're going to agree to my plan, and in a week, you will be riding with Klaus and me in the wagon to Berlin. And if not?"

She watched him, scarcely daring to breathe.

Willem came close again and touched her cheek gently. The feel of his warm fingers against her skin made her want to empty her stomach. "And if not," he said again, very low, "I'm going to see that the council gives *you* a trial, too."

20

"Elva, are you all right?" her mother asked.

Elva looked up from her untouched breakfast. "Yes, Mama. Why?"

"You haven't been eating much all week." Mama tucked a strand of hair behind Elva's ear. "And it looks like you haven't been sleeping enough, either. I know you're worried about Mathilda, but whatever happens at the trial today will happen. And between you and me, I don't think she'll let them lay a finger on her. How strange," she added, with a faraway look in her eyes, "that I'll be seeing her again today after all this time."

"I don't think Mathilda will let them touch her, either."

"Is there something else, then?" Her mother hesitated. "I haven't seen much of Willem around here lately. Did the two of you quarrel?"

Elva bit back her frustration, wishing Mama would stop hovering and fretting over her. "Let's just get through today, and I'll be back to normal," she said with a forced smile, grateful when Rayner came clumping down the stairs and gave her mother someone else to fuss over.

"Is Papa already outside?" her brother asked.

Mama handed him a heaping plate of eggs and sausage, which he began shoveling into his mouth. "He's with the farmhands, going over the plans for today. He wanted to let you sleep in, since you'll be over-seer today when he's at the trial. You've done good work this week."

"Everything looks very nice and secure," Elva agreed, glancing out of the window. The farm looked as sturdy and strong as she could want. "How long do you think it will take to finish everything? I mean to build the underground shelters and gather and seed the crops?"

"Just another few days," Rayner said, his mouth full of food.

"Good. Even if the storm I saw came tonight, we'd be more ready than we were before," Elva said, and he quickly lowered his eyes, gobbling down his eggs without answering. Rayner was worse than Papa when it came to things he couldn't understand or see with his own eyes. "Where's Cay? Did you see him upstairs?"

Mama frowned. "Yes, where *is* that boy? His food is getting cold."

"His door was still closed when I came down," Rayner said.

"It's not like him to sleep in. Should I go wake him?" Elva asked.

"No, I'll go," Mama said. "You eat. I have to bring down the washing, anyway." It was a long while before she came back down, and when she did, her eyes were round with worry and she had forgotten the basket of laundry. "Cay isn't in his room, and his bed hasn't been slept in."

Elva dropped her fork. "What? Where is he?"

"He went to bed around the same time we did, didn't he?" Rayner asked.

Mama shook her head. "No, he wasn't home last night. He begged to be excused from supper, remember? He had research to do and wanted me to pack him a basket of food."

At that moment, Papa joined them inside and they told him about Cay. "Oh, don't worry," he said cheerily. "He must have come home after we had all gone to bed and left again at sunrise. He's a perfect farmer in that regard, always up before the sun. Too bad he isn't more interested in the actual farming."

But Mama shook her head again, her face pale. "I left a shirt I had mended for him on his pillow and it's still there. He would have moved it if he had gone to sleep. No, Oskar, I'm sure he never came home." She turned to Elva. "Did he tell you anything? He always confides in you."

"No, Mama, he said nothing," Elva said, trying to quell her rising panic, but it was no good. All she could see in her mind's eye was the well in the forest, and the body lying beside it.

"I'll run out and ask if any of the workers have seen him," Papa offered, his face sobering at their alarm. "Rayner, you'd better come, too. We can split up."

Rayner was already on his feet. "I'll run over to Herr Bauer's. His farmhands are always out and about and they may have seen Cay walking around."

"Oh, Elva," Mama said, turning to her, "you don't think he's gone to the North Woods?"

Elva blinked away the image of the crumpled body. "If he has, we'll find him," she said stoutly, steering her mother toward the door. "He probably just lost track of time. I wouldn't be surprised if he came home in a minute and found us looking for him."

"No. Something's wrong," Mama murmured. "Or something *will* go wrong. I may not have your ability, Elva, but I can feel it in my bones. He's hurt."

"Don't think like that," Elva urged her, though the words sent a chill down her spine. She thought of what Willem had once said about intuition and its similarity to magic, and felt Mama's anxiety catching like illness, spreading slowly through her body.

Outside, Papa left the barn, his face grim. "The workers saw Cay walking toward the river yesterday, but no one knows where he went after that. Let's wait for Rayner and see."

It didn't take long for Rayner to run back. "They saw Cay yesterday at suppertime," he said breathlessly. "He was crossing the bridge toward the forest with a basket in his hand."

Elva and Mama exchanged glances, and in her mother's eyes was the same fear growing in Elva's heart. Her hand was ice-cold in Elva's as they began hurrying toward the river, followed by Papa, Rayner, and the farmhands they had rallied to help them search.

"Run back to Bauer's and ask for a few men to come with us," Papa instructed Rayner, then put a reassuring arm around Mama. "We'll spread out and Cay will certainly hear one of us calling. I'm sure he's fine, Agnes, but I don't want to take any chances. Not with so many . . ."

He trailed off, but Elva knew his mind was on the children who had gone missing in the woods, never to return. All of them were thinking it. They marched toward the river, coming across many neighbors who asked what was going on. Most of them ended up joining the group and offering whatever services they could, whether it was helping them search, running home to get a horse, or bringing food for Cay in case he was hungry, since he hadn't had his breakfast.

"See how many people adore Cay?" Elva whispered to Mama. "He will be found."

Her mother only pressed her hand silently, her face blanched with fear.

They headed for the North Woods on the path Elva had so often taken in Mathilda's silent red shoes. *Mathilda.* Elva looked up at the sky, which was still pale with morning light, praying that the search would end happily before noon. She had vowed to be with Mathilda at the trial, and there she would be. *We will find Cay*, she repeated to herself over and over, *and the trial will go well.* The words didn't do much to comfort her, but it was something to occupy her mind.

Venturing through the forest had always felt to Elva like walking into a fairy tale, like she could be stopped by a princess or a lost knight at any time. But today, faced as she was with the need to find Cay safe and well, the atmosphere of the woods seemed different. She had never noticed how sharp the branches were, with jagged edges for catching a small boy's shirt or scratching at his eyes, nor had she ever realized that the ground was so full of perilous pits and mischievous roots.

Rayner caught up to them, followed by Herr Bauer and a dozen of his farmhands.

"Cay!" the search party cried, like a monster with thirty heads. "Cay, where are you?"

Their voices rang throughout the woodlands, but no cheerful voice answered and no Cay appeared with sheepish excuses about how the time had gotten away from him. And with every minute that passed, Elva felt sicker in her belief that something terrible *had* happened to her beloved brother. She could have choked on her guilt. All summer long, she had neglected poor Cay, too busy with her own concerns to spend time with him. She could barely look at Mama's face, which was sunken with anxiety. Papa talked in a low voice with Herr Bauer, but his movements were abrupt and uneasy and showed that he had caught Mama's fear, too, no matter how he tried to hide it. Everyone fanned out and swept through piles of leaves, calling Cay's name.

Elva shouted with them, but in her heart, she knew it was useless.

She knew, with growing certainty, that they would not find Cay until they had found a well of rough gray stone, something she had never come across in all of her wanderings through the forest. If Cay had been with them, his uncanny knack for finding water might have alerted them to its presence at once—but then they wouldn't need to be searching for him.

"Cay!" they shouted. "Cay, we're here!"

Elva did not know how much time had passed. It seemed they might spend forever in the woods, searching in vain for Cay. She forced herself to remain calm for poor Mama and tried to take comfort in the sight of dozens and dozens of people sweeping the forest, helping them look. Surely, with so many eyes, they would not miss anything.

"Look here!" a man shouted.

"Oh, Elva," Mama gasped, squeezing her hand as the search party clustered around one of the farmhands. He lifted a small brown wool cloak in the air. Mama pushed to the front of the group, looking faint. "That's my boy's. I made it for him. Oh, he was here!"

"But how long ago?" Elva heard someone murmur.

The urgency of the search intensified. Elva chewed on her bottom lip as they moved on through the forest, peering through the brush and lifting fallen logs. Several men even climbed trees to see better through the woods. The sun rose higher and higher in the sky until Elva could stand it no longer. She found her mother and spoke to her in an undertone.

"Mama, I'm going to see if Mathilda is still home. Maybe she can help us find Cay."

Relief washed over her mother's face. "Yes, go. Surely the trial can't take place today, not with Papa and Herr Bauer and so many neighbors here. I'll make excuses and ensure you aren't missed," she whispered. "Tell her I'm grateful for anything she can do."

Elva spotted the great willow and headed toward it. Everyone was so intent on searching that no one noticed when she slipped away to the witch's cottage. But the place was empty, and Mathilda had evidently left for town bright and early. The cat, however, sat on the windowsill, gazing at Elva with its sea-glass eyes, and something glittered beside it: Mathilda's mirror. In her fear and worry, Elva had not even thought to consult her own mirror, and now it seemed absurd that the idea hadn't occurred to her right away.

She grabbed the mirror and stared into it desperately. "Cay," she said, closing her eyes and directing all of her thought and energy toward him. "Please, I need to find Cay." She cleared her mind of everything but him, and when she opened her eyes, the mirror was showing her the outside of the cottage. Slowly, the scene glided to the right, going in the opposite direction of the willow tree. Mathilda had never taken Elva back there. The vision plunged forward into an empty clearing, where a well of weathered gray stone, with a little roof of granite shingles, sat alone.

Elva didn't wait to see any more. She put down the mirror and raced out the door, listening for the voices of the search party all around her, but she heard not a sound—clearly, Mathilda's boundary prevented any noise from entering or escaping. She wondered if Mama and Papa were close enough to touch her but could neither see nor hear her through the invisible curtain.

"Cay!" she shouted, her heart pounding in her ears. "Can you hear me?"

For several minutes she ran until something tickled her face like a spiderweb, and she realized she had reached the edge of Mathilda's boundary. She lifted the curtain as she had seen the witch do, and it rose easily over her head as she kept running, aiming for the location the mirror had shown. On and on her feet took her for an interminable distance, until finally the clearing came into view. Elva plunged toward the well. Its stones had faded with time, and a blanket of moss and cobwebs draped over its edges. On the edge of the well perched a stack of three volumes that Elva recognized as Mama's storybooks.

"Cay!" she screamed.

Her little brother was sprawled on the forest floor, eyes closed and blood trickling from a cut on his forehead. His right leg was bent at an unnatural angle. A cracked wooden bucket lay near him, its rusted steel chain anchored to the roof of the well. Elva burst into tears and frantically felt his hands and face, which were as cold as death. She pressed her ear to his chest and nose and sobbed with relief when she felt his weak breath on her skin.

"Cay, wake up," she begged. "Please, please wake up."

His eyes fluttered open. "Elva?"

She wrapped her arms around him, holding him tight to her heart. "I'm here," she said, tears streaming down her face. "Oh, Cay, I was so scared. Where do you hurt?"

"M-my leg, mostly." He lifted his head to look at it and grimaced. "I think I broke it."

"What happened?"

"I threw a pebble in the well and didn't hear a splash, so I decided to go down in the bucket. It was plenty large enough for me," Cay said defensively, when Elva groaned at his daring. "I knew I could lift myself back up, and I wanted to see how deep it went. But the chain got stuck and I yanked too hard on it, and my leg got trapped between the bucket and the wall."

"Oh, Cay, when will you learn?" Elva cried, stripping off her apron and wrapping it around his head to stanch the bleeding. Cay winced but lay still.

"I pulled myself back up and climbed out. But I must have pulled too hard, because the bucket flew after me and caught me in the head. I don't feel dizzy or sick, though."

"That's something, at least. How long have you been here?"

"Since supper yesterday. That was when I found the well. I wanted to come home and surprise you with the discovery. Ouch," he grumbled, when Elva pressed a fierce kiss to his head.

"Silly, stubborn, *unlucky* boy. You were just far enough away from Mathilda's boundary that she wouldn't have been able to sense you."

Cay raised his eyebrows, intrigued. "The witch lives nearby?"

"Yes, and if you had been five minutes that way," Elva said, pointing, "she would have come out to help you. Thank goodness I went to her cottage and used her mirror to find you."

"A magic mirror? Is that how you walked around without leaving any tracks?"

Elva shook her head. "She gave me a pair of red slippers to hide my footprints."

"Can I see them?" Cay asked urgently. "Maybe they can help with my research—"

"No!" she exclaimed, exasperated. "Only you could be injured and hungry and still want to do research. I'm taking you straight to Mama. Everyone's sick with worry over you. Why did you ignore my warning?"

"I'm sorry. I was angry that you had kept such a big secret from me," he said quietly. "And I thought if I found a wishing well that somehow worked, I could wish our curse away. So I made a carefully worded wish, just like the books say to do. But nothing happened."

Elva couldn't help hugging him again.

"I found this clearing ages ago and it made me think of that story about the fairy queen who loved a human, but she could never be with him, so she turned the wedding ring she meant to wear into a circle of trees." He gestured to the slim white birches surrounding the clearing. "That's what I thought of when I saw this place. It was empty, but I kept coming back to it. I had a feeling there was more to it than met the eye. And yesterday, that well suddenly appeared."

Elva shivered. "It wasn't here before?"

He shook his head. "No, and I came three or four times. Something kept pulling me back. I guess I could sense that there was water here. Maybe the well was testing me to see if I was worthy, and I was!" He tried to sit up again and winced when his leg moved. "Do you think Mathilda can help with my leg? It hurts something terrible."

"Here, put your arm around my neck." Slowly, painfully, Elva helped him get up on his uninjured leg. As she did so, she heard the voices of the search party calling faintly and shouted back at them. "Mama! Papa! I found Cay!"

They heard leaves rustling and twigs crackling under approaching footsteps, and within a minute, Herr Bauer and two of his farmhands appeared with Mama and Papa right on their heels.

"Oh, Cay!" Mama sobbed.

"I'm fine," he told her brightly, as she put her hands on either side of his bleeding face, kissing him. "My leg's just broken, that's all."

The tension lifted as the searchers let out sighs of relief and shook their heads at Cay's incorrigible cheer. Papa lifted Cay carefully in his arms and carried him to a wheelbarrow one of the men had brought. Cay was wheeled out of the forest with Mama and Papa half running, half walking by his side. Elva put Mama's books back into Cay's basket, knowing he would want them, and followed the group back onto the path.

But no sooner had they emerged from the North Woods than a red-faced Peter Bauer appeared, panting. "Pa, the trial," he managed to gasp to Herr Bauer. "They went ahead with it and it's pandemonium. They're calling for the witch's immediate execution."

"What?" Elva cried, her stomach sinking like a stone. They had been wrong, then: The trial had gone on, even without Papa and Herr Bauer present. And Mathilda had been there all alone.

"They're taking her to the gallows," Peter said, and then Elva was running like the wind. She heard voices calling after her as she tore down the path and across the bridge into town.

21

It was pandemonium, just as Peter had said.

Elva arrived at the town hall to see the building crammed with people, all pushing and shouting. She forced her way through the crowd to the center of the room. The councilmen were on their feet, their benches abandoned, all talking loudly at once. Herr Werner, the head of the council, banged a gavel and yelled for quiet, but no one heard him in the commotion. Finally, he picked up the end of one bench and dropped it on the floor with a crash. "Silence!" he roared.

That seemed to do the trick, at least with the people closest to him. Elva pushed past them and saw Mathilda facing the councilmen with her head held high, eyes full of rage.

"You heard her!" someone in the crowd screeched. "She admitted to all of her crimes!"

"She tried to kill those boys!"

"Witch! Murderess!"

Disturbed, Elva tore her gaze from the councilmen nodding at these awful exclamations. The crowd was so thick, she couldn't find a way to get through it. "Mathilda!" she called, and the witch glanced at her as Herr Werner dropped the bench again for attention.

"Woman! You stand accused of poisoning good citizens of Hanau," he said to Mathilda, his voice hoarse. "Mere boys who were only having a bit of fun. Do you deny this charge?"

"No." Mathilda did not speak loudly, but her voice carried throughout the noisy room.

"You also stand accused of cursing Frau Lina Bergmann with . . . erm . . . reptiles in the throat when she was a young woman. Do you deny this charge?"

Mathilda's eyes sparked. "No."

"You have also knowingly sold wart potions that you claimed to be love tonics to people you considered your enemies. Do you deny this charge?"

"No," Mathilda said defiantly, "and I would do it again if I could!"

The crowd exploded with anger. Two men burst from the sides of the room and grabbed Mathilda by the arms, roughly. One of them had a fistful of her hair. The sight of it incensed Elva. She pushed the people in front of her with all her strength and rushed toward the witch.

"Let her go!" she screamed, and her heart nearly stopped when she saw that the two men were none other than Willem and Klaus. "Don't touch her!"

"Drag the hag to the gallows!" the crowd shouted.

Herr Werner grabbed Elva. "Stay back, my girl. You don't want to get involved in this."

"Oh, but she *is* involved. More than you know, sir," Willem told him, his hand still clenched like a vise around the witch's arm. His eyes glittered at Elva, and she swallowed hard. She fully believed him capable of revealing her secret, right then and there. "Why do you look so frightened, Elva? I only meant you were supposed to be a witness for her," he said icily.

Elva thought that if she had the power, she would open a hole in the earth to swallow him. She looked desperately at Herr Werner. "Let me speak on Mathilda's behalf, please!"

"It's too late," he said excitedly. "Don't you hear the crowd? They've given the verdict."

"Gallows! The gallows!" people screamed, and the councilmen did nothing but nod, some of them smiling at the sight of the witch trapped between Willem and Klaus.

"You heard them! Take her to the gallows, boys!" Herr Werner cried.

Klaus's cold gray eyes met Elva's as he and Willem dragged Mathilda toward an open set of doors overlooking the back of the town hall. Through them, Elva saw the sharp edges of the gallows against the blinding sky, the nooses dangling in the breeze like flags of deadly surrender.

"Mathilda, get out of here!" she shouted.

The witch struggled between the two men, breathing hard, her face bright red and furious. Her long dark hair had come out of its bun and hung over her cheeks in limp, tangled waves. She shook them aside and glared at Elva. "Where were you?" she cried, her anguished face streaked with tears. "You promised to be here! You were supposed to be here for me!"

Elva's heart broke over and over, looking into Mathilda's devastated eyes. "I'm sorry," she wept. "I'm sorry! Let her go!" She pulled at Willem, but he reached out with one hand and shoved her away. She fell onto the floor, landing painfully on her elbow.

Suddenly Papa was there. He grabbed Willem by his work shirt, yanking him away from the witch, and held him to his face. "Don't you ever touch my daughter like that!" he roared.

Herr Bauer was there, too, yelling at the councilmen. "What on earth is happening here?"

Elva cradled her elbow on the floor, spotting a heavy wooden bench rising into the air by itself. The crowd screamed as the bench floated for a few seconds, then moved forward at lightning speed, mercilessly knocking down several councilmen in its path. It headed straight for Klaus, who turned just before it crashed into his head. He fell without uttering a sound.

Now free, Mathilda looked at Elva again, her eyes full of tears and quiet fury, and then she spun in place. One moment the witch was standing there, and the next, there was nothing but empty space beside Klaus's unconscious body.

The townspeople began stampeding out of the hall, braying with fear.

"She's gone!" Herr Werner sputtered, looking around him in bewilderment.

Elva leaped to her feet, still cradling her hurt elbow. "Papa, I have to go to her," she said, and without waiting for a response, she hurried outside with the crowd. She needed to get to Mathilda at once, to find her and explain why she had not been there to defend her.

The path blurred before Elva's eyes as she ran, her hair plastered to her tear-streaked face. It had all been a mistake, this horrible plan of hers. She didn't know why she had ever thought it would work. She had torn Mathilda from her home in the woods and thrown her to the wolves. She might as well have been dragging the witch to the gallows with her own hands.

Hanau was no place for people like them.

She had thought differently, *hoped* differently once. And perhaps elsewhere in the world, they would not have to hide. But this town would never accept them, no matter how much her heart dreamed otherwise. It would always see them the way that Willem saw them, and even the way Papa saw them: as unnatural creatures to be feared.

We'll go, Mathilda and I, Elva thought feverishly, as her footsteps thundered over the bridge. She took the path back to the North Woods, running as fast as she could. *We'll pack our bags and find some safe place to live, far away.* She would make it up to the witch somehow.

Mathilda's cottage still looked empty. The only signs that she had come back were the open door and the wagon outside, hitched to a small donkey that stared accusingly at Elva. It had a ginger coat and eyes like green sea glass, and Elva blinked at it in shocked recognition—it was Mathilda's cat, enchanted into a different form. The wagon behind it contained an assortment of boxes and bundles, and one crate held porcelain dishes, bowls, and cups cushioned with straw. The two cozy chairs that had sat by the fire were upside down on the kitchen table, with Mathilda's leather-bound diary tucked securely between them.

Elva's stomach clenched as she hurried inside. "Mathilda! What are you doing?"

The woman did not answer, nor did she look at her. She was sweeping as though her life depended on it, getting the straw of her broom into every crack in the floorboards. She had not tidied her hair, which was half in her disheveled bun and half flying into her eyes.

"I know you're angry with me," Elva said, trembling. "You were waiting for me, and you were all alone at the trial, and I'm so sorry I couldn't be there."

The witch's head flew up. "You're *sorry*?"

"Y-yes," Elva stammered, taking a step back at the blazing look in her eyes. "Cay got lost in the woods and we were searching for him. When Peter Bauer came and told us about the trial going wrong, I ran. I'm so desperately sorry about everything."

Mathilda snorted. "I don't know why I listened to you, or why I even *wanted* to be a part of this cesspool of a town," she said, sweeping furiously. "If that council is made up of your finest, upstanding citizens, then it's an incredibly poor sample of humanity."

"What happened?" Elva asked, very low.

"I came to the town hall an hour early, hoping to collect my nerves and to see you there. I thought if I could get people used to my presence and show them I could be quiet and harmless, they would be more comfortable." The witch threw her head back and laughed. "All my life, I have worried about *them*. I have lowered my voice, I have bowed my head, I have made myself smaller. I hid myself in this cottage in the middle of nowhere to please them. No more!"

Elva stayed silent, her heart aching.

"Do you want to know what else you missed?" Mathilda spat at her. "When the councilmen came in, they all started snickering and whispering behind their hands like overgrown schoolboys. Their words grew louder and louder, and I can hardly *think* of what they said without feeling sick. It doesn't deserve to be repeated. But rest assured, they covered everything about me, including my face and body, in sordid detail. Like I was meat in a butcher's shop!"

"Oh, Mathilda," Elva whispered.

"They accused me of breaking up several betrothals and marriages. Such skill and talent as they gave me, considering I had never seen any of them in my life!" Mathilda ranted on. "And when they had finished talking about me, they talked *at* me. Asking me what love potions I had used to poison the brew at the pub, which animals I had killed lately, how many times I had flown naked to the moon. There were one or two men who looked uncomfortable and didn't join in, but they never once spoke up in my defense, either."

"I'm so sorry," Elva said, her eyes burning with tears. "So sorry you endured that alone."

Mathilda's voice grew quiet. "I sat like a statue in the corner. I didn't look at any of them. I told myself words could do nothing to me and I had heard much worse before. I reminded myself, over and over, that you would come and I would not be alone. I would have someone who truly cared about me there." Her eyes met Elva's, cold and empty. "But you did not come."

"You were on my mind the whole time," Elva sobbed. "I meant to walk to the town hall directly after breakfast, but Mama found Cay's bed empty. We were so frightened for him."

The witch leaned her broom against the wall in silence.

"Remember that vision I had of the well in the forest, and the body I was bent over? It was Cay after all, and I was afraid the worst had happened," Elva said shakily. "When Papa and Herr Bauer and all of our neighbors were searching the forest, I came to your cottage to find you, but you were gone. Your mirror helped me find Cay."

Mathilda's gaze darkened. "If so many people were out searching for him, he would have been found eventually," she said through clenched teeth. "So many eyes could not fail to turn him up. You could have left the search to them and come to the town hall. You swore you would be by my side. You made it sound like it was important to you, like *I* was important to you."

"It was important, and so are you! But I thought my brother's life was at stake...."

"Cay would have been found!" the witch shouted. "All that time, I sat alone, waiting and waiting for you. I took their hatred and abuse because the thought of you coming kept me strong. And time slipped by and you didn't care to show your face. . . ."

"He was by the old well with a broken leg and a head injury!"

"There were dozens of people there to take care of him!"

"I don't know what you want me to say," Elva cried. "I'm sorry, all right?"

"For god's sake, stop saying you're sorry!" Mathilda screamed.

They stared at each for a moment, breathing hard.

"You were worried about your brother's safety," the witch went on, her voice cracking. "I understand that. But what about me and *my* safety? What about when the councilmen's insults became threats? When they told me they had never planned to have a trial at all but had lured me there to kill me, once and for all? To see me swinging from my neck before all of Hanau?"

Elva swallowed hard, pressing her hands over her eyes.

"Those were the men who were supposed to be keeping the peace, and instead, they incensed the crowd. You heard a little of what people were saying. You saw how those men grabbed me by the hair." Mathilda gave a low, bitter laugh. "So you don't need to tell me you're sorry. Everyone is always so sorry when they've broken a promise. However much you look like Agnes, I used to think you were different. . . ."

"Please don't bring Mama into this."

"You always kept your word. I thought I could rely on you," Mathilda went on, ignoring her. "But the apple doesn't fall far from the tree. It seems I was mistaken about you."

"If by being like Mama, you mean that I put my family first, then yes, I do," Elva said, low and pleading. "But that doesn't mean I don't care about you. I would have come, of course, if I hadn't been sure my brother was in danger."

The witch shook her head slowly. "A conditional promise. Which, if you think about it, isn't really a promise at all. It's a *maybe*. It's contingent on people who matter more to you."

They stared at each other, and then all of the fight seemed to go out of Mathilda. Her shoulders sagged, weary and heartbroken. The distance between them was only about the length of the kitchen table, but somehow Elva could feel it growing in the silence that followed the witch's words. The broom against the wall suddenly crashed to the floor, shattering the quiet.

Elva jumped, but Mathilda didn't so much as flinch.

"I told you that when I met Alfred, the woodcutter," the witch said quietly, "and when I met your mother, I thought they would turn out to be different, too. Every time I dared to open myself up to someone, I hoped for the same thing. And in return, I always got the same thing: pain. You may have meant well, but my heart can't take any more,

Elva." And then, without another word, she picked up the broom and walked out of the cottage.

"Wait!" Elva cried, following her out to the wagon. "Mathilda, please!"

"Go home and don't bother coming back," Mathilda told her, taking hold of the donkey's harness. "I won't be here, and neither will the cottage."

Elva's heart clenched like a fist. "You're ending our friendship over this?"

"I'm tired of being let down," Mathilda said, her voice thick with tears. "I'm tired of being an afterthought, the person people go to when they have no one else, and when they've gotten what they needed, they forget me. I'm too old to keep doing this with my life." She wiped her face. "I'm exhausted, Elva. Let me go. I've helped you however I could. My work is done."

"Is that all you think I wanted from you?" Elva cried. "You thought I came every evening for months, sat by your fire, learned from you, ate cake with you, and asked about your life . . . because I wanted to use you? All because I couldn't keep my word today?"

The witch did not respond.

Elva ran her eyes over the wagon full of the possessions of a solitary life. She thought of the vision she had first seen of Mathilda in the mirror, a young woman surrounded by scattered belongings, weeping in the forest. "You don't have to do this," she pleaded. "You don't have to go. I want you to stay here so we can go on as we have, together. Or better yet, I will go with you. I'm not wanted here any more than you are."

Still, the witch made no answer.

"I can make today up to you," Elva vowed. "You won't ever have to teach me anything ever again. I won't ask for anything more from you than sitting and talking with me."

Mathilda tugged gently on the donkey's harness and it moved forward at once, pulling the wagon behind it. "Go back to your life," she said, without looking back. "Go back to your family and pretend I never existed. I wish with all my heart that Hanau will never find out about your powers and treat you the way they have treated me."

Elva tried to grab her arm, but something like a thick, invisible curtain hung in the air between them. She flailed against the magical boundary helplessly. "Please, don't go!"

"Good-bye, Elva."

"This is what you do!" Elva shouted after her, pushing against the boundary in vain. "Don't you see? You put up all these walls around yourself, magical or otherwise, and when someone manages to get past, you find ways to put them up again. Mathilda!"

The witch, the donkey, and the wagon passed the willow tree and vanished. Immediately, the boundary dissolved and Elva tumbled onto the grass, facedown. "Mathilda, come back!" she sobbed, but there was no sign of her. And when she climbed to her feet and looked behind her, there was nothing there except an empty clearing in the woods.

It was all over—a friendship that had meant the world to her. She had lost the one person who had understood her, and she couldn't even tell her family about it. Nor could she confide in Willem anymore.

"Oh, but she is involved. More than you know, sir," he had said at the trial. There was no telling what he might do or say against her—and he could sully her family's reputation as well. Perhaps they would have to leave Hanau, too, which would devastate Mama and Papa. Even that terrible storm would be better than giving up their farm and the life they had built.

Elva buried her face in her hands, weeping, wondering how it had all gone so wrong. As useless as she knew it would be, she wanted to run back to the well where she had found Cay. She longed, with all her heart, that it would appear for her as it had for him so she could look down into the darkness and shout the most desperate wish of her soul: that none of this—Willem's betrayal, Mathilda's trial, and Cay's disappearance—had ever happened.

It was all her fault.

If she hadn't been so trusting and careless, Willem would never have known her secret.

If she had been a better sister, Cay would never have gone off alone and hurt himself.

If she had been a better friend, Mathilda would still be here, safe and snug in her cottage.

"Come back, come back," Elva muttered under her breath, pinching her eyes shut, as though she could will the witch and the cottage and the wagon all back into existence. But no matter how hard she wished, she was all alone and Mathilda was gone. She wiped her face and got to her feet, feeling more exhausted and drained than she ever had after using her magic.

Elva froze.

Her magic.

Her heart beat faster, skipping along the edges of an impossible thought. She still had her own mirror, the sister to Mathilda's looking glass. She knew how to open the willow tree door. The last time she had done it, she had almost kept that farmhand from tripping over the rake. He had still tripped, but she had delayed it. Despite Mathilda's skepticism, Elva was certain that she'd had a hand in changing that future. All she had to do was try again. She would call up what she wanted most to change: her prediction at the Easter party that Willem would catch the Blue Mermaid, the night she had suggested that Mathilda rejoin society, and the first day Cay had talked about the wishing well. She would imagine herself making different choices this time.

How many times had she heard Mathilda praise her natural skill?

She would clear her mind of everything else but turning back the hands of the clock and feeling the rise and fall of the sun in her bones. Mathilda had warned that it was dangerous, that it was folly and madness to play with time, and it would take more energy than Elva had ever dared give before to her magic. But it was the only thing she could do.

She had to protect her family.

She would go back and change everything: keep Willem a stranger; keep Cay whole and unhurt; and keep Mathilda by her side where she belonged.

"I'm going to fix this." Elva clenched her fists, turning her face to the sky, and her whisper became a shout. "I'm going to fix this!"

Her voice echoed through the trees as she ran into the forest, her hair flying out behind her. She was going to make this all disappear. She would make it right.

22

That night, Elva stopped by Cay's room to check on him. She found him sleeping with his injured leg wrapped and laid upon some pillows. His bedside table was littered with tea, soup, medicine, and the candy Mama never let him have except on special occasions. Elva looked down at his face, framed by feathery tendrils of hair. His eyelids were a constellation of deep blue veins, just as they had been when he was a baby. Even then, he had looked up at her with clear, bright eyes, as though he had already known and loved her as his big sister.

Elva stroked the hair off his forehead, thinking of all the stories they had told and the adventures they'd had. It would be more than worth the risk of playing with time, just for him.

His eyes opened. "Elva?"

"How are you?" she whispered, kneeling down beside the bed.

"Honestly? Bored."

Elva laughed. "You've been laid up for only half a day."

"The physician said my leg will heal fast." He peered at her. "How are *you*? Did you find Mathilda? I heard Mama and Papa talking about what happened to her at the trial."

"She was angry with me." Elva laid her weary head on his pillow. "I broke my promise to be at the town hall with her. She left Hanau and won't be back."

"It's my fault," Cay said quietly. "I should have listened when you warned me about the woods. If I hadn't gone to the well by myself, you would have been with her."

"It is *not* your fault. I should have been there for you."

"I saw how hard you were trying to protect us," he said. "I just wanted to help you. And I thought I'd able to if I could somehow find a real wishing well."

"Did you see anything when you went down the one you found?"

"Not much. It was more of a feeling." Cay hesitated. "The same feeling I get when I know there's water nearby, like a tingling on my skin. It looked like a dried-up old well, but when I touched the stones, they were wet and there was something strange about them. Like they were talking to me, but I couldn't hear voices or see their mouths moving."

Elva shivered. "What did they say to you?"

"I'm not sure. But it was like they knew me. I called hello and my voice echoed, and I thought if I went all the way down, I might end up somewhere new. A different world."

"But you didn't go all the way down."

"I got nervous. I was afraid I would get there and find myself all alone in that world. And I wanted you to come with me." He paused. "I did make a wish, though."

She draped an arm over him. "That the curse would be lifted?"

Cay shook his head wearily. "I thought I would ask for that, but when I was hanging there, it felt wrong. Like it was too easy. I felt like the well was trying to tell me that you can't just wish away your problems. Does that sound strange?"

"Yes," Elva said. "But I believe you. What did you wish for, then?"

"I wished that our family would be brave enough and strong enough to get through anything." He gave an enormous yawn that showed every one of his teeth.

"I think that's a very good wish. And I think it's time for me to go so you can rest."

But Cay held on tight to her hand. "Elva?"

"Yes?"

"Mathilda will come back."

Elva's throat tightened. "How do you know that?"

"Because that's what real friends do." Cay let go of her hand and snuggled deeper into his blankets. His eyes closed, and within seconds his breathing grew slow and even.

Elva watched him sleep, thinking that she had never loved anyone as much as this courageous brother of hers. She owed it to him, as much as to Mathilda, to do what she planned.

In her own room, she pulled the mirror out from its hiding place beneath her bed. She closed her eyes at the feel of the cool glass against her skin, not wanting to look into it just yet. Her heart rattled against her rib cage like a prisoner longing for freedom. She had been so sure she wanted to do this, but now that the moment was here, she kept hearing Mathilda's voice warning her against it. *"Magic-wielders have tried to play games with time in the past, and they have always lost. They have killed others or died in the process, or worse."*

Elva would be experimenting with a branch of magic that not even Mathilda knew well. Still, the longing to have her mentor by her side again was so powerful, it was almost painful.

I'm doing this to bring her back, she told herself.

This was not a choice. This was the only way she could make it all right. She had to force back the hands of time, send the sun and moon backward in their circular dance over the North Woods, and fix everything. And this time, she would be there for *both* Cay and Mathilda.

She tilted her face to the window and felt the moonlight wash over her. She steeled her nerves, slowly opened her eyes, and looked right into the mirror.

Perhaps it was only a trick of light and shadow, but her reflection seemed to belong to a stranger. The moon made her skin glow and her hair shine white-gold, and her eyes were dark and inscrutable. She looked every inch a witch: powerful and unknowable, with a heart like the sea and a will like the force that kept the stars in the heavens. She looked like someone who would sing the universe to sleep and bend time itself if it meant achieving her greatest wish.

Elva let her breathing slow and deepen. Practice eased the process of erasing the room around her and any consciousness of her family sleeping down the hall. She let go of her awareness of the floorboards beneath her and the slight ripple of her curtain in the breeze. She allowed herself to forget where she was in time and space, until there was only her and the mirror in her hands. She thought of Mathilda, her face strong and lovely with eyes like a bonfire, like an approaching storm. Mathilda making sarcastic comments, Mathilda turning fireflies into flowers, Mathilda remembering the handsome woodcutter whose heart had nearly been hers.

A vision appeared in the mirror: the witch turning and leading her wagon away.

Go back, Elva thought, straining with the urge to reverse time the way one could flip back the pages of a book. The willow tree symbol flashed, and then Elva saw herself bursting into the witch's cottage, saying, "I have news!" It was the night she had told Mathilda about the trial. *Go back*, she thought again, and the willow tree became a scene of her and Mathilda in the North Woods, listening to Willem and his companions talk. *Go back*, she thought once more.

Scene after scene, lesson after lesson, until she saw an image of Mathilda holding a pink-and-gold flower in her hand. The blossom opened and closed its petals, then turned a rich purple. She heard herself say, "It's beautiful, what you can do with magic. I wish more people could see this," to which Mathilda replied, "If they could, I'd likely be killed on sight. But thank you."

This is it, Elva thought, her pulse picking up.

The Elva in the mirror asked if Mathilda had ever thought about disguising herself and walking in the village, if she ever got lonely. "Let's be clear on two points," the witch said, setting the jar of flowers on the table with a loud clunk. "I *choose* to be alone. I chose it a long time ago. And as for disguising myself, I'm not ashamed of who I am. I won't walk around this town that hates me unless I get to be myself."

"I understand that, but—"

"And I'm not lonely. I don't need people."

"Everyone needs someone," said the Elva in the mirror.

"Not me. And this conversation is over. It's time for you to get home."

The moment the willow tree flashed, Elva reached out without hesitation and slid her fingers around the edge. The door opened, and the scene replayed. "It's beautiful, what you can do with magic," she heard herself say, and she focused with all her might on erasing the next sentence. *I never said it*, she thought furiously, as the familiar pain tugged at her temples. *I never put the idea into her mind of people accepting magic.* And it was just as she imagined: Mathilda put the vase of flowers on the table and gave her a half smile, and they talked of something else.

One by one, Elva summoned every scene, every lesson in her memory, and wiped from each of them the mention of the outside world. Instead of talking of Hanau or bringing the witch out into the woods, she imagined them sitting side by side in the safety of Mathilda's cottage, making jars float and chairs move, whipping up potions with herbs from the garden, eating cake and drinking tea by the fire. They laughed and talked and were happy, and never once did either allude to the existence of a world outside and whether it might accept them. There was no mention of a trial, and Elva said nothing to Papa, and the council knew nothing of Mathilda.

Beads of sweat slipped down Elva's face as she worked, trickling under the neck of her nightgown, which itched against her skin. *Concentrate*, she told her mind sternly, and the sweat and itching vanished from her awareness at once. She closed herself once more in her thoughts.

Willem came into her mind next. She called up the memories of them together, from that moment at Mathilda's trial and the argument in the barn all the way up to the Easter party, when he had found the copper ring, claimed her kiss, and walked her to the river, where she had foreseen that he would catch the Blue Mermaid. She imagined, with all her might, that she had remained silent throughout the vision. "Did you see something in the river?" she heard Willem ask, to which she smiled and replied, "No, of course not. Excuse me, I better hurry back. My parents will be looking for me." And then she took off the ring, gave it back to him, and returned to the party alone.

The glass grew warmer and warmer in Elva's hands. It slipped a little in her clammy fingers and she tightened her grip, ignoring her aching head as she forced herself to focus.

Cay, next. She pictured her brother with his sunshine smile, eccentric ways, and limitless heart, embroidering a skirt with her and telling her his dreams. She imagined taking him out into the North Woods dappled with sunlight, the sway of the treetops like green lace above them as they searched for the wishing well. She could almost smell the moss beneath their feet as Cay turned back to look at her. "Hurry up!" he shouted, and raced her to the well. They stood side by side, hands braced on the stone lip, and looked in together. The vision suddenly wavered, as though she was looking into a pool of water and someone had dropped in a pebble.

A sharp spark of pain pierced her temple. Elva felt a deep cold seeping through her body, bleeding into her arms and legs, and the edge of her bedroom curtains brushed her face. *No*, she told herself feverishly. *You are not in your room. You are not anywhere.*

She sank again into the nothingness her magic required, but the effort required felt monumentally greater. In the mirror, Elva imagined herself grabbing Cay's arm to keep him from falling into the well. They looked at each other, laughed, and shouted a wish together, their words blending until neither could tell what the other had asked for. And that was just as well. "Wishes aren't always meant to be shared," said the Cay in the mirror.

The mirror felt almost unbearably hot in Elva's hands, and the bedroom floor seemed to shift beneath her. Though she was sitting, she felt herself almost lose her balance and had to put out a hand to steady herself on the floorboards. Her whole body shook uncontrollably, as though she had gone swimming in the river on a winter's night. A cricket sang outside her window, and somewhere down the hall, Papa was snoring. *No*, she thought angrily, *this won't do. Focus.*

But try as she might, she couldn't get back to that peaceful, empty state of mind.

Another powerful tremor snaked through her body. Her nightgown was damp with sweat and clung unpleasantly to her skin, and her back ached from having sat too long on the hard floorboards. How long had she been looking into the mirror?

The mirror pulsed with heat, burning her fingers. Elva cried out in pain, but her hands seemed to be stuck to it. She could not let it go, nor could she tear her eyes away from it as it went blank and showed her pale, exhausted reflection. In the glass, the night sky outside her window was boiling like a poisonous black soup studded with sharp stars. Elva watched in horror as the clouds swirled and tossed, waves in a cruel ocean, and extinguished the sickly moon. A great rumble of thunder shook the earth, and then a heavy, pelting rain began to throw itself against her window with frantic violence. Drop after drop of water, large and weighty as onyx pearls, plummeted to the earth as furious light ripped open the sky.

What was real? What was only a vision?

She found, with increasing panic, that she could not be sure her eyes were open. Perhaps they were closed. Perhaps she was envisioning all this, and the strength of her magic had called forth the storm. *I'm imagining it*, she told herself frantically, even as the lightning raged and the thunder screamed and the rain beat upon the window.

Elva tried to drop the mirror again, but it seemed to be stuck to her skin. Her hands blistered and burned with the heat of the glass, but she could not release her fingers or her eyes from it. She was trapped in her own fever dream. She tried to cry out again, but her lips were every bit as disobedient as her hands and eyes. She had lost control of her body.

At that moment, her reflection in the looking glass disappeared.

In its place, Elva saw the willow tree in the North Woods, the first landmark that would lead her to Mathilda. Her soul ached at the sight of it. She wanted desperately to wrap her arms around it and press her face to its warm, rough bark, and as this thought crossed her mind, Elva felt herself drifting upward. A strange force was lifting her, tugging her with unimaginable strength off the floor of her bedroom and straight into the mirror toward the image of the tree.

The willow drew her toward it. It wrapped loving arms of bark around her and whispered comfort into her ears with a voice that sounded like rustling leaves. Elva felt the earth-scented breeze of the North Woods brush against her face, and the smell of soil and rain and wildflowers seeped into her pores as she grew rooted to the earth. She laid her head upon the heart of the willow and closed her eyes, and her last waking, human thoughts were of Mama and Papa and Rayner, but especially Cay. She even thought of Willem as he had once been in her heart, and finally, Mathilda, strong and loving and proud.

Their faces were the last images Elva saw as the tree swallowed her whole.

23

Matilda sat alone before the dying fire. Her diary lay open in her lap, but she couldn't muster the energy to do anything other than flip through its pages. She closed it, running a hand over the spreading willow tree etched into the thick leather cover, then set it aside with a sigh. A gloomy, unseasonable chill had settled over the woods and hills as the sun went down, and she poked listlessly at the embers to draw out the heat. *Yet another hearth*, she thought. *Yet another lonely night.*

The day before, she had gone straight to the cottage that had belonged to her aunt Louisa and Josefine. It was larger than any of the other homes she had ever lived in, with three spacious bedrooms and a bright kitchen wrapped in red brick, and when its owners had been alive, it had been full of love and joy and good cooking. Every corner held a memory: Here, Aunt Louisa had taught her how to churn butter and put it in a strawberry-shaped mold. Over there, Josefine had taught her about all the mushrooms they had gathered. "You can eat any one you like," Josefine had said, her dark eyes twinkling, "as long as you don't choose the ones you can only eat once."

In this house, Mathilda had learned to love magic. She had seen its beauty firsthand and so, too, had grown to understand its fickle, unpredictable nature. Aunt Louisa had loved her and fussed over her, and Josefine had made her mind and body strong. But now that they were both gone, the joyous memories were only that: memories. It was why Mathilda had decided never to live here again, even though she visited from time to time to pay tribute. A person could not live on the ghost of happiness forever, no matter how much she longed to.

But I did have happiness, Mathilda thought. *A spark of it, when Elva came.*

And now she had lost it forever, just as she had lost everyone else.

She threw the poker back into its holder with a loud clang, startling the cat, which had been sleeping nearby on a cushion. Its eyes narrowed at her as she buried her head into her arms, sick with shame for the way she had behaved. She knew now that she had been stubborn and resentful, and that she ought to go back and beg Elva's forgiveness. The girl had been terrified for her brother's life, that much was clear. It wasn't her fault that she couldn't be with Mathilda, nor was it her fault that the councilmen had chosen to be so cruel.

Not for the first time that evening, Mathilda glanced at her mirror on the kitchen table. It was the sister of Elva's looking glass, forever connected by magical bonds, and if she looked into it, they might be able to see each other. *But she might not want to see me,* Mathilda thought miserably. Perhaps Elva had washed her hands of her, after the way Mathilda had spoken to her.

All her life, Mathilda had blamed the world for pushing her away. But hadn't she done the same to it? Hadn't she built up a wall of thorns around her heart, constructed from hurts and resentments amassed over the years? And anytime someone tried to climb over it, she would find a reason to keep them out. It was her own curse, the punishment she bore for the gift of magic.

What was the use of having such a gift if she couldn't share it with anyone? What was the point of great power granted only in complete isolation?

Mathilda looked at the hearth, where the final ember coughed out a dying breath, and decided to go to bed. Moping was best done on a feather-stuffed mattress beneath thick blankets and plush pillows, and Aunt Louisa and Josefine had stocked their cottage well. She got up, her bones crackling in protest, and went into the room that had once been hers. She slid into bed and closed her eyes, feeling the warmth of the cat as it followed and curled up beside her.

"Everything always looks better on the other side of sleep," Josefine used to say.

But despite how comfortable she was, Mathilda couldn't sleep. Not when her heart ached unbearably for her cozy cottage in the North Woods, for Elva to sit and talk with her by the fire, for her aunt and the woman who had loved them both, for the look in Alfred's eyes before he had known who she was, and for a thousand other nameless things her soul could not describe.

And underneath it all, there was a current of . . . wrongness.

Something tugged at the strings of her consciousness, jarring her like an out-of-place note in a chord of music. Even the cat, which usually slept like a log, stirred restlessly beside her. She put a hand on its trembling back, her skin tingling with unease. The air felt charged, like an invisible bolt of lightning had shot through it, making it crackle with frightening dark energy.

And then the sky lit up.

Mathilda sat up, shivering, her eyes on the window. The night sky did not look right: It was black as jet, smothering the moon and stars.

It swirled like a cauldron of poisonous soup coming to a boil, and any minute now, the steam would burn the earth to blackened rubble. A low, dark rumble of thunder echoed across the land, and then enormous raindrops pelted the roof. It was so loud and furious that Mathilda's shaking hands flew over her ears.

The cat got onto all fours, arching its back and hissing.

"Hush, it's all right," Mathilda said, speaking loudly over the torrents of rain beating down. She climbed out of bed as another ferocious roar of thunder cracked open the night, and at once her mind went to the disaster Elva had predicted in her visions. This *had* to be what the girl had foreseen. Every nerve ending in Mathilda's body felt charged and alert, for she could sense in her bones that this was no ordinary storm—it had been caused by magic. A very powerful magic, indeed, and from the intensity of it, it had come from not far away.

There was only one other person Mathilda knew of who could have produced it.

"Elva," she whispered, as lightning scissored across the sky. Her shoulders shook with the force of her galloping heartbeat. "What have you done?"

The rain came down so violently that Mathilda could not see the row of apple trees her bedroom window looked out on. The walls of the house creaked and groaned against the heavy wind, and a sharp crack sounded out as the gust smashed a branch against the roof.

The anger and malevolence of the storm betrayed Elva's state of mind. She had clearly been in immense distress and in almost certain danger. But what had she been attempting to do that had caused such a powerful act of nature?

Mathilda ran out of her bedroom. She needed to use the mirror and communicate with the girl, or at least see what had happened so she could help. Her heartbeat seemed to cry, *Elva, Elva*, as she sprinted into the hallway with the cat on her heels. But no sooner had she reached the door to the main room than another gust of wind rocked the skeleton of the house.

One by one, with a deafening crash, each of the six long glass windows in the main room shattered, pushed inward by an indescribable force. Mathilda dropped to her knees, gathering the cat to her heart and protecting it from the deadly whirlwind of glass shards.

And then all was quiet.

Breathing hard, Mathilda lifted her head. The storm had vanished as quickly as it had come. The boiling black clouds receded to reveal the moon, shining down upon trees drooping with exhaustion, several of them cracked and missing branches. The chill, too, had gone, and a warm, gentle summer breeze lifted the curtains as though it had been there all along. The moonlight illuminated the mess of broken glass, glinting on every surface.

"Elva," Mathilda uttered, hurrying through the shards, which crunched under her slippers.

Her mirror had been destroyed where it lay, crushed by falling pieces of window glass and ground to a fine powder in some places. Only one jagged fragment was big enough to use. She seized it and held it up to her face, staring hard at the reflection of her right eye.

The shard of mirror cleared to reveal images of Elva and herself: their last argument in the woods...the end of that horrid trial... the two of them sitting by the fire. Scene after scene, memory after memory floated by of all the time they had spent together, but with key differences—Mathilda recognized parts of their conversation that had changed, decisions she had never made, words Elva had never spoken. She frowned, uncertain of what she was seeing if not the exact past. And then she saw images of Elva's sweetheart, Willem, flashing back to the two of them standing by the river, where Elva's prediction about the fish had happened. Slowly, the answer took shape in Mathilda's mind as a skinny, towheaded boy—Cay— appeared next. And when she saw Cay and Elva at the wishing well together, Mathilda reeled backward with the realization of what the girl had been attempting. Elva had been trying to redo everything that had happened in order to change the future, exactly as Mathilda had warned her never to do.

"No!" the witch wailed, her eyes on the wreckage of broken trees outside.

Elva had caused the very storm she had predicted.

Such dangerous magic as playing with time would have created an unpredictable surge of energy... and also *taken* energy, in turn. Desperately, Mathilda looked again at the jagged shard of mirror in her hand, shivering from the effort of calling up the visions. Seeing into time had never been her gift, and it was taking too much from her, but still she tried. She needed to see what had happened to Elva.

The looking glass showed a shadowed room. A slender figure lay on the floor, her eyes closed, gold hair spilling around her face, and lips slightly parted like a princess in a tale. But her chest did not rise and fall, and no breath fluttered the lock of hair over her nose.

Mathilda screamed, the shard of mirror shaking uncontrollably in her hand. "It can't be true," she sobbed, as the vision flickered and wavered with her emotions. "She can't be dead."

Elva lay crumpled by the window, and beneath her fingertips something shone in the moonlight. It was the other mirror, blazing as though a fire had been lit within it.

Mathilda sagged against the table, and the fragment of glass slipped from her limp hand. It shattered into a million pieces on the floor, but she neither noticed nor cared. Because there was only one thing that could have happened to make Elva's mirror glow like that.

Long ago, Josefine had explained to her that the cost of magic could occasionally be so dear, so great, that it took parts of the self that the wielder would never willingly give. Mathilda had passed that warning on to Elva herself, never dreaming that it would actually be needed.

Somehow, the girl's attempt to change time had not only created the storm she had foretold, but it had also drawn something valuable from her, dearer than life, and locked it inside the very tool she had been using to work her magic.

The mirror had taken Elva's soul.

24

Cay remembered a toy his parents had brought home for him once, many years ago. They had gone on holiday to Paris, just the two of them, leaving Elva, Rayner, and Cay in the Bauers' care. Elva and Rayner hadn't minded because they'd had Freida and the Bauer boys to play with, but Cay had been only six and had cried every night until Mama and Papa returned. They came back with a wagonload of gifts: books and paint for Elva and wooden toy soldiers for Rayner.

For Cay, Mama had brought a small globe filled with water. One side of it had clear glass so he could look in at a miniature Parisian street of baked-clay cobblestone, porcelain shops and people, and neat gas lamps painted bright yellow. Whenever someone shook the toy, a thousand tiny snowflakes danced around the scene in a hypnotizing whirlwind. Despite the chaotic flurry, the tiny painted people stayed still, unaware that their world had been turned upside down.

Now Cay knew what it was like to be one of them.

He sat in Papa's armchair, his broken leg propped up on a cushioned stool, motionless in a storm of activity. Neighbors rushed around him, all busy, all speaking in hushed voices as though Elva were only sleeping in her room upstairs.

Not dead.

A low, heartrending wail sounded out, so guttural that Cay barely recognized his own mother's voice. "The price of breaking a promise . . . the price of breaking a promise," she sobbed, before her words melted into something undecipherable. Mama had been crying like that since they had discovered his sister's body early yesterday morning, but the sound still shocked him every time. Her deep, unabated grief was the only thing that made him sure this wasn't an endless nightmare he alone was having.

As soon as Elva had been found, Rayner had run to get help, bringing back with him the physician, Frau Bauer, and several neighbors. It had taken Papa and a few other people to hold Mama down as the others gently laid Elva on her bed, all bright golden hair and rosy cheeks like a cursed fairy-tale maiden. "Why are you carrying her?" Mama had screamed at them. "She can get up herself, she doesn't need you to lift her like that. Elva, get up! Get up!"

Downstairs, Cay listened as his mother's wail went on and on. For a moment, the bustle around him quieted as everyone paused and looked upward with faces full of grief and pity. But soon they were hurrying around again, snowflakes swirling around a porcelain boy.

"How's your leg?"

Cay looked up to see Rayner beside him. "It's fine," he said, surprised. He and Rayner had always been more like two boys who happened to live in the same house and less like brothers. Neither had ever made much of an effort to change that, but now Rayner cleared his throat and took the chair beside Cay's, his eyes on the whirlwind of people.

"I don't know why there are so many of them here," he said helplessly.

Together, they watched as two women nearly collided, one sweeping the floor and the other dusting the table. Frau Bauer and Freida led the charge in the kitchen, where an army of neighbors kneaded bread, stirred soup, and made endless pots of tea they had to drink themselves because Mama wanted nothing. A constant procession of men came in and out of the house, for Herr Bauer and Papa had combined their farmhands to help clean up the wreckage of the storm.

The disaster had ripped through Hanau at terrifying speed last night, uprooting farms and destroying buildings all over town before coming to an eerie halt just before dawn. The farmers had been lending animals or an extra hand to one another and anyone else in need, but even with a cooperative effort, the work seemed endless.

"Why aren't you out there helping Papa?" Cay asked. "Isn't there still a lot of work?"

"He insisted we take it in shifts and make sure to rest, so here I am." Rayner shrugged. "We've mended our fences and cleared away most of the trees, and the crops and animals are fine, so we'll go help those who weren't so fortunate. Thank goodness we reinforced our barns."

"Thank Elva, you mean," Cay corrected him, and Rayner nodded, his face falling.

"What do you think happened to her? Did the shock of the storm really kill her?"

"Of course not," Cay scoffed. "That's just a lie Papa told the neighbors. I think she was doing magic, because that mirror was next to her, but I don't know what she was trying to do. She didn't tell me anything." He wished with all his might that he had asked his sister to stay with him last night. She would have slept in the chair by his bed, and she would still be here. Maybe she would have even talked to him and told him her secrets, the way she used to.

"You all right?" Rayner asked, watching him.

"Can guilt make your stomach hurt?"

"Maybe. What are you guilty for?"

Cay sighed and looked down at his leg, wrapped in a full inch of bandages. "For not being as understanding as I should have been to Elva. I was angry with her for keeping secrets with other people. That's why I went into the woods by myself."

Rayner shifted in his seat, looking awkward. "I don't think you should feel bad. You two have always been so close," he said. "I . . . I think I've always been kind of jealous of that."

"Really?"

"Yes. You were always off in corners whispering and making up stories and imagining things. You're a lot alike." Rayner chewed on his lip, thinking. "Look, you don't have to tell me your secrets, but since you're so much like Elva, if you have an, um, ability or something, you could . . . maybe find out what happened to her?"

Cay shook his head. "I don't have Elva's ability. Honest," he said, and Rayner blew out a breath, looking both relieved and disappointed. "But I keep thinking if I had that mirror, I could look at it and try to figure it out. And she's got a pair of red shoes, too, that Mathilda gave her. Problem is, Mama won't let anyone into Elva's room, much less touch her things."

"I can sneak in."

Cay stared at him. "What?"

"I can sneak in," Rayner repeated. He bowed his head, his eyes darting around the way Elva's used to whenever she was thinking hard about something. "Mama's got to be exhausted. She'll have to sleep sometime. And I can get in there and get the mirror and shoes for you."

"Would you really?"

"I'd better do it soon. Tonight, maybe. I heard Papa and Herr Bauer talking about burying Elva within the next day or so." Rayner looked down at his folded hands. "Papa wants to get rid of all her things first, so they won't hurt Mama so much."

"Burying Elva," Cay echoed softly.

He hadn't cried once since they had found her. Her death didn't seem real. Any minute now, he expected her to get out of bed, hug Mama, and explain that it had all been some mistake. His guilt was worse than he had let on to Rayner because he also didn't feel sad the way he knew he should. Yesterday, Freida—who hadn't been able to stop weeping herself—had sat with him and taken the time to explain that it was all right to just feel numb. "People can be sad in different ways," she had told him. "It doesn't mean you loved her any less."

But now it struck him that this was really happening: Elva was gone, and they would put her in the ground and she would never, ever come back.

Suddenly there it was: his grief, gushing out at last. Cay lowered his head as he cried, his nose wet, tears splashing onto his shirt. He felt Rayner's arm wrap around him, and they sat like that for a long time. Finally, when Cay fell quiet, Rayner sighed and got up, his shoulders drooping as he wiped his eyes with the back of his hand.

"I'd better get back outside and see what I can do for Papa."

"Rayner?"

"What?"

"I'm sorry we left you out. Elva and me."

Rayner reached out a tentative hand and ruffled Cay's hair. "I'm sorry, too. For making fun of you. Maybe sometime you can take me exploring for fairy rings and wishing wells or whatever it is you look for?"

Despite the hard knot of grief in his chest, Cay couldn't help smiling. "I'd like that," he said, and a smile flickered across Rayner's face, too. "Just the two of us?"

He didn't realize what he had said until Rayner's mouth crumpled with grief. "That's all there is left," he said, then hurried away, leaving Cay alone in the armchair.

Mama finally came downstairs at supper that night. Papa got up at once and folded her into a hug, and they stayed like that for a long moment before breaking apart. Mama kissed the top of Rayner's head and wrapped her arms around Cay. "How are my boys?" she asked.

"We're fine," Cay said, looking worriedly up at her. "Will you eat something with us?"

Papa filled a plate for her, piling on the ham and baked potatoes. "Hans and his daughters came over earlier to cook and bake. They left a cinnamon honey cake in the oven."

"They've all been so kind," Mama said, picking at the food. "How goes it outdoors?"

"We're almost done, aren't we, Rayner?" Papa asked, forcing a smile. "The fields were destroyed and there's no saving that row of crops nearest the fence, but we managed to store almost all of the harvest underground. We'll be able to replant and regrow."

"And Flower had her baby," Cay added, and was rewarded with a smile from Mama at the mention of her favorite goat. "I wish Honey was still around to be its great-grandmother."

"I'm glad for this good news, and thankful we could prepare in time." Mama's smile slipped away, and they knew she was thinking of

Elva again. Her fork dropped onto the plate, forgotten, and Papa and Rayner looked at each other, struggling for a new topic of conversation. They were both rescued by a tentative knock on the door.

"That must be Bauer checking on us again. I told him we wouldn't need anything tonight." Papa pushed back his chair and was gone for several long minutes. He came back with an odd look on his face and a bundle of pure white starflowers in his hand. "That was Willem Roth. He left these for Elva. He looks like he hasn't slept at all."

"The poor boy," Mama murmured, taking the flowers from him.

"He looked terrified. Still guilty about pushing my girl like that at the trial," Papa said grimly. "He nearly shredded his hat in his hands as he talked to me. He's leaving for Berlin in the morning, never to return, and good riddance." He hesitated, looking at Mama.

"Is there something else, Oskar?"

"He told me there's something at our gate. A big package, tied with blue ribbon."

Rayner and Cay watched in confusion as Mama's mouth opened and closed. "Blue ribbon?" she whispered, staring at Papa. And then she put the flowers on the table and got up.

Papa followed her, and Rayner helped Cay gather his crutches and trail after them. By the time the boys made it to the gate, their parents were already unwrapping a long, rectangular object covered in brown paper. It was about as long as Papa was tall, but it seemed light, moving easily when he gave it a nudge. A length of shining frost-blue ribbon fell away with the paper, and Mama gave a little cry when she saw the note underneath it. She tore it open.

"What is it, Mama?" Cay asked, frightened by her stillness. "Who is it from?"

"Mathilda," she breathed. "This is a present for Elva."

The boys exchanged glances. "She doesn't know about Elva," Rayner said dully, but when Papa tore away the last of the paper, it was clear that Mathilda *did* know.

The witch had sent them a coffin made of glass. But it wasn't made of sheets of glass, like a window, but of thousands of shards and fragments and slivers. A spiderweb of delicate cracks covered the whole surface where the pieces had been joined together, yet the coffin looked as perfect as if it had been made by a master glass blower. *It's magic*, Cay thought, awed, looking at Mama. Papa and Rayner were watching her, too, their faces full of worry.

But the sight of Mathilda's gift hadn't upset her at all. In fact, Cay hadn't seen her so composed all day. She knelt down and ran a steady hand over the surface of the beautiful coffin.

"I can get rid of it," Papa said uncertainly. "The witch would never know."

"No, Oskar. Mathilda made this for Elva, and to Elva it will go." Mama's lips trembled, but she kept her composure as she lifted the lid.

Mathilda had lined the bottom of the coffin with rich, deep purple velvet and placed a small pillow of the same material at the head. "We'll bury my darling daughter tomorrow," Mama added, a tear gliding down her cheek, "and we'll do it in this."

Papa put his hands on her shoulders. "It will be done."

"I wish I had told her how proud I was of her," Mama said, her voice breaking. "She helped us save our farm. We wouldn't have known about that storm, if not for her."

"And she saved me," Cay said softly. "She saw in the mirror that I was hurt by the well. Who knows if I would have been found without her."

Mama wiped her face. "All these years, we made her hide her visions. I'm glad she met Mathilda. I'm glad they had each other, and that Mathilda gets to say good-bye in this way."

Cay swallowed hard, and for the second time that day he felt Rayner's arm wrap tightly around his shoulders.

Elva was gone, really gone. She would never read fairy tales or embroider fantastical creatures with him again. She would never go on adventures with him, travel the world with him, or see him grow up and become a great explorer and maybe have a daughter of his own someday, a beautiful girl with golden hair who was also named Elva.

Cay leaned heavily on his crutches, the ache in his leg nothing compared to the pain in his heart, and looked at the sunset spreading fiery colors across the sky.

Tomorrow, this glass coffin would be Elva's new home. She would lie there, forever a sleeping beauty in the North Woods, while the world moved on and everyone else grew old and gray.

A few days earlier, when she had left Hanau behind, Mathilda
had vowed never to come back. And yet here she was, hidden
behind one of the trees still standing on the Heinrich farm, watching
Oskar and his son carry the glass coffin into the house. The younger
boy, Cay, followed on his crutches, but Agnes stayed a moment longer,
looking out over the land with the frost-blue ribbon in her hand. The
color in her cheeks had faded, yet she looked almost the same as when

she and Mathilda had met all those years ago. For a second, her eyes swept over the tree that hid the witch, as though she could see her, before she turned and went back inside with her family.

Mathilda sighed and sat down to wait for morning.

"The funeral is at dawn in the North Woods," she had overheard a farmer say, when she had driven through town on her wagon. "I guess Oskar and Agnes think that's what she'd want."

And so Elva would return to the forest. She would take the same path she had always taken to see Mathilda, but this time, she would not come out again.

The witch blinked away hot tears as night fell over the farmland. There was no use in wishing things had been different—that instead of moping, she had used her own mirror to communicate with Elva and protect her from this catastrophe. There was no satisfaction in regret, and yet Mathilda couldn't help thinking, *If only, if only, if only.*

Yesterday, while cleaning the broken glass, she had admired the sun shining on the shards and slivers and had gotten the idea to merge them with magic. It seemed appropriate to surround Elva in glass touched by the sun, when the girl had brought so much sunlight into Mathilda's lonely life.

Hours passed, and when dawn lit the horizon, Mathilda saw several neighbors come and knock on the Heinrichs' door. Oskar and his son came out with the coffin, covered with a thick cloth, and laid it on a wagon. Cay came next, then Agnes, leaning on another woman, and the whole procession slowly made its way toward the river.

Quickly, Mathilda left her hiding place and went into the empty house.

It was bigger than her cottage, but it had a cozy feel. There were signs everywhere that a family lived there: a boy's mud-splattered boots by the door, piles of laundry in a woven basket, and books scattered around a parlor where all the chairs were worn from use. Elva had grown up here, and Agnes had been happy. Mathilda's hungry eyes took all of it in, even as she stayed alert. Room by room, corner by corner, she searched for Elva's mirror.

If the girl's soul was trapped inside, there *had* to be a way to free it. She had to try—but no matter how hard she looked, no table, no drawer, no space beneath the furniture revealed it.

"Where is it?" Mathilda muttered, frustrated. Perhaps Agnes and Oskar had decided to bury it with Elva. And now the witch would have to run after them or miss the funeral entirely. She slipped her hood back over her head and left, moving quickly over the bridge to the woods.

Elva had been well-loved, for fifty or sixty people altogether stood in a half circle around the great willow that had served as Mathilda's first landmark. The men bowed their heads and the women leaned on one another, and even the children were quiet, holding bouquets of vibrant wildflowers as the pastor spoke solemnly and read passages aloud from a book.

Mathilda stood apart, hidden behind an oak tree. Through the crowd, she could just see Oskar and his tall son standing close to the tree. Agnes and Cay had to be nearby, and Elva, too, in her glass coffin. The witch swallowed hard, pressing her forehead against the rough bark of the oak as she waited for the service to be over.

She tried desperately to think of what Josefine would do or advise in her situation. But all she knew was that when a magic-wielder gave their soul as the price of magic, it was impossible to reverse. Consequences always were. "Where magic gives, it can also take—in ways that no one can foresee," she had told Agnes once, the very words Josefine had taught her long ago. Mathilda raked her hands through her hair, listening to the pastor drone on and on in his low, deep voice. Even if she could find the mirror, trying to free Elva's soul from it would be downright dangerous—every bit as dangerous as trying to turn back the hands of time.

A strangled sob escaped from her throat, and Mathilda pressed her hands over her mouth. There was no way to pull Elva's soul out of the mirror that wouldn't be potentially as destructive—or even more so—than the storm. It would be an impossible feat.

At last, the mourners began to disperse, heading back out of the forest to a Hanau that would never again have Elva or her sunshine in it. When they were all gone, Mathilda peered out and saw Agnes and Cay still talking by the tree, with the glass coffin lying beside them.

"I'll give you a moment with her," Agnes told her son. "But don't take too long. The men have to come back to put Elva...to put the coffin in the ground." Her voice cracked on the final words.

"Yes, Mama," Cay said. Agnes kissed his forehead, took one final look at her daughter, and walked away very fast, her face crumpled with grief.

The scrawny, fair-haired boy leaned one of his crutches against the willow tree. With his free hand, he lowered a satchel off his back. "Hello, Elva," he said, with a catch in his throat. "You heard Mama. I don't have a lot of time before the men come back." When he moved to set the satchel on the ground, Mathilda got her first good look at Elva. She thought her heart couldn't possibly hurt more if she had stabbed it with a glass shard.

The girl looked like a young fairy queen on her bed of deep purple velvet, with a crown of white starflowers in her long, rippling hair. Her hands had been folded over a bouquet of wildflowers, and her cheeks were as pink as they had been when she was full of life.

The witch buried her face in her hands, so overcome with grief that she nearly missed Cay's next words. "I brought something for you," he told his sister. To Mathilda's shock, he reached into the satchel and pulled out not only the mirror but also the red silk slippers she had given Elva. "Rayner went into your room and got them for me. He says he wants to go exploring with me. I'm glad, but... I wish you were here so you could come with us, too."

He was silent for a long moment, bending his head over the objects in his hands, and Mathilda had to bite her lip hard to keep from sobbing with him. *This is my fault*, she thought. *If I hadn't been so stubborn, this boy would still have his sister.*

"Don't worry about Mama and Papa," Cay went on, his voice thick with tears. "I'll take care of them, I promise. I'll make sure Mama eats something. And I'm going to keep studying and sewing and exploring, and I'll try to do great things when I grow up, so you'll be proud of me. That's a promise, too." He wiped a sleeve across his face and gently laid the slippers on top of the coffin. "You should have your shoes back. And this."

He unwrapped the mirror from its velvet cloth and lowered it to the coffin.

And then he gave a scream of fright.

Mathilda gasped, but Cay was shrieking too loudly to hear her. He dropped the mirror and fell backward on a patch of moss. The glass, too, was lucky to have a soft landing among the ferns and grass. It fell against a small boulder, which tilted the angle so that the witch could see what had terrified Cay so: The mirror was not reflecting its surroundings. Even though it was facing away from Elva, it showed her coffin, draped in a shroud of darkness. Mathilda could just see the silhouette of the girl's body in the dimness, her slender shoulders and the edge of her elbows, but all else—including her face and hair—was obscured in the shadows.

The hair rose on Mathilda's neck and arms.

Cay Heinrich had called up a vision. He, too, had something of his sister's gift of sight. Elva had never spoken of it, but perhaps she had not known. Perhaps *he* had not known.

"E-Elva?" Cay whimpered.

The image changed. They saw Elva sitting on her bedroom floor as a storm raged outside, gazing into her looking glass. Suddenly the girl collapsed, and something like a miniature sun, glowing bright gold, emerged from her body just over her heart and sank into the mirror. They were witnessing the moment Elva had paid the price for her attempt to change the past.

"No!" Cay shouted, as the mirror glowed gold before him. He crawled over to it and grabbed it with both hands, shaking it frantically as though that might dislodge his sister's soul. "Elva! Elva, can you hear me? Are you inside?" But the glow faded at once and the mirror went back to its normal state. Cay clutched it to his chest and wept and wept, his body rocking with the force of his sobs as he called his sister's name.

Mathilda longed to go and comfort him, but her limbs would not obey her. She stood frozen with grief as Cay slowly got onto his uninjured leg and tucked the crutches beneath his arms. He stayed still for a while, thinking, and then slipped the mirror back into his satchel before moving away through the trees, glancing back several times at his sister in the coffin.

The witch pressed her lips together but made no move to stop him. She had longed to find that mirror earlier, but now she was certain that any attempt to free Elva would be fruitless and maybe even deadly. And in any case, it felt right that Cay should have it to remember his sister by.

Finally it was Mathilda's turn to say good-bye.

She moved forward, kneeling beside the coffin, with apologies on her lips. She wanted to tell Elva how their friendship had changed her life, and that the trial had not been in vain, as painful as it had been. And she longed to say that deciding to open up to Elva—after so many hurts and disappointments—had been worth it, and she would live the rest of her life with that lesson. *I will try again*, she thought. *I will let someone else into my heart.* But kneeling beside the coffin, with the freshly dug grave nearby, Mathilda could not find her voice. She could only lay a gentle hand on the glass and hope Elva knew everything she couldn't put into words.

The witch gathered some ferns and held them in her hands, drawing her magic from the earth around her. The energy flowed from the soil, to her body, to the greens she held, and it felt warm like the sun on her back. The ferns transformed into a bouquet of bright, cheerful flowers.

"Yellow roses for friendship," Mathilda whispered, laying them atop the coffin. "And for the sunshine you gave me. Good-bye, Elva."

Her eyes filled with fresh tears as her hand brushed against the red silk slippers. Elva had been the last one to wear them and had used them to come to see her. Elva had cared; she had liked and accepted Mathilda for who she was, and that had made every bit of pain worthwhile.

Mathilda took the red slippers and hugged them against her chest. Cay had taken the mirror to keep Elva close, and she would take the shoes for the same reason.

Men's voices sounded from a distance. They were coming back to bury Elva.

The witch touched the glass coffin one last time and looked at the girl's beautiful, peaceful face, filling her memory with the sight of it.

And then, with the slippers clutched to her heart, Mathilda went back out of the North Woods and left it and Hanau behind forever. She would go back to Josefine and Aunt Louisa's house. She would collect her cat and all of her possessions, and she would go somewhere far, far away—perhaps the New World that Elva had seen in her visions.

She would create a new home of her own, a new place where she could make memories.

She would live her life, as best as she could. She would take risks and open her heart and let someone else care about her if they wanted to.

Just the way Elva had taught her.

ACKNOWLEDGMENTS

I've been a Disney kid since the day I was born, and met Mickey in person at the age of three, so it was an immense honor to write this book full of fairy tales and magic for Disney!

Thank you to my family for buying me giant volumes of Grimms' tales every birthday and Christmas growing up, and for never batting an eye whenever I sang to bewildered birds in the backyard, like an off-key Princess Aurora. I love you guys!

The book is dedicated to my dear friends Marisa Hopkins and Melody Marshall, who have walked beside me for years on this journey through the dark and magical publishing woods. Thank you for the gift of your friendship!

Thank you to my editors, Brittany Rubiano and Kieran Viola, for granting me this wonderful opportunity. Whether or not I ever come across a pair of red dancing shoes, I have done and will do many happy jigs in your honor! Much gratitude to the entire team at Disney for everything they do, from copyediting, art and design, publicity, sales and marketing, and beyond. Forever grateful that I got to take part in this series and be a part of your family.

No book acknowledgments section would be complete without my stalwart agent and real-life fairy godmother, Tamar Rydzinski. Thanks as always for your advice and friendship!

No magical wishing well could have given me a better group of authors and rock stars to write with than Dhonielle Clayton, Jen Cervantes, and L. L. McKinney. Thanks for all the phone chats and for helping me think more deeply about my story!

Seven is a powerful number. I'm beyond thankful for these seven friends who have seen me through many a treacherous bramble and thorny briar: Rebecca Caprara, Mara Fitzgerald, Kati Gardner, Austin Gilkeson, Heather Kaczynski, Jessica Rubinkowski, and Kevin van Whye.

Thank you to all of the amazing friends and fellow writers and book lovers who brighten my life, especially Samira Ahmed, Theresa Baker, Patrice Caldwell, Natalie Mae, and Tochi Onyebuchi. I'm so lucky to have you with me on this crazy pumpkin-carriage ride.

A million thanks to the booksellers, educators, and librarians who have supported me and my books from the beginning. I can't thank you enough for your kindness.

And my last thanks goes to every Disney kid, fairy-tale lover, and big dreamer out there. Don't stop striving for the happily-ever-afters you deserve!

AGNES'S FAMILY

MATHILDA'S FAMILY

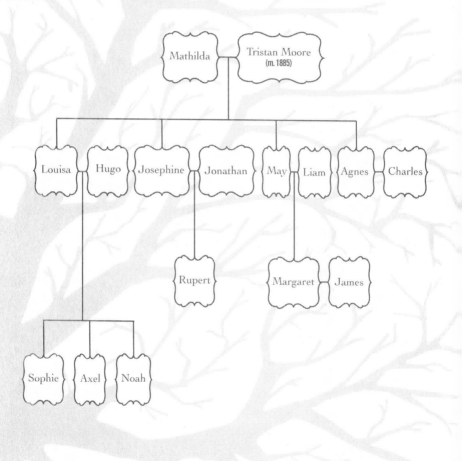

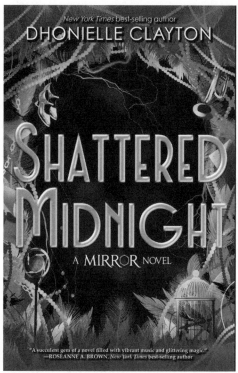

AUGUST 1928. NEW ORLEANS, LOUISIANA.

ew Orleans was a place people went to disappear. Maybe
it was the sticky heat, a thick cloak wrapping you up and
never letting go. Maybe it was all the peculiar people swelling the
French Quarter day and night, easy to fold into and hide. Maybe
it was the never-ending jazz music—trumpets and tubas and sharp
pianos—luring many down cobblestone streets and into alleys, never
to be seen again. Or maybe...just maybe...it was all the dead folks

buried aboveground and the whispers about the Crescent City being a crossroads town, a place where unseen worlds kissed.

That was what Zora had figured out in the two months she'd been living here with her aunt Celine—who had agreed to hide her because she'd gotten into a pile of trouble back home in New York City. She thought maybe this was why her mama sent her down here in the first place. Zora wasn't even her real name, and she still hadn't gotten used to answering to it. But she'd wanted . . . *needed* . . . to vanish. Arms, legs, and feet fading like a pencil sketch erased from a notebook so no one would ever know what she did back in Harlem.

"Mama said you're supposed to be trying on that dress so she can fix the seam before dinner," her cousin Ana snapped. "Everything is about the fit, you know." Willowy and small, Ana twirled before the family's full-length mirror in the bedroom they all shared, leaning in to inspect the new freckles she'd gotten since the start of the summer.

"She's too busy staring out that window again," Ana's sister, Evelyn, replied, sitting at the vanity and fussing with her tight curls. They were barely a year apart yet seemed like twins. A deep blush pushed through her rich brown cheeks. "Always gawking like you never seen nothing. You're from New York City—you've seen *everything*!"

"There's another parade," Zora answered, eyes still glued to the train of bodies, the ginger cat in her lap also perking up to look out the window. She loved the bright parasols and how the blasts of trumpets sent ripples across her skin. The beat of a distant drum mingled with the clash of cymbals and the squeal of trumpets. She tapped the beat on the sill. The jazz here was different than at home: a little wilder, a little less tidy, a little more unpredictable. Each evening, she felt like she was part of it all, the melodies of the parades; rhythms and timbres and crescendos of sound she'd never heard before captured her full attention. She'd fall asleep to the sound of music and revelry somewhere outside the window.

This was the best thing about this city so far. The constant music. The constant dancing. The constant frivolity. The way even the cobblestones seemed to hold rhythms and rumbles. People said it was born in this peculiar city. And she could believe that. Her heart reached for the songs, shaking loose something deep in her bones, the thing she wanted to hide.

Evelyn craned over her to see outside. "That's a second line. We do that when someone dies. Just wait until Mardi Gras. The parades will be happening for weeks. People on stilts, floats, and all the masks to look at."

"The krewes will try to outdo one another," Ana added. "We won't be able to sleep. It'll be terrible. I'll have bags under my eyes again. By the time February comes, I'll have a permanent migraine."

"You don't have parades in New York City? You're supposed to have it all," Evelyn scoffed.

"Most folks are too busy working," Zora replied. "If you danced in the street, you would get flattened like a hotcake by a taxi. But there's some." She continued. "Like on St. Paddy's Day. Or a ticker-tape parade, if someone important visits. Mostly for white folks."

"I can't believe Mama gave her the nice one." Evelyn held up Zora's party dress, and the golden beads and silk chiffon caught the sunlight. Celine, a dressmaker, had made it just for Zora. Evelyn ran her plump fingers over its drop waist. "One of the best Broussard originals to date."

"You can have it." Zora turned back to the window. "I'd rather stay up here, anyway."

Ana snatched it from Evelyn. "But she's our guest for a little while," she mimicked, putting on her mama's thick French accent. "But she's had it rough.... But she's here to convalesce.... But she has a *strange affliction*."

Zora had gotten used to them ganging up on her. The insults had frayed her nerves when she'd first arrived, scraping across her skin like sandpaper. Now she let the words drift out the window to be swallowed by the big brass melodies. She had to.

"What happened in New York? You never did tell us," Ana pressed for the thousandth time, as if that would make Zora suddenly change her mind and spill the whole story.

"I don't want to talk about it."

"You never want to talk about anything," Evelyn spat back. "It's been two months and you won't even tell us about what it's like to live in New York. We're cousins. We're supposed to know things about each other, and we don't know squat."

"I'd rather—"

"Be playing the trumpet," the two said in unison.

"Or the bass guitar. I can play that, too. Even the trombone," she barked back.

Their frowns deepened.

"That's why your lips are so red and puffy. Mama says women have no business playing brass. You'll look like a dried-up fish when you get old," Evelyn said. "Mark my words."

Ana chuckled at Evelyn's barb. "You can't mope around forever," she said, and blew a kiss. She pointed at her house clothes—the simple blue cotton dress Zora loved. "You better get dressed. Mama set up this dinner for you to meet all the important people. Miss Annabelle has to like you. Did you know that the Original Carolina Krewe only accepts the best?" Ana did a twirl across the room to make the beads on her dress click-clack. "The boys fight over who courts you first."

"I don't want to be a debutante." Zora sucked her teeth. If the accident in New York City hadn't happened, she'd planned on becoming the most famous female jazz musician who ever lived. She was a quadruple threat. She could sing, act, dance, and play any instrument she touched. She'd show the men that women were just as good, if not better. "It's fussy and silly, if you ask me."

Evelyn gasped.

"Lucky nobody did," Ana shouted back.

Zora sighed as her cousins listed out all the things that were wrong with her for not being excited. If they knew—*really* knew—what was truly wrong with her and what she'd done, they'd scream and cower in fear. They'd get her aunt to kick her out into the streets. They'd look at her like a monster.

And maybe they'd be right.

Even now, she could feel the hum of her gifts just beneath her skin, like the vibration of a song she used to love. One that felt like her own little secret. But now she hated it.

As the last of the second line eased past the house, a young white man paused. He wore a boater hat, had a face full of freckles, and stared in the window with a strange, clever grin. He looked too perfect and put together to be standing on their corner. He didn't belong. Zora sat up straight, a jolt up her spine. They made eye contact. He lifted a tentative hand and waved.

The bedroom door snapped open. Aunt Celine pounded in, her heels making the floor tremble. Zora's ginger cat cowered and tucked himself deeper into the nook beside her.

With thick dark hair pulled into a perfect chignon, Aunt Celine was a passé-blanc, her skin the shade of steamed milk sprinkled with almond powder. Her aunt pursed her lips in disappointment, and she clapped. "Girls, didn't y'all hear me calling you? I don't holler for my own health." Her honey-colored eyes narrowed, inspecting each of them. "Why aren't any of you dressed? The Colliers and the Bechets will be arriving any moment. I need you downstairs to flash your pretty smiles and remind them that the Broussards throw the best parties in the back-a-town. Mabel is setting out the oyster already."

"Our *houseguest* doesn't want to come," Ana reported with a smug grin.

Before Zora could get a word out, her aunt stomped over and grabbed her arm, yanking her from the small nook, the only spot she felt comfortable in this house.

The cat screeched.

"Get that creature off my furniture. Didn't I tell you about cats? Bad luck. Count your blessings I don't have it stuffed." She tightened her grip. "In the Broussard household, we don't turn down perfectly good invitations to parties thrown in our honor."

Zora tried to wrench away. Her heart fluttered wildly, a humming-bird trapped in her chest, as her aunt's manicured nails dug deeper into her flesh.

"Glad you felt it. Something to knock you out of this rut. You've been skulking around like you can't do nothing."

The warning signs flickered: the flash of heat through her, a thunder beneath her chest, a crackling across her skin as if lightning were about to strike. It hadn't always been like this. She let her eyes close. She only had a few more hours, then she'd be outside and engulfed in music—*just* music, the kind that healed instead of hurt.

Stay calm, she whispered to herself. *Stay calm.*

Her aunt scowled. "What's wrong with you, baby girl? I don't know what my cousin let you get away with in New York City, but this ain't the Big Apple and you best start acting like it."

Zora's eyes snapped open. She gritted her teeth and blinked back tears.

Evelyn and Ana hid satisfied grins behind their hands. Zora felt bruised. The mention of home usually flooded her with memories: a summer Sunday in Harlem, taxis honking, newsboys running up and down West 125th with the latest, the Apollo's lights spilling stardust on the sidewalks, the grocers sweeping and chasing children away from their storefronts, the folks sitting on stoops playing cards or trading gossip when it got too hot inside their apartments . . .

But that was long gone because of what she did. Now the memories were crowded out by the sounds of falling bricks and cracking wood, the snap of broken bones, and the roar of fire mingled with piercing screams. This woke her every night.

"Mabel said you sent her away earlier. It's your turn for a bath. Don't make me have to come back in here, because I'll be bringing a switch. Eighteen is not too old for a good lashing."

Zora flinched.

"You hear me?"

"Yes," Zora mumbled.

"Yes, what?"

"Ma'am. Yes, ma'am, I heard you, and I understand."

"You better." Aunt Celine pulled an envelope from her apron pocket. "This came from your mama. Maybe it'll help set you straight. I told her how you've lost the good sense the Lord gave you, that's what. How lucky you got it, to have kin to take you in when things get rough. Should be more grateful—and gracious . . ."

Zora stammered out an apology. She didn't want to disappoint her mama. She took the letter and traced her fingers over the looping cursive.

"None of that funny business, you hear?" Aunt Celine sucked her teeth and waited for Zora to nod before turning to her daughters and inspecting them. "Ana and Evelyn, wipe all that off your cheeks. This is *not* the Tenderloin. Come with me. You need to entertain our guests as they arrive." She attacked their cheeks with her handkerchief, then strutted out, leaving behind the heat of her words and the scent of her cloying perfume.

While the housekeeper, Mabel, drew her bath, Zora retuned to the window nook. The young white man in the hat was gone.

She unfolded the letter.

August 15, 1928

My dearest,

I miss you so very much, my little love. Your aunt Celine as always full of complaints and commentary. But she's just a honeybee—no real stinger. Give her a few flowers and make her feel like the queen of the hive, and she'll leave you be. She's not much different than the women I cook for.

I wish you were still home with me. And I'm sorry I couldn't prepare you or protect you from this. I'm the one to blame. I should have told you more.

But don't worry—like I said at the train station, the veil is complete. No one will ever know what happened with Mrs. Abernathy and no one will be able to find you. Not as long as I live. I promise.

I'll take a peek in on you. But you cannot write to me. Try to forget about us for a while. Tell others who ask that we are gone. You are gone, in a sense. You're Zora Broussard, and not my little girl anymore.

This storm shall pass. I have faith. Cling tight to the music. It is both a blessing and a curse, but you must use it.

We will be all right. You will be all right. I hope one day we will be together again.

Love,

your mama

Zora held back tears. What would her white, German grandmother think if she could see Zora, her Black granddaughter, now a fugitive in New Orleans? What would she think of the gifts that she'd taught Zora so little about, of what Zora had done with them? What disappointment might Zora see in her eyes?

She was a murderer.

She was a monster.

All because of magic.

2

hen Zora was very little, in their Harlem brownstone, magic was as normal as the jars of spices on her mama's kitchen countertop, folded in like butter in biscuit dough. She'd pick up her father's horn and play a tune, and clusters of notes would flutter in the air as if they'd been lifted from the bars and lines of a music sheet. They also leaked out of her when she'd use her magic, her conduit. Anything she wanted to move with her mind would be swarmed with those ladybug-size notes and carried away.

One day, Oma sat in the small apothecary room, where she mixed tonics for neighbors. She took some lilies from the porcelain white of her wrinkled hands to the brown of Zora's own. "Try," she'd challenged little Zora.

Zora had squeezed her eyes shut, clenched her teeth, and imagined the flower changing colors with all her might.

Oma had chuckled. "Liebling, remember the music. Sing me the song your papa always plays on Sundays."

Zora's eyes lit up, and the happy lyrics burst out of her. And as they did, the soft petals of the lily turned crimson.

Oma smiled. "Each one of us has magic that comes most easily. The one that rises to the surface like cream on fresh milk. Mine is potions—potions that helped others, and that helped me live so long and give birth to your mother and aunts.

"Your mama's is food—she can enchant a kernel of pepper, make dirt taste like the most divine chocolate. But yours..." Oma continued. "Yours is music."

Zora remembered how much fun it had been using her magic as a little girl. Pointing tiny, fat fingers and moving her dolls. Floating spice jars over bubbling pots on the stove, adding a pinch of salt and a dash of cayenne to the simmering liquid under her mama's watchful eye. Clouds of music notes transformed into trays lifting fine china and cast-iron skillets as Mama pulled her latest pie from the oven, blowing over it to cool and enchant it with love and luck. It felt like a stream of melodies flowing outward from her heart, helping her mother make her glorious creations.

And then, just after her seventh birthday, Oma died. Her mother forbade her to use the magic anymore. Said it made her feel too sad. Said the magic could be used against them if they were ever found out—they could be hunted for it.

So Zora had thrown herself into becoming a serious musician. Her soul demanded it. Her truest joy. She buried the magic deep inside the best she could, letting only the notes soar out of her. But the magic buzzed right behind them, waiting, wanting out.

And now she knew just what it could do if she wasn't careful.

"Your bath is almost ready, sugah," Mabel called out.

Zora bit her bottom lip. Watching Mabel's round bottom bent over the tub, she hummed the tune she'd just heard outside. The notes leaked from her fingers like tiny drops of blood. The sensation felt like uncorking a shaken champagne bottle, the magic eager to rush out. The drops stretched into strings, then looped around her mama's letter in a protective ribbon before carrying it to the bed.

She loved knowing that it was still buzzing in her veins, a reminder of Oma. But it also felt like a sharp memory of what she'd done back home, what she was capable of.

"I put a little lavender oil in the tub, baby. Gonna be a long night.

Need a little calm 'round here." Mabel stood in the doorway, hands on her hips, a smile lighting up her brown face. The warmth of her voice always felt like a quilt ready to swaddle Zora. It was like Mabel understood how badly she needed kindness.

Zora kissed Mabel's cheek and went into the bathroom. After a long soak, Mabel helped her squeeze into her dress and sprayed her with enough rose water that even if she sweated in the heat, no one would ever know. She eased down to the dining room and lurked beside its double french doors, clutching Oma's cat to her chest like a shield she hoped would protect her from whatever would happen in that room. She'd successfully avoided all her aunt Celine's parties and attempts to fold her into the colored high society of the city so that maybe by the beginning of next year she'd be ready for debutante season. But everyone had headaches from the Louisiana heat. Everyone had upset stomachs from the rich food. Everyone was a little homesick at first before getting adjusted. Her excuses had run out.

Laughter escaped and Zora could feel the thick electricity of conversation even from her hiding spot.

She stole a glance into the room. The chandelier twinkled over a long table set for ten. The best china had been washed and laid out beside the silver she'd seen Mabel polish during breakfast. The piano sat in front of a large window, its stark white-and-black keys begging to be played. Everything shone under the chandelier, and even she thought it would make her look cleaner and prettier than she ever had. Aunt Celine only liked beautiful things in her house.

Zora took a deep breath and stepped into the room. Evelyn cleared her throat and Ana snickered. The table was full of well-dressed people who reminded her of perfect little brown dolls in matching sets—husbands and wives and their pretty children.

Aunt Celine stood. "Let me introduce my niece, Zora Broussard. She might be rude and late to every party, but she's very pretty."

Zora flashed her best smile. A trail of sweat skated down her back. Another group of people to meet and charm. She would need to make the best impression so that when debutante season started, she'd be accepted.

She still hadn't gotten used to these sorts of folks—fussy and nosy, with a comment for everything. She missed how no one paid her much mind in New York City. Here, she lived under a microscope, her every move up for scrutiny, always woefully failing.

Dr. and Mrs. Bechet sat closest to her aunt, looking like plump figurines atop a wedding cake. Their two sons gawked. Mr. and Mrs. Collier and their son wore ridiculous matching pinstriped outfits and sat sandwiched between Ava and Evelyn. Zora felt like she'd entered a circus masquerading as a dinner party.

"Zora, have you lost your tongue?" her aunt chided. "Say hello.

And did you bring that animal down for dinner? Nobody wants cat étouffée, honey." Her aunt grinned at everyone, and chuckles rippled through the room. She stood and walked over to Zora, grabbed her arm, dug her nails into her skin, and whispered hard in her ear: "I thought we discussed no cat outside of your bedroom. Now send it back upstairs and put a smile on."

Zora put the cat on the floor and sent him back upstairs to her room before turning to face the group. "Hello...I mean hi....Um, good afternoon," she stuttered out, and a flush of embarrassment warmed her cheeks.

"She's come all the way from New York to spend some time down south and away from that noisy place. Though I suppose New Orleans also has quite a bit of ruckus," her aunt added.

The men at the table rose from their seats and waited for Zora to take hers. She eased into a chair beside Evelyn. "I'm sorry it took me so long."

"I told them all how despite being from New York City, you move slow as cane syrup," Aunt Celine said, earning raucous laughter.

Zora grimaced, biting down on her lip to stop a rude remark from slipping out. Mabel wheeled out a spread—fire-red crawfish étouffée, jambalaya bursting with shrimp and sausages, red beans and rice, a steaming cauldron of gumbo, and a pyramid of biscuits.

"It's magnificent, Celine. Truly. You didn't have to go to all this trouble," Mrs. Bechet remarked, her pretty eyes large and wide as she inspected the food.

"Trouble is my middle name on Sundays. And I aim to spoil."

"Must've been holed up in the kitchen," Mrs. Collier added.

Aunt Celine showed her three old oven burns on the inside of her forearm. "Kitchen battle scars."

The look of the thick brown stripes sent a chill up Zora's spine. When she closed her eyes, she saw the ones on Mama's arm, and the buried anger shook itself loose. She swallowed with a gulp.

"Something wrong?" one of the Bechet boys asked Zora. He had the light mustache of a man, but a young boy's squeak still lingered in his voice. His mother called him Jean-Claude.

"No," Zora said, clipped.

Ana and Evelyn guzzled the fizzy champagne their mother let them have on special occasions. Even with the bootlegging happening, New Orleans seemed to always be fully stocked with wine and liquor if you knew the right people.

Mrs. Collier spoke the world's longest prayer and Zora thought the food might turn cold before she was done with all her *amen*s and *hallelujah*s and *thank you, Lord*s.

Aunt Celine lifted her glass and toasted. "To a new season of gloves and gowns and good fortune."

Zora was in desperate need of that. A new fortune. A new start.
Everyone took bites of the delicious food, oohing and ahhing and giving Aunt Celine praise even though Mabel had made it all.

"It's never too early to prepare for our debutante season. Before you know it, November will be here, then Christmas, and then New Year's and Mardi Gras. So much to do. It's only August, and the stress is showing up in my shoulders," Mrs. Bechet said.

Mrs. Collier nodded as Aunt Celine hummed in agreement.

"Zora, tell me, does New York City have as many rats as the papers say?" Dr. Bechet asked, his raspy voice booming.

A series of chuckles followed. His wife playfully slapped his arm.

"As many as I've seen here in the French Quarter. Also, you have more cockroaches than any city should. They even fly here. It's very odd and unfortunate." Zora felt her aunt's hot gaze as she spoke.

"Touché, touché. Those pesky water bugs cling to these streets. I swear they'd survive the end times." He rubbed his salt-and-pepper beard, and his nose crinkled, making Zora brace for another rude question. She gripped her water goblet, taking a nervous sip.

His delicate wife, Mrs. Bechet, flashed Zora a pitying smile, a crease of worry appearing on her forehead. "What do your folks do, Zora?"

"My mama's a chef."

"A cook?" she replied.

"No, a *chef*. She took classes at the only culinary school in all of America. Up in Boston," Zora responded without thinking, puffing out her chest. "And she's worked with many famous chefs."

Aunt Celine flapped her fan aggressively. "She's very, very, very talented," Zora continued. "Always in the papers for this or that. She'll probably be famous one day for whipping up a biscuit that can melt in your mouth and not leave anything on your hips."

Laughter rippled out all around the table.

"Everyone loves her pies and cakes. They can make you forget your own name," Zora boasted, but then swallowed, remembering her mother's warning in her letter about distancing herself from them . . . and what happened.

"Wonder what she'd think of our Louisiana cuisine. It's a mix, like the people who live here and made this fine city. I've done my fair share of traveling, and I swear, there's nothing like a good pot of gumbo and a king cake," Dr. Bechet said.

"What's a king cake?" Zora asked.

A chorus of gasps exploded across the table, followed by more laughter.

"Junior"—Dr. Bechet turned to his son and winked—"you'll have to show Zora around and make sure she gets the best slice from Mama Sugar's Bakery."

The young man nodded, dabbing sweat off his glistening forehead. "Yes, sir," Christophe Jr. said.

Dr. Bechet licked his spoon. "Celine, teach this girl about our ways down here *and* how to make a good étouffée. You put your foot in it, I must say."

"Mabel made that," Zora grumbled under her breath. "All of it."

"What was that?" he asked.

"Nothing," she replied. "Nothing at all."

Her aunt shot her a burning look, the threat of severe punishment in her gaze. Maybe if Zora showed her aunt that she was a terrible dinner guest, she'd let her stay in her room next time. Maybe she'd give up this fool's errand of turning her into a stuffy, boring girl to present like a gift box to eligible men. Maybe she would write her off as hopeless and leave her be.

Stay calm, she told herself. If she made it through dinner, she would have her reward. It wouldn't be much longer.

"If she wants to get married down here, she'll have to learn, too. To be a good wife, one needs to know one's way around the kitchen," Mrs. Collier added.

"I don't want to be a wife—good or bad." The words slipped from Zora's mouth before she could catch them.

Her aunt's gaze turned into a scowl. Her cousins hid their giggles behind fans.

"She has peculiar ideas," her aunt said. "Don't mind them. This good Louisiana air will fix her right up . . . and some good old-fashioned Southern home training."

"I just mean—I mean—I'm not so sure," Zora said.

Mrs. Bechet pressed a hand to her chest, elegant nails tapping her pearls. "Marriage is a sacrament, petite. It is our divine lot—the thing women must do to ensure God's children are brought into this world." She turned to Aunt Celine. "I see you need more of the Lord's word in this house."

"Trust me, Adele, we have plenty. That sinful city she came from teaches young women that they can gallivant around and neglect their duties. But not down here. We still have Jesus. She will walk the righteous path one way or another."

The table exploded with chatter about how Zora might not have been raised right with the church at the heart of her household and how her marriage prospects would no doubt suffer from this neglect. They blamed New York City. They blamed the 1920s jazz and too-short skirts and the fast fancy women in old Storyville and loose morals. They blamed alcohol even while sipping their bootlegged champagne.

Then they blamed her mama and daddy.

She could no longer keep it all in. The calm left her and the little bit of magic she'd let out earlier rushed forward to her fingertips, releasing a high, ringing pitch. The glass in her hand turned midnight black before it shattered.

The women at the table screamed. The young men gawked, mouths ready to lure flies.

"Jesus Christ Almighty!" one said.

"How'd that break?" another replied.

Aunt Celine leapt to her feet; horror and distress marred her beautiful face. "Zora has a mighty grip, is all," she said. "She will be excused. Her constitution is still adjusting to our rich food." She swept Zora from the room, and as soon as they were out of earshot of the party guests, her voice dropped an octave. "I told you about funny business. I'll have none of that in my house. You hear me? Not one bit." She lifted her rosary and kissed it, then dug her vial of holy water out of her pocket and sprinkled it over Zora. "I warned you. This is the last time. The little money your mama and daddy are sending me is *not* enough to take on this burden. Now—out of my sight."

Zora dragged herself back up the stairs, hearing her aunt's excuses trailing her up the steps.

"Her grip is extraordinary. . . . It's from my cousin—her father—who taught her to play the trumpet. Though we all know that girls should not be using those kinds of instruments. Makes hands and mouth indelicate. Strong like a man's. Unladylike. Very, very much so."

Zora's cat greeted her, rubbing his long ginger tail along her leg.

"Another mistake," Zora told him. "Made a pile of trouble again."

Her heart felt sore with disappointment. When she'd first arrived, she'd tuned and played her aunt's piano, hoping music would make her feel a little closer to home. But her cousins made remarks about the types of women who played jazz music, and thick notes poured out of her like torrential rain, choking the room, knocking the portraits off the walls and toppling the lamps. Aunt Celine had a fit. She swatted the notes out the windows like flies, and Mabel ran around in hysterics trying to sweep up broken glass and set objects upright. Her aunt forbade her from singing or using any instrument in the house.

She didn't understand. It wasn't the *music* that was to blame.

The cat stared back with huge sea-glass-green eyes and led her to the window nook. She had so many questions and so much anger about the fact that she didn't have the answers. Why had Mama refused to let her use magic all these years? Was it because she knew deep down it was bad? Why hadn't she told her anything about it?

Everything was just so unpredictable and off-kilter after what had happened with Mrs. Abernathy in New York City. Now it all rushed out violent and sharp as Mama's chef knives, and she had to focus on staying calm so she could control it.

The moon rose outside the window. Zora stuffed pillows beneath her blankets and arranged a silk headscarf in the shape of her head. Her cat sat on the mound to keep watch as she arranged everything into a familiar form.

"Good job." She kissed his wet nose and pulled the sheer bed curtains closed. They would not only protect that lump from mosquitoes, but from the prying eyes of her cousins and aunt. *This* stomachache would last all night.

Turning to her wardrobe, she slid on a pair of crimson T-strap heels and buckled them around her ankles. She took a few steps through the room, admiring herself in front of the mirror. Her step was light, and her feet made no sound on the floorboards. Not that anyone would be able to hear her through the laughter drifting upstairs.

Zora remembered the night her mother gave them to her.

Then, the street noises had pushed through the window of her small bedroom in their Harlem brownstone: the blaring of taxi horns, the fussing of men rolling dice and wishing for better fortunes, the trickle of jazz refrains from nearby speakeasies, the sounds of working men and women dragging their tired bodies up staircases.

Her mama's light brown hands, wrinkled and dry from scouring pans and washing vegetables, had lifted a fragile satin covering in the deepest of reds to reveal a pair of the most beautiful slippers Zora had ever seen. Even better than those that sat in the windows of shops she was never allowed into.

"I got these from Oma." Heirlooms passed down to the women in her family.

Tears had lingered in her mother's voice, her words gravelly and muffled. The mention of her mother always sent her into a deep well of sadness. "They may change."

"Change how?" Zora had asked.

"Watch and see." Her mother untied Zora's shoes and pulled them off, along with her socks. She slid the delicate slippers on her bare feet. "They should adjust. They did for me, but I haven't worn them since she died. They'll let you come and go places without so much as a footprint left behind."

As Zora watched, the soles warmed as if she'd been curled up in front of their living room fireplace with her feet near the hearth. The backs lifted from the floor, exposing tiny new heels. Zora gasped. The ribbons transformed into a T-strap that curled around her ankle and sprouted a small golden clasp.

"No footprints?" Zora had sat forward on the bed.

"Not a single trace of you. It'll be as if you aren't even there. When you secure them tight"—her mother had fastened the hook—"you will remain unheard."

"They're beautiful," Zora said as she fastened the straps. "But why are you giving them to me now?"

"You need to remain unseen until this whole thing goes away. I don't know how long that will take—weeks, months, maybe even a year or two. I will hide you for as long as it takes for folks to forget and make up stories about why that woman died. Enough time for the stories to spin on themselves." Her thick eyebrows furrowed, and sadness left lines across her forehead. "I feel like this is my fault." A single tear skated down her cheek; a deep blush set beneath the milky brown. "The magic in our blood is complicated. . . ."

Zora caught the tear with her thumb. "No, Mama, it's my fault. My anger got the best of me. I am so very sorry. I just couldn't . . ."

Her mother had shushed her. A knock had rattled the door. "Baby girl, it's time." Her papa's warm voice eased in.

Mama had kissed Zora's forehead, slipped the heels off, and repacked them. "Keep these close. Use them when you need to. Everything will settle again soon. The whole world is a bone knocked out of place. God'll make it right."

They were the last things her mother had packed in her suitcase.

Now, Zora eased into the hallway and down the back staircase, the one that led to the kitchen, knowing her steps would be silent. Mabel leaned over a hot stove, dropping dollops of dough into oil to make fluffy beignets. With two quick leaps, Zora opened the back door.

"Who's there?" Mabel spun around, fear consuming her deep brown face.

Zora blew a kiss at her from the window and Mabel waved. She'd always kept Zora's secrets. So far. Sometimes Zora wore the heels and sneaked up behind Mabel to have a look at what she was cooking for dinner. Mabel would get all flustered and chase her out of the kitchen with a broom. Or Zora would sneak into her shared bedroom and tug one of Ana's long corkscrew curls while she was primping and complaining about having to lend things to Zora. She loved hearing her cousin scream, then run around like a startled chicken after realizing Zora was right there.

Her T-straps left a melody only she could hear. As she darted out into the sticky night, Mabel threw salt over her shoulder and slammed the door.

JULIE C. DAO is the author of the acclaimed Rise of the Empress duology, including *Forest of a Thousand Lanterns* and *Kingdom of the Blazing Phoenix*, as well as the follow-up novel, *Song of the Crimson Flower*. A proud Vietnamese American who was born in Upstate New York, she now lives in New England. Follow her on Twitter @jules_writes.